The Beckets of Romney Marsh

Ainsley Becket (formerly Geoffrey Baskin)
Patriarch of the Family Becket
Born in Cornwall, spent time in Caribbean before
returning to England in 1798
Wife: Isabella Becket, died 1798
One child: Cassandra Becket, born 1798

The accumulated children of Ainsley Becket in order of their adoption:

Chance Becket, born approximately 1784
Possibly child of tavern keeper and
unknown female
A Gentleman by Any Other Name

Courtland Becket, born approximately 1785
Rescued by Geoffrey Baskin, remained
mute for several years
Becket's Last Stand – coming soon from
Mills & Boon® Super Historical Romance!

Spencer Becket, born approximately 1788
Possibly child of deceased sailor/pirate
A Most Unsuitable Groom

Morgan Becket, born 1794
Sold to Geoffrey Baskin by prostitute
mother on day of birth
The Dangerous Debutante

Rian Becket, born approximately 1789
Parents killed in pirate raid on a Caribbean island
The Return of the Prodigal – coming soon from
Mills & Boon® Super Historical Romance!

Fanny Becket, born approximately 1795
Parents killed in the same raid as Rian's parents
A Reckless Beauty

Eleanor Becket, born approximately 1792
Sole survivor of an attack at sea
Beware of Virtuous Women

A RECKLESS BEAUTY

Kasey Michaels

MILLS & BOON

Pure reading pleasure

First published in Great Britain 2008
by Harlequin Mills & Boon Limited,
Eton House, 18-24 Paradise Road, Richmond, Surrey TW9 1SR

ISBN: 978 0 263 86564 6

037-0508

Harlequin Mills & Boon policy is to use papers that are
natural, renewable and recyclable products and made from
wood grown in sustainable forests. The logging and
manufacturing processes conform to the legal environmental
regulations of the country of origin.

Printed and bound in Spain
by Litografia Rosés S.A., Barcelona

*Available from **Kasey Michaels**
and Mills & Boon*

THE BUTLER DID IT
IN HIS LORDSHIP'S BED
(short story in *The Wedding Chase*)

SHALL WE DANCE?
IMPETUOUS MISSES
MARRIAGEABLE MISSES

and in the Beckets of Romney Marsh series

A GENTLEMAN BY ANY OTHER NAME
THE DANGEROUS DEBUTANTE
BEWARE OF VIRTUOUS WOMEN
A MOST UNSUITABLE GROOM

To Joseph Charles Groller
Welcome to the world, Joey

PROLOGUE

March 1815

FRENCH SOIL ONCE MORE, so long denied him. Paris awaits!

Napoleon Bonaparte, by the grace of God, Emperor of France, King of Italy, etc., etc., halts at the head of his army of less than one thousand of the Old Guard who had chosen to be exiled with him on Elba for more than a year.

The moment is here. He comes face-to-face with an equal number of royal troops that have appeared with orders to exterminate him and his "band of brigands."

Bonaparte dismounts and walks forward ten precise paces on the dusty road. One slight, small man, alone between two armies. Unarmed. Vulnerable.

"Soldiers of the fifth army corps!" he shouts defiantly to the royal troops, his voice carrying in the still air. "Don't you know me? Is there one among you who wishes to kill his Emperor, let him come forward and do so. *Here I am!*"

And, in a move so daring it brings gasps of dismay from both sides of the line, he throws wide the simple gray cloak covering his chest.

After a tense silence, the cry goes up from all sides. *"Vive l'Empereur! Vive l'Empereur!"*

The one thousand are now two thousand. Bonaparte remounts and surveys his new army from atop his charger, and then stands straight in the stirrups.

Solemnly, silently, he points toward Paris.

And the world trembles...

CHAPTER ONE

Becket Hall, Romney Marsh

DINNER OVER, Ainsley Becket relaxed in his favorite chair in the drawing room, listening to his children as they discussed Bonaparte's adventures since escaping Elba several weeks earlier.

Breakfast, luncheon, dinner, the conversation never seemed to vary. What will Bonaparte do? Where will he strike first? Will the Allies cede all command to the Iron Duke? Will Wellington be able to defeat the man he had, remarkably, never before met in battle?

Ainsley let their individual voices fade into the background as he concentrated on his children.

Such a disparate group, all eight of his children; seven of them the children of his heart, and now all of them grown, some of them already gone their own way, with his blessing.

Morgan, a wife and mother now, lived on her husband's estate near London, her Ethan Tanner,

Earl of Aylesford, undoubtedly laboring very long hours at the War Office.

Chance, Ainsley knew from the letter he'd received from his oldest son a week ago, was also back at work in the War Office, as all of England braced itself for the inevitable clash with the man they'd believed vanquished.

Ainsley sipped at his snifter of brandy, selfishly content that these two men had found a way to serve the Crown without exposing themselves to battle, and stole a look at his son Spencer, who was bouncing his young son, William, on his leg as Mariah Becket smiled at them both.

Would Spencer willingly leave his small family and go to war again? Ainsley planned a quiet talk with the boy, who had sacrificed enough in America, and needed to think first of his wife and son, and the second child Mariah now carried.

Eleanor and her husband, Jack, sat close together near the fireplace, a stack of Paris newspapers Ainsley had acquired in his usual secretive, inventive ways piled in Eleanor's lap. There still was no baby to be held in her arms, a sorrow she hid most times, but one that Ainsley knew ate at his oldest daughter's heart.

Callie, the youngest, and the only child born to Ainsley and his lost Isabella, continued her argument with her brother Courtland about the latter's assertion that he should buy a commission in the army Wellington was hastily forming to confront the French emperor, now that the majority of the Field Marshal's troops had been sent to fight the Americans. As it was, foreign troops would out-number English troops two-to-one.

Courtland, always the solid one, the rock of the Beckets, firmly believed in duty.

Callie, with all the surety of a seventeen-year-old, firmly believed Courtland belonged to her.

"You and Jack have enough on your plates, Court," Ainsley said quietly now, making his point without overtly referring to the roles the two men played aiding the local smugglers, and Courtland nodded his reluctant agreement.

"I know, sir, but I believe you and Jacko are still reasonably capable and can run Becket Hall in our absence. Besides, we'll have Boney corralled and in a cage in a few months, if not weeks."

Callie, always sharp, sharper than most females were raised to be, spoke up. "In a cage, you say, Court? I believe—you'll correct me if I'm wrong, Papa—that it was Marshal Ney who promised the now displaced King Louis that he would bring Bonaparte to him in an iron cage and place him be-fore Louis's throne."

She grinned at Court. "Would that be the same iron cage, Courtland, hmm? Especially now that

Ney is back to perching on a cushion at Bonaparte's feet, apologetically licking his boots?"

Mariah Becket laughed as she took young William from her husband and lifted him into her arms. "She's got you there, Court. You men. So much bluster, so many promises. Spencer? I'll see you upstairs, and meet you with a book tossed at your head if you dare to even hint that you'll attempt to follow the drum again."

Everyone waited until Mariah had left the drawing room before bursting into laughter at Spencer's expense.

"Well and truly tied to the apron strings, aren't you, old fellow?" Jack Eastwood asked, earning himself a speaking look from the love of his life. Morgan or Mariah would have delivered a sharp jab to his ribs, but the petite, ladylike Eleanor needed only to send a level look from her speaking eyes, and Jack subsided, murmuring a quiet, "Sorry, Spence."

"It's all right," Spencer said, walking over to the drinks table to pour himself a glass of wine. "I know I can't go. And neither can you two, not when the Black Ghost has to ride out with regularity, and definitely not when we still don't know where our old friend Edmund Beales might next show his face—and recognize yours. What if he's acting as Talleyrand has, and has now thrown in his lot with the Alliance, abandoning Bonaparte after the fiasco that was his attempt to free him from Elba last August? Bonaparte might not be quite in love with the man now, you know?"

Mention of Edmund Beales cast the room into silence for some moments, and Ainsley was, as always, thrown back in time, remembering the days when he'd considered Edmund his best friend and partner. Before Edmund's betrayal. Before Isabella's death at Edmund's hands. Before the massacre on the island that had brought them all to England and the protective isolation of Romney Marsh seventeen years ago. Before they'd learned that Edmund still lived, and had taken his study of Machiavelli's mad genius to heart, believing himself destined to control the destinies of half the world. Before…before…before…

"It's true," Callie said, breaking the silence, as she saw the shadows in her papa's eyes, and wanted them gone. "None of you can be seen by Beales, as he may have seen all of your faces at one time or another. So you can relax, Papa, nobody is running off to war. Except Rian, of course," she added, her pretty face marred by a frown as she thought about the day, a few weeks earlier, Rian had made his farewells and ridden away with an eagerness he couldn't quite disguise, his commission in his pocket.

"Our brother is so damn hot to play the hero, the fool," Spencer said, shaking his head. "We can only hope he'll stay cooling his heels in Belgium, and never even set foot on French soil."

"Amen to that, Spencer. I still find it difficult to believe the way the French have embraced Bonaparte, after damning him just over a year ago," Eleanor said, paging through the newspapers she'd been holding on her lap. "Just look at these, for pity's sake. Let me read the titles of the articles written over the course of the past weeks by the *Moniteur,* once so loyal to the Emperor. Here, darling, help me before they all slide to the floor."

She passed some of the newspapers to Jack, whom she asked to read the oldest one first.

"It would be my pleasure. Ah, here we go. 'The Corsican werewolf has landed at Cannes.'"

"Yes, the *werewolf,*" Eleanor said. "Now this one is next, only a few short days later. 'The tiger appeared at Gap, troops were sent against him, the wretched adventurer ended his career in the mountains.' They said he'd been killed, for pity's sake."

Jack reached for another newspaper. "And were forced to eat their own words. 'The fiend has actually, thanks to treachery, been able to get as far as Grenoble.'"

Eleanor continued with the title of a later article, "'The tyrant has reached Lyons, where horror paralyzed all attempts at resistance.' But, Papa, haven't your agents in France already told you Bonaparte was greeted with cheers and bouquets?"

Ainsley nodded. "Eleanor, you really expect truth from a newspaper controlled by the state? I thought I'd taught you to be more discerning than that. Read the rest, if you please. They are amusing, in a rather macabre way."

Jack lifted another newspaper, scanned it and smiled ruefully. "Ah, no longer the werewolf, tiger or tyrant, I see, but actually at last referred to by name. And in just a few days time. 'Bonaparte moves northward with rapid strides, but he will never reach Paris.'"

"And these last two," Eleanor said, shaking her head. "'Tomorrow Napoleon will be at our gates.' And, lastly, this, 'His Majesty is at Fontainebleau.' His Majesty, is it? Hypocrites, all of them! But if that's how rapidly the French can turn their coats, can Bonaparte sleep easy at night?"

Ainsley drained the last of his brandy and stood, ready to return to his study and the maps he'd been poring over since first he heard of Bonaparte's escape, comparing those maps to the steady stream of information his money so cleverly bought. He'd correctly picked Cannes as the man's initial destination. Now he looked north, to the area around Brussels, feeling that to be the logical ground for Wellington and the Emperor to at last meet across a battlefield. He'd already forwarded his thoughts to Chance and Ethan, with little hope such an necessarily anonymous warning would be heeded by their superiors.

And Rian, God help them, was already in Belgium.

"Remy," he said, referring to his informant in Paris, "has written me that Bonaparte paused on the steps of his palace the day of his arrival, to look out on the quiet city, and said, 'They have let me come, just as they let the others go.' So, if that answers your question, Eleanor, I would say that the man knows his rule is tenuous, at best. Which I believe, sadly, means he will march out of Paris soon, to confront the Allies, rather than wait for them to come to him. He has to prove that he is still the strongest man in Europe."

Courtland, who had spent many hours poring over the same communiqués and maps as Ainsley, disagreed. "It will be the end of July before the Russians and Austrians can meet up with our own army, and neither we English nor the Prussians will be fool enough to engage Bonaparte until all of the Allies are together."

Ainsley smiled indulgently. "Don't think of rosy scenarios, where the world works to your hopes, Court. Better to think like your enemy. Can you conceive of a better reason for Bonaparte to move now? His people will want to see a victory, a bit of the old soldier in his battle-worn green greatcoat, even if that means coming out with a smaller army than he'd like. And I do not believe he wants that initial fight to be a defensive action, one that takes place on French soil. No, Bonaparte is first and foremost a soldier. War may have been declared on him by the Alliance, but he will take the initiative, attack. If only the fools in the War Office could understand this."

"Pray God they will, Papa. So…so Rian could be closer to this first battle, when it comes, than we believe?" Eleanor asked, slipping her hand into Jack's.

"That blasted girl!"

All heads turned to look at Mariah, who was standing in the doorway, her cheeks flushed, and clutching a thick lock of light blond hair. She held it aloft, shook it with some fury.

Ainsley looked at the hank of hair and felt a frightening chill, as if a goose had just walked over his grave. "Fanny?"

Mariah nodded, scarcely able to speak. Fanny Becket had pushed back from the dinner table the previous evening, complaining of the headache, and gone to her room. "I knocked on her door a few times today, but there was no answer. You know how can she can be, sulking ever since Rian left, and I decided—Eleanor and I decided—to simply let her stay locked up in there until her stomach finally forced her out again. But tonight, well, enough is enough, so I commandeered a key and...and she's not there."

Callie turned in her chair to ask, "She's run away? Did she leave a note?"

"She didn't have to," Ainsley said, sitting down heavily, feeling all of his years. "We all know where your sister has gone."

CHAPTER TWO

FANNY BECKET hid herself just at the entrance to a foul-smelling alley fronting on the bustling wharf where soldiers and horses milled about as dusk fell, waiting for the order to take ship. She nervously fingered the *gad* hanging around her neck from a gold chain, one of the especially prepared alligator teeth her old nurse and Voodoo priestess, Odette, insisted all the Beckets wear.

It was a silly thing, but Odette renewed the protective magic in each *gad* every spring, and how could Fanny leave such a potent weapon against the bad *loa*, the bad spirits, behind as she went off to war?

Dear God, she was going to war!

She'd ridden through the night and day to make Dover before anyone could catch her, drag her home, but she'd been standing in this alley for the past two hours, not knowing what to do next. Because Dover wasn't Ostend, and she knew she had to get herself across the Channel to Ostend before she could travel inland, to Brussels.

To Rian.

Her mare, Molly, stood obediently behind her, nuzzling at Fanny's neck, hoping for a treat, and she absently dug into the pocket of Rian's cloak for the last broken bit of carrot she had brought with her, handing it up to the horse.

It was a mad scheme she was considering now as she peeked out at the milling soldiers, but desperate times called for desperate actions. After all, Rian had told her she was pretty, even as he laughed at her, pretended not to love her as anything more than his sister, even though they were not related by blood.

But they'd always been together, for as long as Fanny could remember. From that day when, at no more than three years old, she had knelt beside her mother in the pretty, whitewashed island church, and the priest was holding up the chalice, and her mother bowed her head, striking her breast three times, once for each time the bell was rung on the altar.

Just as the bell rang that third time, the cannon had exploded all around them, and Fanny had looked up, seen the blue sky, seen bits of the roof raining down on them before being pushed to the floor, her mother lying on top of her, protecting her.

That's where the man later to christen himself Ainsley Becket had found her, still half-crushed beneath her mother's lifeless body. There were others, other survivors of the Spanish pirate's attack that had come from the sea without warning, Rian among them. Three of the women still lived in Becket Village, but other mothers and their children, and the four other orphans of that day, had survived only to die several months later, when Edmund Beales attacked their island.

Pirates. Brigands. Warm white sands and clear blue waters. Death. Death everywhere; once, and then again. Fanny barely remembered any of it. Just watching her mother beat at her breast as the bell rang, calling down the roof onto their heads…and Rian, only a few years her senior, but always there, always holding her hand, protecting her, swooping her up into his own thin arms that last day and carrying her deep into the trees, away from Edmund Beales's treachery.

She'd do anything to protect him, as well.

Even see if he was right, that she was pretty. A pretty girl.

Fanny tested the knot holding the colored scarf around her head, hiding her badly butchered blond hair, and flipped the edges of her cloak back over her shoulders, the better to display the rumpled gown she'd donned over her breeches once reaching Dover.

"Don't follow me, Molly," she admonished the mare that hung her head as if she understood, and she probably did, for Molly was very intelligent, and Fanny had trained her well.

Then Fanny stepped out of the shadows, heading directly toward the slim young boy in the scarlet uniform of the 13th Regiment cavalry. She'd chosen him for his regiment, for his youth, for his size.

"You're to be sailin' off tonight, is it, you pretty thing?" she asked him, circling around both him and his horse, effectively cutting the youth from the herd of his fellow soldiers, all of them exhausted after sailing from Cove, their ship damaged enough that they'd had to put in at Dover for both repairs and provisions before following their two other ships to Ostend.

It had been unbelievable good luck, an omen, Odette would have said, that she'd found some of the 13th here, on this overcrowded dock. Rian's own regiment; fine, brave Irishmen from County Cork, and beyond. It had seemed fitting to Rian that he fight with the Irish, even if the only thing still Irish about him was his blood, and his name. For the past seventeen years, since the age of nine, since that bell had rung a third time, he had been a Becket.

The young boy Fanny had singled out—he seemed such a child—dipped his head at Fanny's question, swallowing down so hard that his Adam's apple seemed ready to collide with his chin. "And that we are, Miss. Off to chase Boney back where he belongs, give him what for."

Fanny measured him with her eyes. Yes, this was

good. He topped her own not inconsiderable height by only a few inches. "Well, God bless you then, boyo," she said, pushing even more of a lilt into her voice. "And would you be wanting somethin' to take with you then? A last kiss from a grateful lass late of County Clare? Mayhap a bit more than a kiss?"

The young soldier looked about him, wetting his lips. "I'm not supposin' you'd be offerin' such a thing for free."

Fanny smiled. "And what are you takin' me for, boyo? One of them loose wimmen?" She reached up, stroked his smooth cheek that had only a hint of peach fuzz. What was he? Sixteen? "No brave man should be goin' off to fight without first bein' with a willin' lass, now should he?"

"I been," the soldier protested, his cheeks going red. "I been plenty." He clasped his rifle with one hand and took her elbow with the other, even as she deftly grabbed on to his mount's bridle, steering her toward the alleyway, which was right where she wanted to go. "But it's quick we'll be, a'fore the Sergeant-Major misses me, you hear?"

Fanny felt herself pushed rather roughly against the wet brick as the boy fumbled, one hand holding her still even as he propped his rifle against the wall and began unbuttoning his breeches.

That was helpful. He was giving her a head start, in a way, or so Fanny thought as she closed her eyes, whispered a quick "I'm so sorry" and brought the heel of the pistol she'd extracted from the pocket of her cloak down hard on the soldier's temple.

Fanny might be young, and slim, but she was also tall, and fairly strong. Bending only slightly beneath the dead weight of the soldier, she dragged him deeper into the alleyway and lowered him gently to the ground.

She worked quickly, stripping the boy to his last little bit of clothing, for she was wearing Rian's underclothes, and didn't much care to exchange them for drawers that looked, even in this dim light, capable of standing up by themselves.

Five minutes later, leaving behind a small purse of coins, as well as a rough pair of trousers and a shirt for the boy to cover himself with when he awoke, and with her white braces in place across her now red-coated chest, the rifle slung over her shoulder, as well as the heavy pack containing the best of the soldier's gear and her own, Fanny emerged from the alleyway once more, leading Molly and the black gelding by the reins of their bridles.

She stayed between the two horses and kept her head down as she joined the men just now being formed up to go aboard, wondering if she'd just saved one young Irish life, but never doubting her own fate.

Ostend awaited. Brussels awaited.

Rian, although he didn't know it yet, awaited.

CHAPTER THREE

RIAN BECKET sat alone at a back table in a small roadside tavern in an area he believed was called something akin to Scendelbeck, the top button of his uniform opened, his overlong black hair damp and plastered against his forehead above bright blue eyes that hadn't seen more than a few hours of sleep in several weeks.

So much for the romance and glory of war.

Thus far, that war consisted of a prodigious amount of parading under a hot sun or a drenching downpour, a good deal of tending to his horse, a measure of drinking, and much too much sitting and waiting.

At least at long last Rian had seen the man he'd been cheated out of meeting last year in London, as the Duke of Wellington himself had just today inspected their forces, along with the Prince of Orange, the Duc de Berri, the Duke of Brunswick and even Field Marshal Blücher, the man, it was said, who had drunk half of London under the table when there last August for, it turned out now, the premature Peace Celebrations.

"Lieutenant Rian Becket?"

Rian looked up at the tall man standing in front of the table, about to rise if that man had been wearing a uniform. But as he wasn't, and looked very much as if the clothes he did stand up in were the same clothes he'd laid down in several nights in a row, Rian only slipped lower on his spine in the wooden chair and motioned for the fellow to join him.

"I'd offer you some of my wine," Rian said, hefting the dark blue bottle in front of him, "but as you can see, alas, I've finished the last of it. You know my name. If you'd now return the favor, perhaps we can then split a new bottle."

The sandy-haired ruffian—he did, truly, look the ruffian—smiled as he sat down and extended his hand. "Valentine Clement, Mr. Becket, at your service. Jack Eastwood wrote to me, asked that I—"

"Jack? Oh, bloody hell," Rian swore, sitting up straight while ignoring the man's outstretched hand. "My brother-in-law thinks I need a nursemaid? No, thank you. And if you're applying for the role of batman, Clement, it should have occurred to you to first clean up your dirt before presenting yourself."

The man withdrew his hand, his light hazel eyes twinkling in amusement. "A thousand pardons, Lieutenant Becket. I'll inform your brother-in-law of your so polite refusal." He pushed back his chair and got to his feet before making a damned graceful bow for a ruffian, a small smile on his face. "Good day to you, sir."

Feeling as if he might have made some sort of mistake, Rian called for another bottle. But, instead of the barmaid, one of his superiors from the 13th Light Dragoons delivered the wine, as well as a second glass clearly meant for himself.

"Remain seated, Lieutenant. That conversation was a mite short," Captain Moray commented, pulling the cork from the bottle and pouring them each a full tumbler of surprisingly good wine. "What did his lordship want? He say anything about what's going on with Boney?"

Rian looked at the older man, the quick flip of his stomach telling him he probably didn't want to hear anything Moray might say next. "His lordship? You're not mistaken? His *lordship?*"

Moray nodded, and then drank deeply from his glass before setting it down again. "I still hate this part, the waiting. One more bloody parade, Becket, and we'll all be busy reshoeing our horses while Boney is driving over us with his cannon. And, right you are, his lordship. That was himself, Valentine Clement. Earl of Brede, you know. Haven't seen him in a while, and us that know are never supposed to let on who he is, but I've been down this road before, and that was him, I'm sure of it. The great bloody Brede himself."

Rian jammed his fingers through his hair, feeling young and stupid. "Oh, well...*hell,*" he said, disgusted, and then slumped back against his chair. "I just turned him down for the position of my batman. And all but told him he smelled, needed a bath. Which he did, damn it all anyway, on both counts."

Moray's braying laugh had heads turning in the tavern. "Cheeky young pup. But he knew you, didn't he, called you by name? Brede's one of Wellington's own, you know, and been with him forever. Hand-picked for being sneaky. Flits around wherever he wants, his ear always to the ground. Odds are his lordship supped with Boney at that fancy Versailles of his three nights ago, and then flirted into the mornin' with all the prettiest *mam-selles.* And you all but served the man his notice? There's bollocks for you, I'll give you that. I think that calls for another bottle, I do." And he leaned back in his chair, snapping his fingers at the barmaid.

Rian drank silently, mentally kicking himself for his own arrogance. Elly's husband had written a letter, sent Brede to him. Jack never spoke much about what he'd done years ago, but they all knew he'd acted as a spy on the Peninsula, among other things. A spy like Brede. So did Jack then break both his hands affixing a seal to the letter to Brede, so that he couldn't send another to his brother-in-law, warning him as to what he'd done?

"That man—Brede—he looked as tired as old death itself, didn't he?" Rian asked his Captain, feeling young and damned foolish. "He's seen things I shouldn't want to see, I think. I thought this all would be…different somehow. Good. Noble."

Moray lifted his head, smacked his lips together a time or two, as the wine, far from his first bottle of the evening, had begun to make his tongue numb and thick. He peered across the tabletop at Rian. "Noble, is it? Then that's your mistake, boy. You never should have set foot from home, not a dreamer like you. Put that dreaming away. If you don't, you'll end up dead, mark my words."

"Then I'll put away the dreams, if that's what it takes. I want to fight, Captain Moray," Rian said, bristling. "And I'm damn good at it."

The captain grinned, his head sort of sliding down between his palms as one cheek made slow, gentle contact with the tabletop. "You can ride like the very devil, I'll give you that. Never miss the straw with your saber, either. But a heap of straw ain't flesh, boy, and that fine, light-footed bay of yours will probably be shot from under you in the first minute of the charge. When you're knee deep in blood and mud, tripping over pieces of the men you drank with the night before, and the Froggies are screaming, running at you—then we'll see how damn good you are. Enough. Jesus, I hate this...I hate this. Too much waiting...too much thinking. Too much remembering the last time. Cursed Boney, he was supposed to be gone...."

CHAPTER FOUR

FANNY SAT WITH her back against the raw wood planks that made up the hold of the small ship, her knees bent as she braced herself against the storm raging in the Channel. Molly, her lead tied to a hook like the other sixty-five horses jammed in together in the cramped space, kept trying to nuzzle Fanny's shoulder, her huge brown eyes wide and frightened.

"It's all right, Molly," Fanny told the mare, reaching up to stroke the horse's velvety muzzle. "Just a little wind, just a little rain."

Her eyelids heavy, Fanny continued to comfort Molly, but the black gelding was becoming anxious, rolling its red-rimmed eyes and jerking back its head, trying to be free of the rope, the dark hold, the ship itself, most probably.

"Shamus Reilly! Control that damn horse before it sets the others off, or I'll have your skinny guts for garters!"

"Yes, sir!" Fanny said, jumping to her feet.

"And, by Jesus, don't be callin' me *sir.* That's Sergeant-Major Hart to you, boyo!"

"Yes, sir—Sergeant-Major Hart!" Fanny repeated, wincing at her mistake. She reached into the pocket of her uniform trousers and pulled out the scarf she'd worn tied around her head only three hours ago, talking softly to the gelding as she reached up to tie the material around those wild, rolling eyes.

"Good work, Private Reilly," the mutton-chopped Sergeant-Major said, prudently standing at Blackie's side, and not directly behind the animal, in case it decided to kick. "You see that, boys? All of you, cover their eyes, keep 'em quiet. *Move!*"

Fanny kept her back to the Sergeant-Major, mumbled a quick thank-you, then wondered if she should have spoken at all.

Probably not, as the Sergeant-Major was still paying entirely too much attention to her.

What did he see? What could he see, in this near-darkness? Why didn't he just go away? Was he about to discover her deception?

She was tall, tall as the real Shamus Reilly. She'd clubbed her hacked-off hair at her nape with a plain black ribbon. Nothing unusual there. And Lord knew her bosom wasn't giving her away, as nature had already snubbed her nose at Fanny and given most of it away to her sister Morgan.

"Private Reilly."

Fanny's spine stiffened. "Yes, Sergeant-Major!"

"How old are, boyo? Fifteen?"

"No, Sergeant-Major!" Fanny, who had just passed her twentieth birthday, denied with what she hoped was the indignation only a lad who had not yet felt the need of a razor could muster. "It's ten and seven I am, come last Boxing Day."

"A poor liar you are, Private Reilly. I'll not have babies in my troop. But I need every man I have, and that includes you. Christ. Ten and seven, my sweet aunt Nellie. Next they'll be saddlin' me with babes in arms."

"Yes, sir—Sergeant-Major!"

By the time they'd finally reached Ostend, Fanny had convinced herself she was safe.

She was wrong.

"Private Reilly!"

Now what did that man want? Fanny fought down a yearning to roll her eyes at the sound of Sergeant-Major Hart's voice as the man edged his mount in close beside hers as they rode out of the city. Did the man have nothing better to do but to hound her, set her heart skipping every time she thought she was safe, anonymous, hopefully invisible?

"Sergeant-Major!"

"We can talk more private now, can't we? Who are you huntin', Private Reilly? A brother? A lover? The father of your unborn child?"

"Sir?" Fanny kept her eyes forward, even as her stomach attempted to drop onto the cobblestones beneath Molly's feet.

"*Sergeant-Major,* damn your eyes! And it's denyin' it that won't work, Private Reilly, not when you're up against a man like me, who's seen it all before."

Fanny swallowed hard, trying to moisten her dry mouth. "Yes…yes, Sergeant-Major."

"Who you after, Private?"

"I'd rather not say, Sergeant-Major."

"Now, see, lass, there's where you'd be wrong. I wasn't *askin'* you. It's not a friendly chat we two are havin' here, you understand?"

Fanny lifted her chin. "He doesn't know I've followed him. It's no fault of his, sir."

"*Sergeant-Major.* How thick would be your head, Private Reilly, that you can't remember such a small thing, such an important thing? You'll stay by yourself, sleep with the horses and keep your yammer shut, even if that means my men think you stupid. Would they be far wrong, Private Reilly, were they to be thinkin' that?"

"No, Sergeant-Major," Fanny said, aware that she was blinking rapidly now, on the verge of angry tears. "It's Lieutenant Rian Becket, cavalry officer in the Thirteenth who I'm searching for, Sergeant-Major. My brother."

Sergeant-Major Hart rubbed at his florid face

with the palm of his hand. "Brother, eh? At least there's no bun in your oven, thank the Virgin. Seen that enough, I have. He'll not be thankin' you for trailin' after him, Private Reilly. Man wants to think he's a man, all on his own."

Fanny nodded, miserable. What had seemed such a grand plan as she'd conjured it up in her bed-chamber, now seemed silly, and impossible. Once out in the sunlight and, according to the Sergeant-Major, even in the dark of the hold, her charade had lasted no longer than the Romney Marsh mist on a sunny August morning.

"He's been here for a bit, sir," Fanny said, giving up any attempt to be soldierlike. "Do you know where he'd be?"

"Right where we're headed in a roundabout way, I'd wager, poor devil. Place called Scendelbeck. You just keep your head down and your yap shut, and you'll be seein' him soon enough. Wouldn't be you, though, lass, when he sees you, not for all the world."

RIAN WATCHED AS the Earl of Uxbridge rode past after a day of reviewing his troops, looking just the sort of romantic hero Rian had dreamed of in his youth, when he'd first thought of war, of soldiering. A rather flamboyant fellow he seemed, the tailoring of his uniform definitely in the first stare, his dark hair waving over his forehead, his brasses twinkling in the sun, the horse beneath him stepping high, seemingly proud of the handsome man on its back.

Wellington had turned command of the cavalry to Uxbridge, but not too happily, Rian had heard, disliking the man's taste for the dash and flash, but as Uxbridge was also the best cavalry general in the whole of the British army, the Iron Duke hadn't really had a choice.

"The dear earl eloped with Wellington's sister-in-law some time ago, you know," said a voice beside Rian…drawled, actually. "A huge scandal, of course, for which the Duke has yet to forgive our handsome Lothario. It speaks to Uxbridge's talents in the field that he isn't still cooling his heels in London, with nothing to do but nag at his tailor."

Rian reluctantly turned his head to see the Earl of Brede next to him, nonchalantly leaning back against the stone fence bordering a sadly trampled wheat field. The man looked no better than he had a few days previously; if anything, he looked worse. Worst of all, those world-weary hazel eyes were still twinkling the way they had in the tavern as Rian dismissed him as a nursemaid, and he still looked more than a little amused.

Rian jumped to the ground and bowed to the man. "My apologies, my lord. I allowed the drink to speak for me."

"That, and your youth." Valentine Clement smiled, running his cool, lazy gaze up and down Rian's well-turned-out figure. Had he ever been this young, this eager? Perhaps before Talavera, before Albuera, Salamanca and the rest. Damn, how he wished this over, and now they were going to have to best Old Boney yet again. "But you've found a batman, perhaps? Neatly pressed, that pretty scarlet coat. Ever pause to think, Becket, what a marvelous target scarlet makes? But you all look so...spiffy, on parade."

Suddenly emboldened, for he was young, after all, Rian gestured at the Earl's filthy greatcoat, the nondescript white shirt and loose trousers. "Better the inconspicuous gray of the field mouse...or the kitchen rat?"

"At times, Lieutenant, yes, it is," Brede drawled, clamping an unlit cheroot into a corner of his mouth, striking a match against the fieldstone, then looking at Rian beneath his brows and the lank, light brown locks that fell over those brows as he put flame to tip. There was something cold, almost calculated, about the man, for all his seeming ease and conversation. He didn't suffer fools gladly, not this Valentine Clement, Earl of Brede and rumpled spy. "We move soon."

"Do we?" Rian said, keeping his own tone even. "And I suppose you know where we're going?"

Brede looked around at the dismissed soldiers, all carrying their rifles inelegantly slung over their shoulders as they headed for any space of ground or comfortable flat rock they could find, still sweating like fatted pigs from another full day of marching about to impress their superiors. He sighed, shook his head. As if marching ever won a battle— although strict discipline did, and that was really the point, wasn't it? Poor bastards, marching straight into cannon fire whenever the order came. Not for him, not for Valentine Clement. He'd live or die on his own merits, using his own wits, making his own decisions.

"Come with me," he said, and then vaulted neatly over the wall, heading for the line of trees at the side of the trampled wheat field, expecting young Becket to follow him.

Rian looked behind him, saw Captain Moray wink at him and carefully secured his sword at his side before hopping onto the wall, sliding his legs over and down, to follow after a man he couldn't quite seem to like. Probably because this man had already proved himself, and Rian knew he still had so much to prove.

They made their way through the cantonment, the neat lines of small white tents, the cooking fires now just coming to life again, and into the trees, at which point Brede turned to Rian, looking hard at him again, measuring him again.

"If you don't want to tell me anything, I—" Rian began, only to be cut off by a wave of the Earl's hand.

Brede inhaled hard on the cheroot, blew out a stream of blue smoke and then said what he'd come to say. Hell of a thing, being beholden to somebody. Even Jack, who'd saved his life for him, twice. But he'd be damned if he'd wrap this pretty boy in cotton wool. Every man has to be given the right to prove himself, sometime.

"Jack swears you've got a good head, can ride anything with four legs or even less, know how to shoot, and how best to use that pretty sticker you've got strapped to that neatly pressed uniform. You know your place, says my old friend, and how to guard a secret. Now, listen to me. You saw Uxbridge today, Becket. Frippery fellow, you'd think, looks useless, but you stay close to him if you can. He knows what he's about, he's as hard as rock at his center. By tomorrow the Eleventh, the Twelfth, the last of the Thirteenth, the Sixteenth and the Twenty-third—they'll all be here. Light Dragoons, mostly. You'll be maneuvered all over hell and back at a field not far from here, eight, possibly ten hours or more a day, until Uxbridge is satisfied. After that, Becket, rest. Rest as much as you can, you and your horse. Stay sober, feed your belly, keep your socks dry—hang the wet ones around your neck, dry them that way, and for God's sake don't lose your extra

pair. Your feet rot off and you're no good to anybody. The next time the men move from here,
Becket, it will be into battle."

Rian felt his blood singing through his veins.
"When? Where?"

Brede smiled, the cheroot still stuck in the corner
of his mouth, and Rian was still having trouble
separating the unkempt clothes from the obvious
intelligence in those piercing hazel eyes. God, he
looked the ruffian. Not an earl at all, at least not at
all like the Earl of Uxbridge. "I'd guess Quatre Bras
or Ligny, somewhere in that direction, although
nobody else does. Not yet. But they will, I can only
hope, once I've made my final report. Now, listen
to me. We can none of us stop this, you understand?
The Alliance won't allow it, Napoleon can't avoid
it. But I can get you out of here."

"Jack asked you to do that?" Rian could barely
see through the bright red of his sudden fury.

Brede smiled. "No. But he holds an affection
for you, and I have an affection for him. I also have
enough consequence to get you reassigned to
Wellington's own staff. He needs good men, with
Pakenham and so many others cut to pieces in New
Orleans, damn that stupid war for the folly it was."

Rian nodded his agreement. "My brother Spencer fought at Moraviantown. He called that battle
considerably less than laudable."

Brede brushed aside the comment. He had places to go before nightfall. "The Duke doesn't hide, so if you're with him, you're not out of danger. But there's more than one way to fight a war, Becket. With your body, thrown into the field against other bodies, or with your brains." He extracted the cheroot from his mouth, stared at the glowing tip now that the sun was sliding toward the horizon and it was growing darker beneath the trees. "I offer this only the once, Rian Becket, and for the sake of an old friend who did me more than one good turn on the Peninsula. As you so rightly said—I'm no nursemaid."

"Thank you, my lord," Rian said, bowing to the man. "I would, of course, be honored."

"Only a damn fool wouldn't be," Brede said, smiling once more. "Two days from now, as I have things to do, things that don't concern you. I'll see you on Monday, exactly here, sometime before noon, with new orders for you in my possession. You will be ready to go, or I'm leaving without you. Understood?"

Rian opened his mouth to answer, but the Earl of Brede had already turned to walk away, taking no more than ten steps back out onto the wheat field before gracefully throwing himself up onto the saddle of a sleek, dappled gray stallion whose head had been held by no less than Captain Moray.

Brede turned the horse, pulled back on the reins so that it reared up on its back legs as the Earl threw Rian a casual salute, and then he was gone, gray figure and gray horse soon fading into the equally gray twilight.

"Uxbridge isn't the only flamboyant one," Rian mumbled as he headed toward a grinning Captain Moray. "He merely dresses better...."

CHAPTER FIVE

THIS WASN'T TOO TERRIBLE. The countryside was beautiful, the air not too uncomfortably warm, and the horses a grand protection. Fanny might miss her soft bed and Bumble's fine way with a chicken, but the adventure made up for that.

And, with every mile, she drew closer to Rian.

"Who will probably attempt to box my ears for me," Fanny muttered quietly behind the scarf she'd tied around her nose and mouth to keep out the dust raised by the horses.

She rode at the back of the troop, which meant that after the dried strip of beef she'd had for breakfast, she was having road dust for luncheon. Mentally, she added the lovely tin tub in her bedchamber at Becket Hall to the list of things she missed most.

"Private Reilly!"

Fanny rolled her eyes and straightened her slim shoulders. Honestly, the man was constantly at her; her own father didn't guard her half so closely. Of course, if he had, she wouldn't be riding across Belgium at the moment, would she? "Yes, Sergeant-Major!"

"We'll be at the cantonment in another few minutes. Just around the next bend, I'm told. Now, here's what I'm doing. You'll see that brother you've come all this way to see, and then you'll be off to Brussels with the rest of the women who had nothin' better to do than follow along with us. No women here for much longer, Private Reilly, to help with the cookin', the washin'. Uxbridge won't allow it. You'll have plenty to do, helpin' with the wounded when the time comes, honest women's work, and then you'll be shipped off home, wherever that is."

"But, Sergeant-Major—"

The Sergeant-Major shook his head, sighing in an exaggerated way. "And here she goes again, dear God, thinkin' she has somethin' to say to any of this. Show me an army of women, and I'll show you pure disaster, every one of them questionin' me, thinkin' she knows best. 'Oh, no, Sergeant-Major Hart, we should camp farther from the stream, it's too damp here. We'll catch a sniffle.'"

Fanny pulled down the scarf and grinned at the man. "When you get to heaven, Sergeant-Major, the good Queen Boadicea may have a word or two to say to you."

For the first time since she'd encountered the

Sergeant-Major, Fanny saw the man smile. "Her? She was only in a snit."

"She raised an army against the Romans, destroyed London and was responsible for killing seventy thousand soldiers. That's a bit more than a *snit,* don't you think? And then we might discuss the Maid of Orleans, the famous Joan—"

"And they don't know when to stifle themselves, women don't," the Sergeant-Major grumbled, pulling on his muttonchops. You'll be goin' on to Brussels, where it's safe, you hear me?"

Fanny was fairly certain she shouldn't ask him to say *please,* and simply nodded her agreement. "I was stupid, sir. I shouldn't have come."

The Sergeant-Major slapped his huge thigh. "Well, now, that's what m'sister shoulda said, back in aught-six. But she chased her Bobby Finnegan all the way to the Peninsula. He didn't thank her for it, any more than this brother of yours will be thankin' you. Dead these eight years, the both of them."

Fanny's stomach clenched. "On the Peninsula?"

He nodded. "Caught a fever, like so many. Private Reilly, I've seen men starve. I've seen men drown in holes they dug to protect themselves from the enemy. I've seen... You do what I say. I'm not to be havin' you on my heart along with my Maureen. I've no one now, no home, no family. So I take good care of you boys...you all."

Fanny pulled up the scarf once more. "I'm sorry, Sergeant-Major, that I've worried you, even as I realize how fortunate I am that you're the fine man you are. When this is over, I know my papa will want to shake your hand, want to thank you. Will you please remember this? Becket Hall, in Romney Marsh. If I could find my way here, you can find your way there. You'll always have a welcome and a home there if you wish it, that's a promise. Papa has a great respect for honest, brave men."

Sergeant-Major Hart looked at her rather incredulously, but then nodded. "Becket Hall, in Romney Marsh. I'll remember. Now, you stay with these horses, tend to them, and I'll find your Lieutenant Becket for you. Mayhap keep him from saying what he should say. And no tears from you, Private Reilly. You hear me?"

"Yes, sir!"

He shook his head in mock dismay. "Such a simple thing, lass. *Sergeant-Major.*"

Fanny grinned behind her scarf as he rode back toward the head of the line. "Such an honorable man—*sir.*"

And then, because she knew she'd been wrong to follow him, because she knew Rian was going to tell her how wrong she'd been to follow him—and at some length—Fanny blinked away her tears and prepared to do battle with the man too stupid to know she loved him. Had always loved him.

RIAN WATCHED the Sergeant-Major walk away and then turned to look at his sister as she sat cross-legged on the ground in front of him. Her face was smudged brown with road dirt from the middle of her cheeks to the top of her butchered blond hair, the whites of her eyes and their emerald-green centers thrown into stark relief above the bottom half of her face, which seemed unnaturally pale.

And she was in uniform. Even the Sergeant-Major, who had been pleading her case for her—if calling her a brainless baby was pleading for her—had been aghast to hear her at last admit how she'd come by that uniform.

Rian stayed seated on a large flat boulder, his elbows over his knees, staring at her, and said nothing.

He was quiet for a long time. He looked so sad to Fanny, so angry. So disappointed in her. She longed to run her hands through his black as night hair, put the blue sky back into his stormy eyes. If, as he'd said, she was pretty, he was beautiful. Like some tragic Irish poet, his brothers had always teased him. Almost too pretty to be real. He'd wondered why she'd worried for him, followed after him?

Her heart broke for him. She swore she could feel it break.

"Rian?" Fanny said at last, as the grass was wet, and her rump was getting cold. That was the difference between them—he felt his own torment, while she, more pragmatic, mostly felt the damp. "I said I was wrong. I said I'd be willing to go to Brussels."

Rian swore sharply and leapt to his feet. "Well, Fanny, isn't that above all things marvelous? You'll go to Brussels. You'll do us all this great favor—after making a bloody mess and having the family out of their minds, worrying about you. Hell, they'll probably all be here by morning, looking for you. Why, we'll have us a party, won't we? *Jesus!*"

"Oh, don't be so dramatic. They won't do that. Will they? Come here? Not Papa, surely. He never goes anywhere."

Rian beat his fists against his chest, reminding Fanny of her mother rhythmically beating her fist against her chest just before the sky fell in on them all. "This is *my* time, Fanny! My turn, damn you. I'm not some infant who needs caring for, and I damn well don't want to be caring about you. Not now. This is *war,* Fanny—not some bloody adventure."

"You always said it was an adventure," Fanny said, then quickly bit her lip. She should keep her mouth shut, Sergeant-Major Hart had warned her. *Take all he throws at you and don't argue with him.* "I…I'm sorry. Go on."

"Go on?" Rian looked around the small clearing, the same clearing he had stood in only days earlier with the Earl of Brede as that man offered him a place on Wellington's staff. Well, Fanny had put paid to that, hadn't she? "Damn you, Fanny! We're not children anymore. We're not on the island. We're not even at Becket Hall, chasing across the Marsh together. And hear this, Fanny—you're my sister. You're my bloody *sister!*"

"No, I'm not," Fanny whispered. "I was never your sister, and you were never my brother. You were my friend. And…and I love you."

Rian turned his back on her, his chest stabbed by a very real, physical pain. "Sweet Jesus," he said, looking up at the trees, seeing the sun almost straight above his head through the leaves. He'd seen this coming, for years, Fanny's infatuation with him. He wasn't an idiot. Or maybe he was, but was this the time for that most important conversation? No, damn it all, it wasn't. Not with Brede showing up at any moment.

He turned back to her, held out his hand to pull her to her feet. "There's no time for this now, Fanny. The Sergeant-Major said he'd make arrangements for you to ride to Brussels with the other women tomorrow or the next day—three at the most. Did you bring a gown with you in that pack you're carrying? You're not staying in uniform. I won't allow it."

Predictably, Fanny's despair flashed into anger. They'd often fought, growing up together. Fought together, as well as laughed together, cried together. "You won't *allow* it? And who are you, Rian Becket? You said you're my brother, you're not Papa. You can't tell me what to do. *I* won't allow it!"

Rian felt his own anger drain out of him, to make more room for the fear—fear for Fanny that she didn't seem to understand. "You do have a gown. You wouldn't be so angry, if you didn't have a gown rolled up in here," he said, grabbing the pack before she could move toward it. He unbuttoned it and dumped the contents onto the grass. "And there it is. I don't suppose you thought to bring a brush— and some soap." He picked up the gown, tossed it at her. "Go back into the trees and put this on."

"No."

"Fanny…"

She held the rolled-up sprigged muslin against her chest and glared at him through slitted eyelids. "I *hate* you."

"Oh, dear me. Have I somehow stumbled over a lovers' quarrel? A thousand pardons, Lieutenant Becket, I'm sure."

Rian swore under his breath. *Brede.* You'd think the man had rags wrapped round his boots, muffling his steps, he moved so quietly.

Fanny whirled about to see a man standing behind her, negligently leaning against a tree trunk. He was dressed all in dark gray, a long white scarf carelessly looped around his throat, his mussed, sunlightened tawny hair falling from a ragged center part to the middle of his cheeks. His brows were low over amused hazel eyes and he had a straight, faintly wide nose; a slight growth of beard smudged those cheeks. The unlit cheroot trapped in the corner of his wide, full-lipped mouth made him seem rakish. Dangerous.

And he was looking at her in a way that made her wish herself back at Becket Hall. In her bed, under the covers. Behind a locked door.

"Lieutenant?" he said, pushing himself away from the tree trunk, and he advanced on them both with a slow, almost insolent grace. "You'll not be introducing me to the…lady?"

Fanny smacked her palms against the sides of her head in frustration. "Have I fooled *no one?* I cut my hair. I'm wearing a uniform. I'm *filthy.*"

The man removed the cheroot from his mouth and leaned close to her ear. "And you most unfortunately smell very like a horse. There's also that, my dear. Becket? An explanation, if you please. Quickly. I'll be in Brussels by nightfall, with or without you. We are at war, if you'll recall the matter? There's no time for private skirmishes."

Fanny looked to Rian to see the telltale flush of

anger in his cheeks. She wasn't an idiot. She knew she'd ruined something for him, and it was up to her to make it right again.

She held out her hand in her forthright way. "My name is Fanny Becket. I'm afraid, sir, that I'm at fault here, entirely. I gave in to impulse and donned this…masquerade, in order to follow my brother. And now, if you'll excuse me, I'll—"

"Your sister, Becket?" Brede said, ignoring her hand. "And I imagine Jack has an affection for her, as well? Christ. He should have just let them shoot me. It would have been a mercy compared to this. I was not fashioned to run herd on an unruly nursery. *Becket?*"

"Sir! Arrangements have been made for her, my lord. I'm free to go whenever you wish."

Free to go, was it? Oh, Rian would pay for this! But she understood his eagerness. Then Fanny frowned as she looked at the strange man once more. *My lord? My lord what? My lord Ratcatcher? And yet there were those eyes, and that cultured voice. And, again, those eyes…*

"You'd leave your sister, Becket? Perhaps you're not the man Wellington needs."

"No! No!" Fanny raced into speech at the sound of the name. Wellington? Rian all but worshipped the Iron Duke. She went to her knees, hastily stuffing her belongings back into the pack. "Truly, my lord, this is all my fault, and Rian has already made arrangements for me. I'll be quite safe. *Please* take him with you."

Rian bent down, put his hands on her shoulders, gently pulling her to her feet even as she was hastily pushing a decidedly feminine undergarment back into the pack. "No, Fanny. Beckets don't grovel, not even to the Earl of Brede. You're my responsibility. My lord, I thank you for your intervention on my behalf, the trouble you've gone to, but I'll be staying here until I know my sister is safely on her way to Brussels with the other women in less than three days time."

Brede stuck the cheroot back into the corner of his mouth and clapped his hands together in mocking applause. "Bravo, Lieutenant Becket. A belated self-sacrifice, but not unappreciated by your sister, I'm sure. Miss Becket, the uniform will suffice for now, but not for long. The two of you—be ready to leave here in twenty minutes, not a moment more."

"But, sir—"

"Becket, don't make me regret this bit of charity even more than I do now, which is considerably, by the way. We go to Brussels, where your sister will be placed in the house I've taken there—locked inside a room there if she protests—and you and I will continue with our business."

Fanny would have hugged the man's neck, except that she'd also rather die than do anything so foolish. "Thank you, my lord."

Brede removed the cheroot once more, smiled down at her—my, he was tall. "Oh, no, Miss Becket. Don't thank me. You'll only regret it later."

CHAPTER SIX

THEY RODE INTO Brussels with the sun just sliding behind the Gothic buildings at the heart of the teeming city filled beyond overflowing with, Valentine thought, imbeciles.

Had half of fashionable London gotten together to say, "Here's a brilliant thought. Bonaparte has escaped, he's marching somewhere on the Continent with a reformed *Grande Armeé,* there will be a terrible battle, perhaps a terrible war—what say we all go watch? What fun! Jolly good time, what?"

Idiots. Fools. Did they plan to ride out in their fine open carriages, picnic on some grassy hill overlooking whatever battlefield might present the best view of the carnage?

There were times Valentine Clement heartily despised his fellow Englishman. Or perhaps he was tired, weary to the heart. Of war. Of the things he had witnessed, things he had done.

He'd not spoken above a few words to young Lieutenant Rian Becket, and less to his sister, in the past several hours, but had turned inward, considering what he'd learned on his last foray into French territory, and how best to present that knowledge to Wellington and the others.

Everyone was so sure the battle was still weeks away, and the Russians and Austrians would have by then swelled the ranks of the British and Prussians, turning that battle into a rout.

But if they were all wrong and he was right? What then? If he was right, even Blücher's Prussians might not arrive in time, leaving Wellington's depleted force alone to face what could be more than seventy thousand Frenchmen. All those French soldiers and, much worse, the most gifted, charismatic commander the world had seen in a long time.

And, while he should be thinking—gathering the right words, the most convincing arguments— Valentine was instead playing nursemaid to a foolish young girl whom he'd deem as having more hair than wit, if it weren't for the fact that she'd damned near shorn herself like a spring sheep in a ludicrous attempt to pretend she was a man.

With eyes like that? Granted, her brother was a shade too handsome to be taken seriously, but at least he was obviously male. This Fanny Becket, with her catlike, tilt-tipped green eyes, could no more conceal her sex than she could climb to the top of that bell tower over there and hang from the steeple while singing verses of "God Save the King."

The coach traffic on the streets had slowed them, and Valentine kept his slouch hat pulled down low over his face to lessen the chance that anyone would recognize him, try to stop him. He needed his house, his valet, a hot tub and a hot meal. He had no time to be corralled by some curious peer who wanted nothing more than a fine bit of gossip with which to regale his companions at tonight's dinner party, tonight's ball.

Valentine heard a muffled giggle from behind him, and turned back sharply to remind Miss Becket that someone in her tenuous position should have precious little to laugh at. But then he smiled, for the young woman who seemed completely at ease in her uniform, riding astride, was pointing toward the public fountain featuring the figure of a small boy urinating into the water.

"The *Mannekin-Pis,* Miss Becket," he told her, and watched as she blushed furiously and dipped her head so that he couldn't see her face. "Very famous. It amuses you?"

"No, my lord," she muttered, and for the first time since Valentine had met with him today, Rian Becket grinned, looking young and eager, and more than happy to join in the joke at his sister's expense.

Good God, Valentine thought, turning front on

his mount once more, *I* am *a nursemaid. Jack, my friend, we are even, more than even.* He touched his heels to the gray's sides and pushed ahead through the congestion, and a few minutes later they arrived at the narrow house he'd rented.

Not waiting for the other two to dismount, he tied Shadow to the black iron railing fronting the street, and bounded up the full flight of stone steps to the bright red door, banging down three times with the knocker.

The door opened to reveal his man, Wiggins, looking comfortable in shirtsleeves, two buttons open at his neck, his usual lace cravat nowhere in place. "My lord! You...you were not expected."

"I should never have guessed," Valentine drawled, stepping past the short, red-haired man and into the infinitesimally small foyer. "Rouse the cook, Wiggins, as I'm starving. Oh," he added, turning back to look at his two charges, "and...do something with these, if you please."

"*Do* something, my lord?" Wiggins asked, but he'd asked it of his lordship's back, as the man had already bounded up the stairs. "Um..." the servant said, turning to smile rather weakly at Fanny and Rian. "Would...um...would you two gentlemen care to follow me?"

"The one gentleman might, Wiggins," Fanny said, used to the free and easy way of the Becket servants—actually referred to as the *crew* by the Becket family, who had all been raised to lend a hand whenever one was needed. The protocol between London society master and servant was totally lost on her. She looked up the empty staircase, longing to know if this small household boasted more than one bathing tub. "However, I, lady that I am beneath this dirt and uniform, would much rather be pointed in the direction of my chamber so I can wash off this dirt. Would that be possible, please, Wiggins?"

The servant pushed his head forward on his short neck and goggled at her. "A lady, sir? Never say so."

Fanny looked to her brother. "At last, Rian, someone who believes my deception. And at entirely the wrong time."

Rian stepped forward, taking the servant by the elbow and walking him to the other end of the foyer—not a large distance. "My sister, Miss Becket, is in dire need of food, a bath and a change of clothing. Mostly, Wiggins, that change of clothing. Now, how do you suppose two intelligent gentlemen like ourselves are going to manage that, hmm?"

While Fanny kept her head lowered, pretending not to hear, Wiggins said worriedly, "Why, sir, I surely don't know. Your sister, you say?"

"Wiggins!"

All three people in the foyer lifted their heads to

look toward the upstairs landing where the Earl of Brede stood, stripped to trousers and shirt. He tossed a folded square of paper over the railing. "Take this to my sister in the *Rue De La Fourche,* if you please, and fetch her back here with you. Don't allow her to say no or I may have you flogged. And where in bloody hell is my supper?"

He disappeared again, that disappearance followed quickly by the sound of a slamming door, and Fanny rolled her eyes in disgust. "What a monster he is," she told Wiggins, who was in the process of hastily rebuttoning his shirt. "Wiggins, do as he says or else he'll most likely bite your head off. My brother and I will find our own way to the kitchens, as we're able to more than *bellow* to fill our bellies. We'll even fill his for him before he tears down the house."

Wiggins looked caught between loyalty to the Earl and his need to take the note he clutched in both his hands to the man's sister. "I…um, that is…thank you, miss. I'd say I shouldn't be a minute, but the good Lord knows Lady Lucie can't so much as say *good day* to a person in less than ten, so I don't know when I'll be back." He pulled a plain brown jacket out from behind a small marble statue of some Greek goddess and slipped his arms into it. "Did his lordship say anything about… That is, he's not usually so…so in his altitudes. The battle comes soon?"

"It would seem so, Wiggins," Rian said, motioning for Fanny to join him, as he'd opened a narrow door, exposing a set of equally narrow stairs leading down, and from the smells emanating from beyond, felt certain he'd found the way to the kitchens. "So, your master isn't always so unfriendly?"

"Oh, no, Mr. Becket, sir, I wouldn't want you to think that," Wiggins said, winking. "He's always so unfriendly. He just usually takes pains to hide it better. We're sorely short-staffed, what with the city so crowded. So I thank you for your help, sir. We'd best feed him. Soon."

FANNY KNEW SHE WASN'T a patch on her sister Elly when it came to organizing a household. But she'd watched her enough, and had spent enough hours in the kitchens at Becket Hall to know the rhythms and routines of that particular area, usually chopping up carrots as punishment for something she'd done and would doubtless go off to do again once Bumble released her from her stool and pile of vegetables.

Within the hour she had struck up a smiling, gesturing friendship with a buxomy old woman named Hilda, who spoke no English. As for herself, she spoke no German or whatever language the woman kept tossing at her. She'd washed her face and hands at the wooden trough in a corner of the narrow kitchen, shoved some lovely fat slices of ham into her cheeks and made certain a heavily loaded tray had been sent up to the Ogre in the Tower, which is how she'd decided to think of the Earl of Brede.

Her filthy scarlet jacket draped over the back of one of the high-backed chairs, Fanny sat cross-legged on her chair—wonderfully comfortable in her uniform trousers—and looked across the scarred wooden kitchen table at her brother, once again urging him to, for pity's sake, stop pouting and eat something. After all, it wasn't the end of the world, was it?

Rian sat back in his chair, shaking his head at her. "You have no bloody idea how difficult you've made things, do you? Just as long as you're happy."

"Rian, that's not true," she said, waving a fork at him, the threat lessened quite a bit by the small roasted potato stuck on the tines. "I said I was sorry, and I am. But we've suffered no major setback, now have we? I've seen you, I'm safely here with the Ogre, and you're to be joining Wellington's staff in the morning, or even later tonight. I know how happy that makes you. I'll pen a note to Papa tomorrow and I'm sure the Ogre will frank it, so there's nothing to worry about there. All in all," she said, pushing the potato into her mouth and maneuvering it against the inside of her cheek, "daring to overlook my punishment when I get back to Becket Hall, I'd consider the exercise a success."

Rian gave up his moody pose and smiled. "As I remember the thing, you also thought coaxing Molly safely over that five-bar fence a success, even if you'd fallen off and broken your arm in the process, and couldn't ride again for the rest of that summer. But Wellington's staff, Fanny! Can you imagine? I'll be right in the thick of things."

Fanny plunked an elbow onto the tabletop and rested her chin in her hand. Although at least six years her senior, he was so, so young. "What do you suppose you'll do?"

"I've thought about that, about how Brede mentioned how Jack told him I can ride anything with four legs—or even three. So I'm thinking, since I really don't know anything about strategy so that the Field Marshal will be soliciting my opinion on matters, I'll just be one of those riding out again and again, taking orders from Wellington to his generals during the battles. Jupiter will be magnificent there. He may not be the fastest of foot, but he's got the best heart, and he'll go forever. You know that."

Fanny speared the last potato on her plate and popped it into her mouth, mumbled her question around it as she chewed. She knew she was being inelegant, as Elly would call it, but real food tasted so *good*. "So, then, you'll be safely behind the lines?"

Rian shook his head. "Would you stop that, Fanny? But, yes, I'll be fairly safe. Except when I'm riding by myself, between our ranks. Then things might become interesting."

"You're just saying that so I'll worry," Fanny said, gathering up her dish and utensils and carrying them over to the sink already piled high with plates and pots. "But if you're not, please remember to ride low on Jupiter's back, your head close down by his neck, so that you don't present too tempting a target."

Rian set his own dishes into the sink and smiled a thank-you to Hilda. "How many times, Fanny, have I outrun the Waterguard on the Marsh?"

Fanny took a quick look at Hilda, not that she thought the woman could understand her, yet when she answered Rian it was in a whisper. Beckets learned early not to trust many people. "Riding with the Black Ghost and outrunning the Waterguard from time to time as you guard the men moving a haul inland is not facing Bonaparte's army, Rian Becket. I'm just saying—don't go riding along the top of a ridge with the sun at your side, waving your hat in the air, that's all."

Rian bent and kissed her cheek. "You're such an old woman. You've been listening to Court entirely too much, you know. I won't let any of Boney's men kill me. I wouldn't give you the satisfaction of believing yourself right."

Fanny shut her eyes, swallowing down a sob. "Oh, Rian…"

He put a finger to her lips as he turned in the direction of the narrow staircase. Moments later a pair of legs appeared, followed closely by the head of Wiggins, who looked none too happy. "His lordship's sister is here and with his lordship in the drawing room. You're to join them, please."

"Is the Ogre still biting off heads, Wiggins?" Fanny asked as she hastily grabbed her uniform jacket and shoved her arms into it. "Or has food soothed the savage beast?"

"That's very funny, miss," Wiggins said, not smiling at all. "If you were please to follow me?"

Rian pushed a nervously giggling Fanny up the stairs ahead of him, then pulled her aside to insist she spit on his hands so that he could attempt to tamp down her butchered and dirty hair with his fingers. "Now, remember, Fanny-panny. Not a word of protest, no matter what the man says. As Sergeant-Major Hart warned us, even the luck of the Irish runs out from time to time."

Fanny nodded quickly, reluctant to tell Rian that her entire insides seemed to be shaking. Would she be back aboard ship by morning, heading to Becket Hall? Had this all been for nothing? Was the Ogre about to send her on her way?

Together, they entered the small drawing room.

"Ah, and here they are again. It wasn't a nightmare and I'm awake now. How unfortunate," Brede said from his place standing in front of the cold fireplace. Rian stopped short to slam his ankles together and smartly salute him. "Yes, yes, very pretty, thank you, Lieutenant. And the redoubtable Miss Fanny Becket, as well. Don't you look—so depressingly the same."

Fanny opened her mouth, but Rian's elbow was in her ribs before any words could come out, so she merely inclined her head slightly, mockingly, in his lordship's direction.

"My stars, Valentine, you weren't funning me, were you? And you expect me to, as you begged me, *do something* with that? My stars!"

Fanny's attention went immediately to the couch and the petite young woman sitting there, at the moment waving a black-edged lace handkerchief beneath her softly rounded chin. The woman was handsome rather than beautiful—there was too much of her brother in her for beautiful—and dressed in the most becoming mourning black London could fashion.

Not that she held a patch on Brede himself, who was also in black, his linen white as a gull's wing, his streaked light brown hair ruthlessly combed back from his face. Rough and tumble, dirty, he was formidable. Dressed as he was now, he was truly frightening. And, again, those eyes. And that dangerous, smiling mouth...

"Ma'am," Fanny said, caught between a bow and a curtsey, so that she nearly tripped over her own two feet, eliciting a short bark of laughter from the Earl.

"Did you see that, Valentine? Oh, my stars!"

"Lucille, if you could dispense with that repetitious and quite annoying exclamation, so that we might move on? Lieutenant Rian Becket, Miss Fanny Becket, you are in the presence of my younger sister, one Lady Lucille Blight, widow of the late and largely unlamented Viscount Whalley, although she is quite enjoying her blacks, aren't you, Lucille? Please, Miss Becket, don't attempt that maneuver again—you may injure yourself."

"Valentine, you're such a wicked tease," the woman said, waving at Fanny. "Please, call me Lucie. Everyone does. Everyone save Valentine, but I pay him no never mind, although he is quite right about poor William. I don't know what possessed me to think I had to have him, and all over my dear brother's objections. He drank like a fish, you understand, and chased anything in skirts. Oh, don't scowl so, Valentine, it's not as if no one knows. And aren't you pretty, Lieutenant? Valentine—isn't the Lieutenant pretty? You couldn't give me him, could you, and just keep the girl for yourself? You go about looking nearly as bedraggled half the time anyway. I mean, she's wearing *trousers*. My stars!"

Fanny, unable to help herself, actually snorted, and Rian rushed into speech to cover her rudeness. "Thank you, ma'am," he said for lack of anything more intelligent springing into his mind, bowing yet again. "My lord, again I apologize for the monstrous inconvenience my sister and I have put you to, and I would like to say that I am more than cognizant of your forbearance and—"

"Oh, for the love of heaven, Becket, shut up," Brede said wearily, looking at Fanny. "Lucille, what do you think? Can you rescue that?"

"In time for the Duchess of Richmond's ball this Saturday night? That's only four days away. Oh, I hardly think so, Valentine. My stars. When have you known me to perform miracles?"

Brede smiled slightly. "A miracle? Surely, Lucille, you don't see Miss Becket here as on a par with loaves and fishes?"

Lucie gnawed on the side of her index finger as she looked at Fanny, who was caught between amusement and longing to wring the Ogre's neck with his own snowy cravat. "I suppose a bath might be of some small help? And then I could have my Frances attempt something with the hair. And there's this lovely little modiste a few blocks from— Yes, all right, Valentine, if I must. I shall gather all of my depleted strength and attempt to do my best."

This last was completed with the tragic pose and half-gulping voice of the truly put-upon, and Fanny looked at Rian, whose shoulders were shaking as he attempted to tamp down his mirth at her expense.

"That's my brave Lucille. The trials you endure for your quarterly allowance," Brede said bracingly, wondering idly if he was right as to Bonaparte's current position, and the possibility of riding there, lashing himself to the mouth of one of the French cannon. "You're dismissed."

Lady Whalley got to her feet, clearly in a huff. "Dismissed, is it? You drag me away from a perfectly marvelous lamb cutlet, just to dismiss me? Oh, very well." She looked to Fanny yet again. "Tomorrow. But no one can see her until I work this miracle you require of me. Bring her round to the servant's entrance tomorrow morning at eleven. *Clean,* if possible."

Fanny didn't bother to either curtsey or bow as Lady Whalley swept out of the small room, trailing her ruffled black skirts and enough scent to make a meal of by itself, and then turned back to glare at the Ogre. "Definitely your sister, my lord. There's no question there."

Brede ignored her, the cheeky brat. When forced to deal with females, ignoring them had always topped his list of the ways preferable to him. "Lieutenant, you will accompany me tomorrow morning at precisely eight of the clock. You'll be quartered with other more junior members of the Duke's staff, which means the food will be good and the beds dry. Take any opportunity to ride out these next few days, familiarize yourself with the topography of the area—I suggest you concentrate on the area south of Brussels, all the way to Quatre Bras, Ligny, and beyond—as I expect you'll be traveling that ground quite often in the next week or two. But keep an eye out for Boney's advance parties. I last spied one only a few miles below Givet. He's been there before with his army, years ago. But he won't wait for us to come to him there, fight on traditionally French soil. For the moment, I suggest you scare up Wiggins from where he's hiding himself and he'll show you to your chamber. The same goes for you, Miss Becket."

"I'll want a bath," Fanny dared.

"If you are applying for my opinion, I completely concur. However, I do not number that among my duties to Jack Eastwood. There are other females in this house—I'm sure I've glimpsed at least two of them. Go find one, Miss Becket, and beg a tub. Difficult as this may be for you to comprehend, I have other things to do."

Fanny watched, her mouth screwed to one side, her fists jammed on her hips, as the Earl of Brede quit the room in much the same way his sister had moments earlier. The sound of the door to the street slamming behind him lent her the happy information that the Ogre was gone.

She turned to Rian and grinned. "Papa would adore him, wouldn't he?"

Rian gave a single shake of his head. "If he didn't kill him, yes."

CHAPTER SEVEN

WIGGINS HAD WORKED a small miracle of his own, Fanny decided the next morning as she donned the freshly laundered and pressed gown she'd rolled up and stuffed in her pack. She'd had a bath last night before slipping in between clean, fresh-smelling sheets, and felt very nearly human again. Her only regret was that she'd slept the sleep of the dead until nine, which meant that Rian had gone off without saying goodbye to her.

But she'd find him again, she had no fears there. After all, she'd found him before, hadn't she?

After breakfasting in her chamber, something she did at Becket Hall only if she was ill or, when younger, when being punished for something or other and temporarily not allowed to "associate with reasonable human beings," she made her way downstairs, leaving her pack and uniform behind her, for Wiggins had promised he'd have the pack sent round to Lady Lucille's later in the day. She'd miss those trousers.

She'd only just entered the small drawing room, wondering when the Ogre would make an appearance and toss her off to his sister, when the Earl, in the act of passing by the entrance, saw her. Stopped. Walked into the room.

She narrowed her eyes, daring him to say anything cutting.

He was dressed in buckskins and a dark blue superfine jacket, and still held a small riding crop in his right hand. He smelled vaguely of horse and tobacco and sunlight, and she knew he'd been out and about, delivering Rian to Wellington's headquarters.

"My lord," she said, dropping into a very abbreviated curtsey. "Rian is now situated with—"

"Hush," he said, using the riding crop to tilt up her chin as he examined her, head-to-toe. He walked slowly around her, and she was rather forced to turn with him until he allowed the riding crop to slide from her chin to her modestly revealed shoulder, skim across her back, and finally come to rest against the base of her throat before he, now standing in front of her once more, removed it. "I was afraid of this," he said at last. "The hair remains an issue, naturally, but you're quite attractive in that gown, Miss Becket."

Would he stop looking at her that way! The way, she realized, her cheeks flushing, she was looking at him!

"And…and that's made you unhappy, my lord?" she asked, unable to tear her gaze from his.

"Uncomfortable, Miss Becket," he said, abruptly turning away from her to pick up a folded newspaper that someone had placed on the table between the couches. Reading whatever ridiculousness the French newspapers were spouting now was much preferable to looking into those exotic green eyes. "There's a difference. How old are you?"

Fanny felt herself bristling. But he'd been nice to Rian, and he still hadn't said anything about sending her back to England, so she bit down her anger. "Twenty, my lord."

Then she lifted her chin, the chin she'd swiped at the moment he'd taken away the riding crop. She had needed the feel of him gone. It had been bad enough, looking into his tired, hazel eyes, and when she'd transferred her gaze to his full mouth that had been…well, that had been worse, although she wasn't sure why. She merely knew that the Earl of Brede bothered her. More than a bit.

"Twenty? My, my," Brede said, dropping the newspaper back onto the tabletop as he looked at her again. "Quite ancient."

"Not nearly as ancient as you, my lord," she said, tiring of this dance he seemed to be doing around her.

"True, Miss Becket. I'm two and thirty, and many mornings feel twice that. This morning, alas, being one of them. Tell me, what did you use to hack at that lovely blond hair? A dull sickle?"

"Frances will fix it."

Brede frowned. "I beg your pardon? Frances?"

"Your sister's maid, or whoever she meant. Lady Whalley mentioned her by name last night. Weren't you listening?"

"I make it a practice to never listen to Lucille," Brede said, smiling at last. "Let that be my advice to you, my dear. You'll thank me for it. Never listen to Lucille. She'll only depress you."

"Really? Oh, my stars!" Fanny exclaimed, her hands to her breast, and then laughed.

And Brede laughed with her.

Which, as it happened, left Wiggins quite nonplussed as he stood at the entrance to the drawing room, clearly unaccustomed to seeing his employer in such a good humor. "Um...my lord?" he asked, as if unsure of the smiling man's identity.

"Wiggins, yes," Brede said, collecting himself. "You're here to say the carriage is waiting, aren't you? But Miss Becket has voiced a desire to see more of the city, so we'll walk to Lady Whalley's instead."

Fanny looked at him quizzically. What on earth was the man about now?

"Um...certainly, sir."

"Ah, my wishes meet with your approval, Wiggins. How reassuring." Brede extended his arm to

Fanny, who hesitated only a moment before slipping her arm through his elbow. "We won't mention your sad lack of a bonnet, Miss Becket."

"*We* just did, my lord Brede," she pointed out cheekily as Wiggins raced ahead to open the door leading down to the flagway. "Oh, what a beautiful day. Look at these grand old buildings. And all the flowers, all the different colors. Everywhere! It's difficult to believe danger could be so close, isn't it?"

"So very close, yes," Brede agreed, looking down at her as she lifted her face to the sun. Smudged, grubby, she had been interesting, different, almost exotic. But the miracle of soap and water seemed to, for the moment, rival that of the loaves and little fishes, for she was now radiant. Young, eager, so very alive. Fearless. And dangerous.

He must be exhausted from too many months spent watching Napoleon's maneuvers around France. He must be old. He must be too long without a woman.

He must be mad.

He must see Fanny Becket smile again. And again. And again…

Fanny was uncomfortably aware of the Earl's closeness to her as they made their way down the flagway crowded with ladies in fine gowns and bonnets, parasols held high over their heads, near hordes of soldiers clad in several different sorts of colorful uniforms, solemn-faced gentlemen walking and talking and gesturing without regard to anyone else on the flagway.

"I've never seen a city this large, my lord," she said, if only to break the strained silence between them.

"You've never been to London?"

"No. I've been to Dover. Just the one time. The largest house I've seen is Becket Hall, which is considerable, but I believe that building just over there, across the square, could make three Becket Halls, with room left over for Becket Village. I'm a bumpkin, aren't I?"

"I'll do my best to forgive you if you promise not to admit to such a terrible sin when we're in company," Brede said, patting her hand as it lay on his forearm. "Jack's signature included the address of Romney Marsh. You'll pardon me my ignorance, but I thought only sheep lived there. And smugglers enjoying the proximity of Calais across the narrow Channel, of course. I imagine your family enjoys French brandy from time to time."

"I wouldn't know," Fanny said quickly. "My father and our family are involved in other pursuits. And Jack now, too, since he married my sister Elly and came to live with us. Have you known Jack for very long? We're all extremely fond of him. And Elly dotes on him, of course."

Brede thought he sensed something almost nervous in Fanny's voice, as if that lighthearted tone was somehow deliberate. Which was ridiculous, as she was young and innocent, and couldn't possibly have anything to hide…other than that atrocious hair, and he was actually beginning to get used to even that. The sun seemed to turn the light, white-gold strands into spun silk. Or spun sugar.

And he was becoming fanciful again.

They were only a few doors from his sister's rented residence now, and Brede knew chances for private conversation with Fanny would be few and far between once Lucille had her teeth in the poor girl. In addition, he'd just received another assignment from Wellington that would take him out of the city until late tomorrow night at the very least.

"Fanny," he said, pulling her over to stand in front of one of the buildings.

"My lord?" she answered, noticing for the first time that he, among all the men on the street, was not wearing a hat. He'd done that for her, she was sure of it; if she had no bonnet, he would wear no hat. She'd thank him, but then he'd probably just say something cutting and sarcastic and make her regret thanking him and long only to box his ears.

"I've written to Jack, explaining that I don't have the time or the wherewithal at the moment to find a way to send you home to your family. Nobody knows where Bonaparte will strike, or when."

"But you said you thought Quatre Bras or Ligny," Fanny reminded him, and then mentally kicked herself, because she probably should not let him know how closely she listened to him.

"He could, I agree. He could also retreat after showing himself, only so that we likewise show him our strength or, at the moment, with no sign of Blücher's forces as yet, our lack of it. He could head west and north, hoping to come at Brussels that way."

"He won't go east, because that's where the Russians and Austrians are advancing against him," Fanny said, as she and Rian had spoken long into the night last night, and Rian had even drawn a small map for her on paper he'd found in the Earl's miniscule study. Then, remembering how much she wanted to remain in Brussels, near Rian, she quickly added, "But he could go west, as you said, skirt around us. No, I certainly can't be riding toward Ostend, can I?"

Brede allowed one side of his mouth to rise in a small smile. "I'm not sending you home, Fanny. Not until this is either over or more manageable than it is now, the situation more stable. You were protected enough, in the eyes of society, with Rian in my house with you last night, but now that he's gone, you'll stay with my sister. I think that's penance enough for chasing your brother across the Channel."

"My sister Morgan says London society ladies are a breed apart. I didn't know what she meant, until I encountered Lady Whalley," Fanny said, smiling. "But please don't worry, I'll manage. Morgan, however, would probably have tied your sister's tongue in a knot at the third 'Oh, my stars'!"

"Your family becomes more and more interesting. I think I'll enjoy escorting you back to them."

Fanny kept her smile in place, even as her stomach did a small flip. The Earl of Brede, at Becket Hall? A man who seemed to see everything, spending time with her family? Clearly, when the time came, she needed to disappear, again. He might follow her; he seemed that obstinate. But at least she'd have time to prepare her family, in case Jack just thought of the man as a friend. "How very... delightful, my lord."

"Valentine," Brede said, watching Fanny's tip-tilted green eyes as shadows seemed to come and go in them. "I have, after all, seen you in trousers."

"I think we can safely forget that memory, thank you," Fanny told him, wishing he would let go of her arm, finish escorting her to his sister's residence. He was beginning to make her very nervous. Not just by what he was saying, but by the way he was looking at her. Rian had never looked at her that way, not ever. As if she was somehow…fascinating to him. She rather liked it.

"Agreed. The memory is consigned to the distant past. However, as you have already shown that you forget nothing you've heard, let me explain about Lady Richmond's ball. It's one of any number of balls, routs, our fellow countrymen are hosting here, as if the world is gathering in Brussels for one large party. Wellington himself hosts at least one a week. I've been fortunate enough to escape most of them, but I can't escape the Duchess of Richmond if I'm in town that night. Barely anyone can. You'll attend, as well, with Lucille, even if I cannot."

"Why? The Duchess of Richmond doesn't even know I'm alive, for pity's sake."

"Ah, but she knows Lucille. And, Fanny, where Lucille goes, you go. She's been warned not to let you out of her sight."

"That's insulting," Fanny told him. "If I give you my word that I won't go…go chasing after Rian again, will I then be able to remain at your sister's? I have no desire to spend an evening standing in a corner, watching people laugh and joke when the world could be turned upside down in an instant."

He felt so damned old. "The world is always poised to go upside down in an instant, Fanny."

She pulled her arm free, turned away from him. "Now you sound like my papa."

Brede smiled at her turned back, fought down the urge to reach out, stroke her sun-bright hair and its poor, chopped ends. "That most assuredly wasn't my intention. In any event, I'll definitely be elsewhere until at least tomorrow evening, so you don't have to fear me barging into my sister's demanding to know your whereabouts."

Fanny turned quickly, putting her hand on his arm, then just as quickly grabbing it back when she realized what she'd done. "You're... Where are you going?"

"And that, my dear, is really none of your business, is it?"

"No, it's not," Fanny agreed, mentally kicking herself for worrying about this arrogant man. She had enough to worry her about Rian, who seemed to have much in common with the Duchess of Richmond and the others, as if Bonaparte marching toward them with unknown thousands of soldiers at his back was just too exciting, too titillatingly delicious for words, and they simply *couldn't* miss out on the fun.

Fanny was very far from titillated. Because she'd been having dreams ever since Rian left Becket Hall. Terrible dreams. Dreams of the island on that last day. She'd been young, too young, to remember that day, and yet, in her dreams, she thought she could hear, as well as see it. Hear the screams of agony. See the white sand, the ghastly red blood soaking into it. Terror then, war coming at them now. Was there a connection? What could that connection be?

She could have gone to Odette, asked her why these dreams, these nightmares, were plaguing her. But then Odette would answer her, and she wasn't sure she wanted to hear that answer.

To Fanny, Rian was the answer. Rian, who had always been her haven of safety. She'd needed to see him, yes. But she'd also fled to him...not that she'd say anything like that to him. He had enough to concern him, what with Bonaparte out there somewhere, planning his attack. But she was frightened about more than Bonaparte. So very frightened...

Brede tipped up her chin with his knuckle, smiling into her eyes. "Such a solemn little face, Fanny. Are you worried about me? How novel. Lucille cares about her quarterly allowance. Of course, Wiggins, bless him, actually seems to have a care or two for my welfare, although he might only worry he won't again find such a congenial employer."

"Yes," Fanny said, banishing her thoughts and forcing some levity into her tone, "I can certainly see that. You are above all things mellow, my lord."

The corners of Brede's mouth twitched in amusement. He didn't understand it. He was feeling younger by the minute, just looking at this girl, just talking to her, teasing with her... having her tease right back at him, just as if she couldn't care a twig about who he was, about his consequence.

He had so damn much consequence; sometimes it hung around his neck like an anvil.

He really did need Bonaparte gone, and himself back in London, where he didn't spend the majority of his time dressed in dirty clothes, with danger all around him and only Shadow for company. "As I was attempting to say before your rude interruption—it's pleasant to believe you might have some small worry for my well-being. Was that what spurred you into asking where I might be going when I leave you?"

What did she feel? Did she feel anything? How could she know? And why would she, for pity's sake? She'd barely met the man. She loved Rian— she'd always loved Rian, ever since she could re- member being alive.

So why was she looking at this man, feeling sud- denly hungry to memorize his every feature? Why was he looking at her in an unsettling mix of amuse- ment and something she felt was far more dangerous?

Perhaps it was the danger itself that hurt her heart, perhaps it was the thought of Bonaparte marching toward them all, turning the world upside down? Everything—the flowers, the sun, Brede's hazel eyes—seemed to be in such sharp relief. *Intense.* "It's… That is, I…"

"Yes, of course," he said, smiling in a way that made her itch to slap the smile from his face. "Exactly as I thought." He offered her his arm once more, and he felt suddenly distant from her, even as he walked beside her….

CHAPTER EIGHT

"YOU'RE NOT AFRAID OF HIM?" Lady Whalley looked at Fanny in some shock, then gave a dismissive wave of her hand as she settled back onto the satin settee she'd earlier sworn had been fashioned by sadistic foreign devils intent on bruising her poor bottom with their outlandishly uncomfortable design. "Oh, you're only saying that to build your own courage. *Everyone* is afraid of Valentine, most especially of his horrid tongue, always so cutting. And that's just the way he likes it. What's worse, Fanny, he absolutely *revels* in their fear. The great, unapproachable Brede. My stars, if I wasn't his sister, I'd cut a wide path around him myself, I vow it."

Fanny was barely listening to the woman. She'd taken Brede's advice, for the most part, and had spent the past two days pleasantly smiling, and nodding, and allowing herself to be guided into gowns, slippers, pelisses, cloaks and several yards of satin ribbon she had no use for at all—although she felt fairly certain Lucie did, and delighted in the fact that all the bills would go to her brother.

Besides, Fanny didn't want to hear about the Earl of Brede. She wanted to *see* him, demand that he take her to see Rian. Rian would have come to her if he could, so obviously he couldn't, which meant she would go to him. Ladies were riding out to the various encampments every day in open carriages, picnic hampers tucked on the facing seat, parasols held high to keep off the warm June sun.

"Are you sure, Lucie," she asked, turning away from the window overlooking the street, where she encamped herself as often as possible, "that you don't wish to ride out to see the troops parade? I'm sure it would be great fun—and you could show off your new bonnet?"

Lucie had lifted her small feet up and onto the settee as she lay back against at least a half-dozen cushions commandeered from every corner of the rented house. "Well," she said, dragging out the word, "I suppose we could. Except—no, Valentine forbade it. He left me very distinct written orders. You are to remain here until he returns. And it hasn't been so long, only yesterday and today. Although I agree, an afternoon can seem a week long, when there's no gaiety. Alas, this is a house of mourning, drat William."

Fanny took up a seat at the very edge of a chair

placed across a low table from the settee, her hands on her knees, about to demonstrate to Lucie the sort of logic that had the rest of the Beckets sighing over her with regularity. "He said I had to remain *here*. Ah, but where is *here*, Lucie? *Here*, as in this house? I don't think so, because we did go out shopping all day yesterday, didn't we? Or did he mean *here*, as in Brussels? Or even *here*, as in Belgium itself? There are so many definitions of *here*. He should have been more clear, don't you think? It wouldn't be your fault that he wasn't more specific, now would it?"

Then Fanny arched her brows, watching the gears begin to turn in Lady Whalley's pleasant but limited brain.

Lucie sat up, sliding her feet to the floor once more. "My stars, yes! He should have been more specific, shouldn't he? That was very lax of him, wasn't it? Exactly where *is* here?"

"I suppose he simply thinks you should *moulder* here, like some warden watching her prisoner," Fanny said, blinking several times in baffled innocence as she turned the screw. "And why he should punish *you*, his dear and loving sister? Why, it passes beyond my imagination, it truly does. Your brother seems to have no consideration for you. Some—not you or I, of course—might even call him a selfish brute."

Lucie drew up her features in a scowl, and then rose quickly, her spine straight, and began to pace.

"Yes, the brute! How *dare* he? Giving me orders, as if he was Wellington himself. My stars! The whole world is here, enjoying the fun, and here I am, *wardening* a perfectly rational young woman who is at least presentable now, no thanks to him, but thanks to *me*. And what is my reward? I'm supposed to just sit here…sit here…"

"Twiddling your thumbs?" Fanny suggested helpfully, then winced, fearing she may have overplayed her hand.

But, with Lady Whalley, Fanny would not only have to overplay her hand, she'd probably have to write on the nearest wall, in foot-high letters: I'm leading you down the garden path, madam.

"Yes! Yes, that's it—twiddling my thumbs," Lucie said, tugging on the bell pull. "The *nerve* of that man! Fanny, run upstairs and have Frances bring me my things. We're going *out!*"

Fanny all but flew up the stairs to alert the maid and fetch her new bonnet—a lovely thing, all buttery-yellow straw, and with cherries on the brim—and was back in the hallway before skidding to a halt, remembering her gloves and shawl, and skidding back into the small bedchamber to retrieve them. Seconds later, and only slightly out of breath, she was descending the stairs in a most ladylike-Elly fashion, a refined young miss about to take the air.

Frances came huffing and puffing from the rear

of the narrow hallway, having had to negotiate the steep servant stairs, and the carriage was waiting for them in the street.

Fanny kept looking to her left and right, sure Brede would show up somehow and ruin all her fine plans, but the carriage, a pretty thing of foreign make, with its leather top folded down so that she and Lucie were sitting in the sun, moved off toward the wide avenue at the corner.

"You forgot your parasol," Lucie scolded as Frances, commandeered to ride along, unfurled Lucie's and held it over her head. "Are you going to make me order the roof put up? Oh, stars, I hope not. Nobody's seen *my* new bonnet as yet, you know." She frowned. "I don't know that I should have let you have that one. I do like those cherries. Perhaps even more than my silk roses. I'm just so glad William's gone six months now and I can wear my lavenders, too. Black is so boring, although I will say I do believe it flatters me."

Fanny smiled and nodded, and Lucie kept on talking, when she wasn't waving at passersby and then making quiet comments to Fanny. "Did you see her cane? My stars, does she think wrapping it in satin ribbon will make anyone forget she's older than dirt? Oh, look, isn't that the Marquess of Daventry? Yes, yes, it is! And doesn't he look marvelous in his uniform? So handsome. Yoo-hoo—Banning!"

"I don't think he heard you, Lucie," Fanny said, biting on the insides of her cheeks, as the man had most definitely heard Lady Whalley, and seen her, but he'd then made a quick business out of stepping into a nearby shop rather than speak to her. She could be wrong in her conclusion, but she was fairly certain that fine London gentlemen did not make it a habit of frequenting *corsetiers*. Lady Whalley could talk the ears off a donkey, and if she, Fanny, saw a handy corset-makers shop, she might duck into it, too, poor man.

"Well, that is too bad. He's single, you know, and quite wealthy. Although cut much in the same pattern as Valentine, so he most probably would feel the need to throttle me within days of the wedding. Oh, well," Lucie said, sighing, "there are so many other lovely men to choose from. Valentine says I should be on the lookout for a deaf one, but he was just being facetious…."

Fanny bit the insides of her cheeks once more, nodded, and then pretended a great interest in her surroundings as Lucie prattled on and on about nothing.

Not that she had to feign interest for long, for Brussels was quite the largest city she'd ever seen, and full of things to look at, admire. Several times she saw scarlet-jacketed soldiers traveling in groups down the flagway, but none of them walked with that certain elegance and grace that came so naturally to Rian.

It was only when the carriage left the city for a smooth path that ran along through greener-than-green grass that Fanny began to despair of finding her brother, for the fields seemed to have grown full regiments of scarlet-jacketed soldiers. They were everywhere, some marching in close formation, others sitting in groups, cleaning their weapons, others cooking over small fires.

"Oh, wait," she said at last. "There, just at the crest of that hill, all those large tents. That must be the Duke's headquarters, don't you think?"

Lucie sat up straight and squinted into the sun. "Yes, I would suppose Wellington could be there. See the flags? Everything looks so…regimental. Do you think your brother is with him? He'd make a lovely excuse to get down and stroll about a bit, don't you think? Unless you think the sight of a widow in her mourning, even her half-mourning, would perhaps be seen as a bad omen? You know, it would have been ever so much better if William had died in battle rather than by simply falling off his horse and cracking his head in the gutter, because then I'd be welcomed as the widow of a hero. That was so inconsiderate of him. But, then, that was William all over, and never a thought for me."

Fanny opened her mouth to say something, but then realized that, as with so many of Lucie's statements, there was just no proper way to comment, to answer. "There—I see Jupiter. Rian has to be here. Please tell your coachman to stop."

"Jupiter? But isn't that a— Oh, my stars, you don't mean a *planet,* do you? And not some ancient God, either, I'd imagine."

"Lucie, *please?*" Fanny said as the carriage moved on along the roadway. "I really want to stop here."

Lucie called an order to the coachman and then looked at her reprovingly. "High-strung, aren't you, my dear? But I can see the grass, Fanny, and it's still wet from last night's rain, so I'll just sit here and you can take Frances with you to— Oh, my stars! Fanny, you should wait for the coachman to put down the stairs."

But Fanny had seen Rian striding toward Jupiter, and she wanted to reach him before he could mount and ride off. She'd fussed with the handle of the low door for a moment, ready to vault over it if the latch wouldn't budge, and then jumped down to the ground, almost immediately feeling the squish of water running into her brand-new black patent slippers. She lifted her skirts and headed up the hill.

"Rian, wait!" she called out when she was half-way there and a Private was holding Jupiter for him to mount. At first she thought he didn't hear her, or was going to ignore her as the Marquess of Daventry had ignored Lucie. But then he turned her way, his fists jammed on his hips, and impatiently waited for her to climb all the way to the top of the hill.

"Well, look at you," he said, his tone not all that welcoming. "Does his lordship know you're off the leash?"

"I don't care what his lordship knows," Fanny said, still holding up her skirts, as the hill was not only wet, but covered in horse manure. "Don't let Jupiter get any of this mess stuck beneath his shoes or he'll—"

"Fanny, I know how to take care of my own horse," Rian interrupted, and then looked past her, toward the carriage. "How's Lady Oh-my-stars? Are you behaving yourself?"

"She's still breathing, isn't she? Although, I'll admit it, yesterday in the shops, and again this morning, it was a pretty close-run thing," Fanny grumbled, and then smiled when Rian laughed out loud. "Have you seen the Duke yet, Rian? Did you talk to him? Are you going to be a courier, or whatever?"

"I'll be taking messages, orders, to our commanders, yes," Rian said, visibly preening. "I spent all day yesterday doing as the Earl said, riding out with Jupiter, all the way to Ligny, as a matter of fact. I'd like to be in the thick of things, smack in the battle, but this is important, Fanny. Deadly important. If only Blücher's army would show itself before Boney does. We're outmanned,

Fanny. We may be the better men, but there aren't enough of us. Not with the news the Earl brought this morning."

Fanny felt her stomach do a small flip. "He's here? He's back?"

"That he is. Rode in here an hour ago, his horse all lathered, and nearly fell out of the saddle. He saw them, Fanny. At least a small party, probably out looking for us. And he got too close, if you ask me. I saw a hole from a ball in his cloak. He's with the Duke now."

"They *shot* at him?" Fanny turned toward the tents, suddenly feeling slightly sick in her stomach. "How do you know he wasn't hit?"

"Because he told me," Rian said, grinning. "Right before he cordially told me to go to hell, asking asinine questions, because he was still walking, wasn't he? I like him, Fanny, so don't pest him out of his mind the way you do the rest of us. He wrote to Jack yesterday, told him you're all right and that he'll act as your guardian until he can get you home again. So you're his ward now, I think it's called, and that means he's in charge of you."

"Oh, he is not," Fanny protested, wishing she felt as confident about that as she sounded. "You're here. You'll act as my guardian."

Rian pushed his spread fingers through his dark hair. "But you see, Fanny, the thing is, I don't want to. I already know you'd drive a monk to drink, but the Earl doesn't. Let him find out for himself."

"And that's fine with you?" Fanny asked him, looking at him narrowly, and in some disappointment. "You'll just hand me over to him, a stranger, and wash your hands of me?"

"I washed my hands of you—no, let me start over before you launch yourself at me. I *said good-bye* to you at Becket Hall, Fanny. I'm here now, where I want to be, and it's not my fault you got it into your head that we…that we…"

"That I love you," Fanny whispered, as three soldiers walked by, on their way to their horses. "That you love me. That you'd want to see me as much as I needed to see you. Rian, I've been having strange—" She clamped her mouth shut, realizing she'd almost blurted out some nonsense about her frightening dreams, had almost added to his worries. "Please, Rian, understand…."

Rian's hair took another raking from his stabbing fingers. "Oh, Christ, Fanny-panny. I *do* love you. You're my sis— My best friend," he corrected quickly. "My very best friend, Fanny. But you're young, and you've never seen the world."

"And you have?" she asked him, blinking back tears as she looked into his beautiful face. His kind eyes. Didn't he know that he was her world?

"I've been to London. Twice," he pointed out,

avoiding her eyes. "All right, I grant you, only for a few days each time. But at least I've been out of Romney Marsh, seen that there is a world out there—out here. You only know us, Fanny. You can't know what you want. *Who* you want."

"I want you to come home, Rian," she said brokenly, a single huge tear spilling down her cheek. "I don't want to lose you. I can't bear to lose you."

"Ah, Fanny-panny," Rian said, gathering her close against his chest. "I'm coming home. Just as soon as we send those Frenchies to hell. I promise."

"Lieutenant Becket? Perhaps I misunderstood. Weren't you ordered to ride to La Haye Sainte and bring word from our forward parties reporting there?"

"Yes, my lord," Rian said, putting his hands on Fanny's arms and gently pushing her away from him. "It's just that…my sister— I'm on my way, sir!"

"Oh, no, Lieutenant," the Earl of Brede drawled. "There's no need to rush off. I'm sure his grace will understand any delay. Why, I'm convinced your sister will be more than happy to explain to the man that it's more important for the two of you to have a lovely coze out here in the sunlight than it is to bring him his information."

Fanny turned about, swiping at her moist eyes as she glared up at him, once against clad in his filthy gray clothes. "Oh, cut line, my lord. Anyone would think you're in love with the sound of your own voice."

"Fanny! My lord, I must apologize—"

Fanny whirled on him. "I can speak for myself, Rian," she told him warningly.

"Yes, you can," he shot back at her. "And you do, don't you? Even when any sane person would know to shut her mouth." Rian sighed, caught between anger and a grudging respect for his sister's tenacity. "Please, Fanny, be good. I know you can, if you apply yourself." He bent and kissed her cheek, hugged her against him for a moment, and then bowed to the Earl and mounted Jupiter. "Behave yourself. For me, Fanny," he said quietly, looking down at her, and then he turned the horse and walked him toward the southern perimeter of the camp.

Fanny watched him go, wondering when she'd see him again, and then straightened her shoulders, feeling as if the Earl of Brede was boring a hole in the center of her back with those strange hazel eyes of his. She began counting, wondering how long it would take before he gave in to his own meanness and said something cutting to her.

"He's as safe as I could get him, Fanny," Brede said after a moment, his tone kind and sympathetic. "But, like all of us in these next days and weeks, nothing can be certain. I'm sorry."

She kept her back to him as she nodded, biting her bottom lip to hold back a sob. He was being nice to her. How dare he? She was angry with the Earl, angry with her brother. Men were so stupid, finding joy in risking their lives.

"I know," she said at last, turning to face him, her eyes dry. "He's so happy. How dare he be so happy?"

Brede smiled, shook his head. "He's young."

"He's six and twenty, old enough to know that war is not a game. After what we've—" She closed her mouth with a snap, knowing she'd been about to say *after what we've seen*. "Rian said he saw a hole in that atrocious cloak of yours. Was he correct?"

"There is?" Brede slipped the cloak from his shoulders and held it up in front of him. "Well, fancy that. And your brother would be incorrect. There appear to be two holes in this atrocious cloak of mine. The French are notoriously bad shots, thank God."

Fanny looked past the cloak, to the man. Who was smiling!

"You're all alike," she all but spat at him, her frustration rising up to nearly choke her with its fury. "And you all *disgust* me."

She picked up her skirts and ran down the long hill, straight to where Lucie's carriage was surrounded by eager young men in their scarlet uniforms.

Fanny tugged at elbows and stepped on toes, fighting her way through to the low door, pulling it open and plopping herself down next to Lucie, crowding her terribly. "We can leave now, Lucie," she said, her gaze concentrated on the blue sky filled with small white clouds—a beautiful summer day. The sky didn't know what it and the sun and the stars would be looking down on in a few days or weeks. The blood, the carnage. The *waste*.

"Oh, but don't be silly, Fanny," Lucie said, fanning herself as Frances held the parasol over her mistress's head, "I'm having a most delightful time!"

"How *delightful* would this time be if I were to stand up in this carriage and begin screaming?" Fanny threatened, her voice low. "Obscenities. I believe I'd like to scream obscenities. I've never done it before, but I do know some *extremely* vile words. Shocking words."

Lucie looked at Fanny's chalk-white face. Looked at the dashing Captain of the Guards, who was in the middle of asking her to reserve a dance for him at Lady Richmond's ball. Looked to Fanny. To the Captain of the Guards.

"Oh, my stars! Driver!" she called out just as Fanny opened her mouth, took a deep breath. "Take us home!"

CHAPTER NINE

THE EARL OF BREDE found Fanny in the small garden tucked behind the house his sister had rented at her own expense rather than being "forced to cohabitate with *you,* Valentine, you *bear.*"

Fanny didn't hear his footsteps, but just sat on an uncomfortable-looking iron bench, her back straight, her hands folded in her lap, looking up intently at the star-dotted sky.

Her profile was amazing, her chin cut so cleanly, proudly, above her long, slender neck, her straight nose lending her the profile of some ancient Greek goddess. Even her butchered hair had been salvaged by some genius with a scissors, and had been pulled back severely from her forehead, a mass of fat curls secured at her nape, all of it shining almost silver in the moonlight.

She was so very young, so obviously pure. Clearly outside his touch. He could only destroy that innocence, dampen that glorious, courageous spirit. She was youth and beauty; he felt as old as time itself.

She didn't fear him, wasn't cowed by him, dared to stand toe-to-toe with him, give as good as she got. She didn't simper, but he was sure she would, if it suited her purposes. She'd risk most anything to get what she wanted, what she believed necessary to her.

He could dismiss her as a child, if it weren't for those deep green eyes of hers, century-old eyes that peered from that young, pure face. Those eyes were full of mystery, full of knowledge, bright with intelligence. And yet shadowed. Eyes that had seen bad things, and recognized what was going on around her now as if she had somehow experienced it all before. Or at least the pain of it.

As if, like him, she had seen war, knew the consequences.

Which, of course, was ridiculous.

Her brother's eyes held no such shadows. Rian Becket was a young man like so many young men, primed and eager for excitement, for adventure… for cannon fodder. He'd seen young men like Rian before, hot and ready on the eve of a battle, recognized his younger self in them. He ached for them, longed to shake them, make them realize that the glory they sought to clasp tight in their hands would only sift through their fingers, like ashes gathered from a funeral pyre.

Fanny Becket seemed to already know that. How, Valentine did not know. He'd think it was a matter of her sex, that all females recognized the horror of war, but then what would explain his sister, and all the women gathered here in Brussels, laughing, dancing, eager for excitement?

No, Fanny wasn't like those women.

She lifted her slim shoulders, let out her breath on a sigh. Valentine stepped closer, almost involuntarily, thinking to comfort her. But he'd already tried that, earlier, at the Duke's headquarters, and been rebuffed for his show of sympathy. Fanny Becket, he believed, did not care to be considered an object of pity. His most especially.

"Ah, there you are," he said jovially, watching her body jump slightly as he interrupted her quiet contemplation. "Lucille told me I might find you here. Plotting another escape, are you?"

Fanny turned on the bench to see the Earl clad once more in well-fitting evening clothes, his over-long sandy hair combed severely back from his face, that face wearing one of his mocking half smiles. He wore civilized clothes, but he was far from civilized, no matter his fine manners.

She wondered how he would look in an unguarded moment. Except the man seemed always on his guard, whether dressed in the height of fashion or like a ragman, a vagabond.

"I didn't escape this afternoon, my lord," she told him tightly. "I merely…rearranged my location. And only so that I could see Rian, who couldn't come to me."

"Really? Is he wearing a leg shackle I missed? All of Wellington's staff have town privileges in the evenings. I know this because they clog up every fine restaurant and then crowd the dance floors at every ridiculous party."

Fanny averted her eyes for a moment, so her hurt wouldn't show in them, before glaring up at him. "Rian didn't know where I am, that I've moved to your sister's house."

"Yes, and I tarried behind that move long enough to cut out Wiggins's tongue, so that he couldn't give your brother Lucille's direction."

"Why?" Fanny asked, unable to resist his taunt. "Why must you point out that Rian doesn't want to see me? Does it delight you somehow? He's made it obvious enough, himself."

Valentine indicated the space beside her and, at her grudging nod, split his coattails and sat down on the hard bench. "Because, dear girl, you don't *listen* to the boy. He's caught up in his own dream at the moment, and has no time to think about anything but the moment he's in, and then the next moment after that. Don't distract him, Fanny. He needs to be doing just as he's doing."

Fanny nodded, her heart still aching. "I know that. A part of me knows that. But I keep thinking of things I want to tell him. To keep his head down. To be sure Jupiter is properly shod. To sleep when he can and eat well whenever possible. To not let his socks become damp. To remember that…that people love him."

Valentine rubbed a hand back and forth across his mouth, a thought that had struck him longing to be said, even as he knew he shouldn't say it. But the urge was too strong. "Your brother is a lucky young man. A lifetime ago, when I left for the Peninsula, my father spared a moment from reading his newspaper to tell me to, for God's sake, not disgrace the family escutcheon."

Fanny impulsively laid a hand on his arm. "Perhaps…perhaps he didn't know what else to say?"

"Perhaps," Valentine told her, very aware of the slight pressure of her hand. "He died while I was gone, so I have no way of knowing." He smiled once more. "Although I am fairly certain a fatted calf wouldn't have been butchered for my return. A very proper man, my late father. I was a sad disappointment to him, choosing to serve the way I did— anonymously—rather than openly leading men into battle. He called me furtive, and that wasn't a compliment."

Fanny spoke without thinking. "Goodness, Brede. If you were a sad disappointment to the man's sense of consequence, what was Lucie? The final nail in his coffin?"

Valentine looked at her for a moment, the corners of his mouth twitching, and then he threw back his head and laughed out loud. "My God, I never thought about that. Lucie was still in the nursery when he died. If she ever got to slip her feet beneath the family dining table and actually *speak* to the man, he probably would have had an apoplexy. A mind filled with feathers—that's what he'd say about females like poor Lucille. And, bless her, not without reason in her case, I suppose."

"But you love her," Fanny said, retracting her hand. He had such a nice smile, one that lit up his eyes. And his laugh was deep and unaffected, although perhaps a bit rusty, as if he didn't laugh often. "She told me how good you are to her. Giving her a quarterly allowance, maintaining her estate and house in London."

"That's only to be expected," Valentine said, unconsciously rubbing at his forearm, missing her casual touch. "She is my sister, and her husband left her not only penniless but deeply in debt. I could hardly have her locked up for debt, dropping a basket down through the bars of her cell, angling for farthings from passersby on the street."

Fanny hid a smile. "Yes. That would be bad for *your* consequence. And she'd probably lose her grip on the string and hit some poor innocent on the head with the basket, and end up being hanged for murder. Considering all the possibilities, I suppose you did the only possible thing to protect yourself, and can't be credited at all."

"Exactly," Valentine said, more than willing to add to the nonsense. "It was completely a selfish decision, as are all my decisions."

"Including helping Rian and me?"

He looked at her sharply. "I owed Jack a favor. In fact, I owe him my life, twice over, for services he did me years ago on the Peninsula when I was discovered somewhere I should not have been. However, when I consider what I have endured these past days, and what I surely will endure until I can get you home to your Romney Marsh, I believe the two of us are now even."

"I haven't been that much of a problem to you," Fanny told him, her temper rising. "And my father will repay you for any expenses you incurred. *You* were the one who wrote to Jack to say that you're my *guardian* now, that I'm your ward. Which is just the most absurd thing I've ever heard. I don't need a guardian. I didn't need a guardian to get myself here, now did I?"

Valentine shifted on the bench so that he was facing her. "No, you didn't. What you needed, Fanny, was a *keeper* to make sure you didn't get yourself here. But," he said, raising a hand to keep her from responding, "now that you're here, we'll make the best of things. Lucille outdid herself, you know. You look more than presentable, and I'll be proud to escort you to Lady Richmond's ball tomorrow night."

"Yes? Well, I'm not going," Fanny said, turning to face him, their bodies now only inches apart. "If Rian doesn't want to see me, I most certainly am not going to *impose* myself on him."

"Really? And here I had just begun to convince myself that you aren't a child."

Fanny's palm itched to slap his smiling face. "No wonder Lucie hides from you whenever possible."

"She hid well enough to elope with Whalley," he told her. "And lived to regret it. Don't live to regret not seeing Rian when you could. I'm sure he'll be happy to see you tomorrow night. He would not be delighted to see you chasing him down at Wellington's headquarters again. You do appreciate the difference, don't you?"

"Yes. Yes, I do. I won't drive out there again, I promise." Having apologized, which hurt tremendously, Fanny then changed the subject. "You saw the French today?"

"Early this morning, yes," he told her, then debated with himself for a moment, deciding to tell her the rest. "They're still some distance away, but moving faster than anyone would suppose, I'm afraid. We've sent word to Blücher that a forced march might be necessary if he's to get his troops here in time."

"For the battle," Fanny said, making things clear in her mind. "So it will come soon? You'd said weeks, didn't you?"

"Days or weeks," Valentine reminded her. "Our Russian and Austrian allies will never arrive in time to do more than either congratulate us or bury us, and we can only pray the Prussians will be faster. Fanny, I want you to promise me something."

He was looking at her so intently, seemed to be measuring her. "I will, if I can," she told him, hoping only to ease the worry evident in his eyes.

He smiled. "Now, there's a woman's answer. Very well. If, and I'm not saying this will happen, if you hear cannonfire, if the battle comes that close to the city, I want you to take Lucille and head straight to Wiggins. He already knows what to do."

Fanny moistened her lips, wishing her mouth hadn't suddenly gone dry. "And what does Wiggins know to do?"

"Get you and Lucille the hell out of Brussels, to my yacht moored at Ostend, and back to England."

"No."

"Fanny," Valentine said dangerously, taking her hands in his. "Rian needs to know you're safe. If things go badly, he needs to be able to concentrate on himself, on his orders, and not be worried that his sister could become a casualty, or a prisoner of the French. I need to know that, too."

"About Lucie. Yes, I understand that. But Wiggins will take care of her, surely. You said he knows what to do."

"Not just Lucille," he said, squeezing her fingers in his. "You're also my responsibility, remember?"

"I didn't ask to be," she told him, attempting to free herself from his grasp. "And I can take care of myself."

"No," Valentine said, his eyes searching her face. "That's not good enough. I need your promise."

"And you're not getting it!" Fanny pulled free of his grip and got to her feet, her back turned to him. "Besides, Wellington will be victorious. He's always victorious. That's what he does. He'll send Bonaparte scurrying back to France, his tail between his legs."

Valentine got to his feet slowly, feeling every bit of the day and night he'd spent in the saddle, not once but twice having to push Shadow into a hard gallop to avoid French patrols. "Murat has come to Bonaparte, and Ney, both of them brilliant generals who also know that to fail will be to be tried and executed by the Alliance. He's got most of his Old Guard, men well-seasoned, obedient and more than competent. We've got a hastily assembled army lacking some of Wellington's finest and most trusted aides, and the Russians and Austrians still on the march, nowhere near to close enough to join us. Wellington has hunted on this land, but has never fought on it. The advantages are all in Bonaparte's favor."

She whirled to face him, saying accusingly, "You think we're going to lose."

"No, Fanny, I'm considering the consequences of losing, even as I work and pray for victory. So is Wellington. And the damnable thing is, he also has to think of all his countrymen and women who have come to Brussels thinking they'll be part of some grand spectacle. God, the man has been hosting balls every week, deliberately keeping his tone light, confident, as we pray for more time. If he has to manage a retreat, it will be with coaches and wagons filled with those men and women clogging the road in front of him, hindering that retreat. To be trapped here, in this city, protecting those who couldn't flee in time, would lead to the worst fighting, the most casualties, the greatest danger."

"I…I didn't think of that." She lifted her chin. "But we'll win. I know we will."

"So speaks youth. And you condemn your brother for his eagerness to fight? Fanny, promise me. I'm not ordering you, I'm asking you. If you sense things going badly for us, take Lucie and go to Wiggins."

Fanny looked down at the bricks at her feet, blinking back tears. Then she lifted her head and looked straight into Valentine's eyes. Those steady, weary, mesmerizing eyes. "Yes. I'll take Lucie to Wiggins. I promise."

She was being qualified in her promise, and he knew it. But he also knew she wouldn't give another inch. When the time came, if the time came, he would only have to hope that she'd finally see the sense of his command.

"Thank you, Fanny," he said, stepping closer to her, putting his hand on her arm.

She tried to look away from him, but couldn't. "Where…where will you be? If there's a battle?"

"Probably doing what your brother would be doing. Taking messages to and from Wellington. Reporting on action beyond his vision. And, because I've done this before, making suggestions as to where to best deploy our forces to counter moves made by Bonaparte and his generals."

"Then you'll be in uniform?" Fanny asked.

Valentine smiled. "Hardly. I'm just a lone man on a horse, moving fast in the distance, just at the edge of sight. I leave that sort of sartorial flamboyance to Uxbridge and the rest."

"I would imagine you'd look…very fine in uniform," Fanny said, wondering why they were talking about uniforms when what she really wanted to say was *be careful, please, be careful.*

"Not half as fine as you, my dear," he told her. "I find myself still thinking fondly of the sight of you in trousers, your face brown with road dust, your expression indignant. Daring."

Fanny felt her cheeks burning. "I think Shamus Reilly had fleas," she told him. "Wiggins told me he was forced to hang the uniform in a burlap bag over a smoky fire."

"I'd rather he'd burned it entirely. Where is that uniform, by the way?"

Fanny looked him straight in the eye. "I left it with Wiggins. He was going to bring it to me, but I told him I had no further use for it."

Lying. The girl is lying. "Very good. I'll order him to dispose of it for you."

"You do that," Fanny shot back at him. "You seem to order everything for everyone anyway. Now, if you'll excuse me, I'm tired, and would like to go upstairs to my bed. With your permission, of course."

She curtsied, turned to leave him, and he tightened his hold on her arm, not knowing when, or if, they could ever be private again.

"Fanny. These are trying times. Nervous times. The world is so…intense. Moving so quickly toward God only knows what. People say—and do—things they wouldn't ordinarily say or do. Think things they wouldn't ordinarily think. Imagine things. Risk things. Not always rational actions. But they seem rational, at the time. Even necessary. Inevitable. Like now, for instance. If you'll forgive me…"

She waited for him to make his point, but he said nothing more. He just looked at her. Stepped closer to her. Bent his head to hers.

Fanny closed her eyes as his lips touched hers, lightly, brushing gently. Lingering a moment, then leaving her.

She was twenty years old. Others her age were already married, already mothers. Yet this was her first kiss on the mouth, freely given, hesitantly accepted.

She kept her eyes closed. "Again," she whispered. "Please."

Valentine slipped his arm around her waist and pulled her closer, slanting his mouth against hers once more. This time bolder, but not daring too much intimacy, as the last thing he wanted was to frighten her.

She tasted young, fresh. Innocent. Three things he hadn't been in a long, long time.

He drew back, cupped her head in his hands, lightly rubbed her cheeks with the pads of his thumbs. "Interesting," he said quietly. "Now who, I wonder, is to guard you from your guardian?"

Fanny opened her eyes at last, suddenly, and very wide. "You're laughing at me, Brede, aren't you?"

"No, sweetings, that's the very last thing I'd do," he told her, dropping his hands to his sides. "I'm cursing myself for the fool that I am. Because the very last thing I need on my mind these next days is you. And yet, here you are."

She watched him leave via the gate at the back of the small garden, and then lifted a hand to her mouth. Not to wipe away the feel of him, but to savor that feeling.

She loved Rian. She always had. She hadn't questioned her feelings, not since she'd been a very young child.

But she'd never before felt like this.

A battle was coming, one Brede wasn't sure they'd win. Wasn't it enough that she was frantic with worry for Rian? Did she now have to fear for Brede, too?

What had he said? *But they seem rational, at the time. Even necessary. Inevitable. Like now, for instance.*

He'd believed kissing her to be rational, inevitable? *Necessary?*

"Yes," Fanny said, settling back down on the bench, hugging her arms around her, as the evening was growing cool. "I suppose it was, wasn't it…"

CHAPTER TEN

FANNY HAD NEVER BEEN to a ball, so she could not know that this one was quite modest compared to London standards, held in a large square room once used to store carriages, its walls hastily papered over in a trellis pattern with roses, the guest list numbering only a few dozen over two hundred.

There were several gaily laughing young ladies clad in virginal white or pale pastels present, along with a sea of men of all ages, dressed in scarlet uniform jackets, gold epaulets, dark trousers and high black boots, and a scattering of more sober evening dress.

Musicians were already sawing away on violins, the center of the floor filled with couples in the dance, when Fanny entered the room a few paces behind Lucie, who was dressed once more in stylish lavender, trailing scent like bread crumbs. Fanny's gown was more sedate, a soft lime silk she thought rather beautiful, if possibly too short, but that, Lucie had told her, was the price a female paid if she not only had forgotten to have her maid pack her own gowns for her, but had also insisted upon growing so unfashionably tall.

Fanny searched the room for any sign of Rian, but he wasn't there. Oh, wait, there he was. On the dance floor, smiling down into the face of some petite red-headed girl who was chattering at him each time the moves of the dance brought them together.

He looked happy, a bit mischievous, and achingly beautiful in his finely brushed uniform. He and the redhead stepped closely together in the move of the dance, their hands held up high between their bodies, and he bent to whisper something in her ear.

The redhead laughed.

Fanny turned her back on the pair of them, pretending an interest in the lavender-tipped feathers stuck in Lady Whalley's hair.

"I shan't dance, of course," Lucie told her, looking wistfully at the couples moving around the floor. "It would be unseemly, with William not yet in the ground a year. But I already have four names scribbled on my card, with each of the gentlemen expressing no reservations about sitting with me rather than dancing. Oh, look, isn't that your brother? Ah, and that's Sally Pitney, making calf's eyes at him. Well, why not? He is delicious. Oh, don't frown, Fanny. My stars, even a sister has to know when her brother is more handsome than even broody Byron himself."

Fanny forced a smile to her face. "My other brothers say he is much too pretty, and needs a few scars. They regularly volunteer to give him some."

"Oh, my stars, no! Mar that handsome face? That would be criminal in the extreme. Ah, but never mind. Look, there's the Duke. Now there is a fine hatchet face for you."

"I think him handsome," Fanny said, looking at the tall man who had paused just inside the doors, to bow over Lady Richmond's hand. "Rather like Brede."

Lucie looked at her owlishly. "Like Valentine? Don't be ridiculous, Fanny. They're nothing alike."

"Not in looks, certainly," Fanny said, her gaze still on the door, as Valentine had just entered behind Wellington. "In manner, in the way their eyes seem to look nowhere, yet see everywhere. They... they've *lived,* experienced things, and you can see that on their faces. My papa would call them both seasoned, I believe. My old nurse, Odette, would call them both dangerous, and delight in that danger."

"Seasoned? Fanny? Is the heat bothering you? I admit, it is close in here. You're saying such odd things."

Fanny drew her gaze away from Valentine, smiled as she shook her head. "I'm sorry, Lucie. I believe I'm having some difficulty comparing the gaiety of the dancers with the rather severe expression on his grace's face. See him? He's smiling, yet he isn't smiling. Do you suppose the French are on the move again?"

"Smiling, not smiling. Not looking, but seeing everything. My stars! If I knew you were going to be so maudlin, girl, I would have left you at home. Now smile, *really* smile, and then laugh as if I've just said something witty. Call some attention to yourself. Bat those absurdly long lashes at one of these scarlet-coated young gentlemen. My stars, I'll not have you sitting like some pale wallflower wilting next to me while I'm flirting with my beaux. It would put a damper on my fun. Think of me, if you can't think of yourself."

"Lucie, you're incorrigible," Fanny said, pulling out a word Elly and others had used on her from time to time. "But the dance is over and Rian has seen me. He'll bear me company."

Fanny held out her skirts and dropped into a small, pert curtsey as Rian bowed to them both. "Well met, brother."

Rian grinned at her. "Don't you look fine as ninepence, Fanny-panny," he said as Lucie wandered off a few minutes later with the soldier she'd been talking to the other day, at Wellington's headquarters. Rian held out his arm to her, and Fanny slipped her gloved arm through his elbow. "His lordship has provided well for you, hasn't he? You're not driving him mad in order to thank him, I hope."

"If I'm driving him mad, Rian, it's only because he's a maddening man," Fanny told him as they walked toward the perimeter of the room, for another set was forming. "Have you heard anything more about the French? Brede says they're moving faster than anyone had hoped, while the Russians and Austrians are still a long march away from joining us."

Rian rolled his eyes. "Not tonight, Fanny. I've ridden Jupiter from here to there and back again, twice, at least a dozen times today. No talk of war tonight, all right? Besides, Wellington won't go out, engage Bonaparte, not until it's absolutely necessary. He needs time for Blücher to get his army to us. Now, did you see that girl I was dancing with a moment ago? What do you think?"

Fanny frowned, her mind still very much on Bonaparte and his *Grand Armée*. "What do I think of what?"

"Of *her,* of course," Rian said, dragging Fanny behind a blatantly fake marble pillar wrapped in ivy. "Granted, she giggles, but she's pretty enough, isn't she?"

"Ah, but if she giggles?" Fanny did her best to smile, keep her tone light. "Could you really abide a woman who giggles?"

"Probably not for long, no," Rian said, frowning. "But they're all being so friendly, Fanny. Driving out to our headquarters, bringing baskets of food and drink. Charles Battenly—he's also an aide—says you pick the flowers when you can in times like these."

"Flowers," Fanny said, looking at him intensely. He was six years her senior. When had become so young? When had she grown so old? "You're comparing these young women to flowers, ready to be *picked?*"

Rian flushed to the roots of his hair. "I knew you wouldn't understand. I never should have said anything. Let's discuss you, instead. His lordship told me you'll take his sister and leave Brussels with Wiggins, if things start going sideways. He said you promised. Did you promise, Fanny?"

"Are you asking me to make sure we take up your Miss Pitney with us?"

"Who?"

"Miss Pitney. The flower you plan to pluck."

Rian grinned, looking abashed. "Is that her name? I don't care a fig about her, Fanny. I was only telling you what my friend Charles said." He took her hands in his. "Don't make me have to worry about you, Fanny-panny. Promise me?"

"Promises. All I seem to do is be asked to make promises," she told him, trying not to look at him as if she was memorizing his features, as if she might never see them again. "Don't worry about me, Rian. I'll be very careful, I *promise*. Now promise me that you'll also be very careful. Promise me you'll come home."

He bent and kissed her cheek. "You know I will, Fanny. We'll go home to Romney Marsh together in triumph once old Boney's been beaten. I promise."

"Home. Becket Hall seems so far away, doesn't it?"

Rian saw the quick shadow in Fanny's eyes. "No. Our lives seem so far away from Becket Hall. Isn't that what you really mean? What seemed so certain there, isn't so certain anymore. Is it?"

Fanny averted her eyes. "You…you mean, how I… How I feel?"

Rian's heart squeezed tight in his chest. She was so young, for all her intelligence. "Yes, Fanny, that's just what I mean. I love you. You love me. We've been close as sticking plaster our whole lives, you and me, out there, in the back of beyond. You're my best friend. That will never change. But there's this whole world out here now, isn't there? So many things we've never even thought of, much less experienced, so many things we've never seen. So many people we haven't met. So—" he spread his arms, fisted his hands as if grabbing something tightly in them "—so much *life* to live, Fanny-panny."

"So many pretty, young, willing redheaded girls," she said, hating to admit the truth in his words, adding silently, *and a man like Brede, who is like nothing or no one I've ever dreamed existed.* "Yes, Rian, you've made your point. I'm a silly little girl who believed something just because I had nothing else to believe. But I still love you, you know."

"You'd better, or I'll just have to go throw myself on the first French sword I see coming toward me," he warned her, lightly striking her chin with his fist. "You're growing up, Fanny. We're spreading our wings, both of us, like birds finally escaping the nest, away from the necessary secrecy of Becket Hall. But you'll always be my sister, and I'll always be your brother. We'll always understand each other as no one else can."

"A special bond," Fanny said, blinking back tears. "Yes. We have that, don't we? Nobody can take that from us."

"Nobody, Fanny," Rian said, looking deeply into her eyes, so proud of her, and realizing that she was no longer the little girl whose hand he'd held, the little girl who'd chased after him everywhere he went, driving him mad, flattering his slightly older self terribly. "Nothing and nobody could ever do that."

"Such serious faces. Am I interrupting a family chat? Good evening, Beckets."

Fanny turned to see Valentine standing beside her, glorious in his evening clothes. "Good evening, Brede," she said, unable to meet his eyes. "As you did not visit your sister today, I had thought you might not be in attendance this evening."

"I said I'd be here," Valentine reminded her. "It was…*necessary*. Lieutenant, I've heard a compliment about you."

Rian pulled himself up very straight. "Yes, sir?"

"Yes, indeed. Sir William Ponsonby told me you aren't half-inept," Valentine said, smiling. "High praise, indeed, from Ponsonby. Fanny? How would you like to meet his grace?"

"The Duke?" She would adore meeting Wellington, at any other time. At the moment, she had no desire to do anything more than go back to Lucie's town house and bury her head under the covers, hope to understand why Rian's defection didn't bother her half so much as Valentine's casual way of speaking to her, as if they'd never kissed last night. "I'd be delighted, of course," she said brightly, accepting his offered arm.

"You go, Fanny," Rian told her. "I've seen enough of the man these past few days."

"Your brother's hot for battle," Valentine told her as they made their way around the perimeter of the large, square room. "And he is doing well, Fanny. He's already made one suggestion Wellington has taken under consideration, pointing out what he believes the best position to make good use of our cavalry if attack should come from the west. I should have known Jack wouldn't have asked me to do a favor for an idiot."

"He's not inept, he's not an idiot," Fanny said, looking up at Valentine. "Such high praise. Is that the best you can do when handing out compliments?"

Valentine stopped, and then guided her behind a potted palm, took her hands in his. "How's this, then, Fanny," he said, his voice low, intimate. "I've thought of you every moment since last night, even during a few moments when I most definitely should have been thinking of anything and anyone but you. And now here you are, looking so young, so fresh, so very beautiful, and I know what a bastard I am to want to take you from here, now, take you back to my own house, and kiss you, hold you, until we're both too exhausted to do anything but sleep. I don't know, Fanny, if you'd consider any of that a compliment, or even know what it means for me to make such an admission. But that's how I feel, and the world is moving so fast, the future is so uncertain for any of us, that I had to say it all, say it now. So you'd understand."

Fanny's heart was pounding so loudly in her ears that his words seemed to come to her from a great distance. She didn't know how to answer him, what to say. So she told him the truth. "You frighten me. I hate that you frighten me."

Valentine sniffed slightly, smiled. He felt young,

foolish, and yet older than time itself. "Well, then, we're even, Fanny. Because you frighten me. Shall we blame it all on the moment? Danger everywhere, Bonaparte on the march? Those damn trousers you were wearing when I first saw your dirty, smudged face? Yes, let's blame it all on that. Now, I believe I was about to introduce you to the Duke."

"Brede, I—"

"No," he said quickly, lightly pressing a finger against her lips. "Don't say anything more, Fanny, please. I've disgraced myself enough as it is now. Another day, another few weeks, the world back where it belongs, Bonaparte back where he belongs, and I'll be sane again, I promise."

"And mean, and cuttingly sarcastic and odiously arrogant?" Fanny asked him, aching to help him climb out of the hole he'd so unexpectedly dug for himself. "In other words, Brede—more like yourself?"

His smile widened. "Unquestionably," he agreed, leading her out from behind the palm. "I'm much happier with myself when I'm biting off heads."

"And you're quite good at it," Fanny told him as they wended their way around the perimeter of the overheated room. "Do you practice?"

He sliced her a look. "I beg your pardon?"

"I asked—do you practice? Being mean, and cutting, that is. Agreeing with me when I said I needed a bath, for instance. That was very mean. I laughed, because it`was also funny. But I imagine you frighten quite a few people, don't you?"

"But not you, I believe," he said as they stopped about two feet away from Wellington and the Duchess of Richmond, who were deep in conversation. "I don't frighten you. Except, of course, for when I'm being a jackass."

"Exactly," she told him, feeling on much firmer ground now. "So we won't do that again, will we? At least not until the world is…back where it belongs. And it will be soon, won't it?"

His smile disappeared. "If I have to personally carry that Corsican bastard back to Elba on my shoulders, yes, it will. If only so that I can decide if I was a jackass to say anything to you, or a jackass for allowing you to change the subject."

Fanny nodded, once again unable to speak, and then quickly pretended a great interest in what Wellington was saying to the Duchess.

"I don't know what they'll do the enemy, but, by God, they frighten me."

The Duchess laughed, waving her fan rather frantically in front of her face. "Your own soldiers? They're the salt of the earth, Arthur."

He shook his head. "Scum. Nothing but beggars and scoundrels, all of them. Gin is the spirit of their patriotism."

"Shame on you, sir!" the Duchess exclaimed as

Fanny and Valentine exchanged looks. "Yet you expect them to die for you?"

The Duke seemed to have lost interest in the conversation, looking past the Duchess. "Mmm-hmm, yes."

Fanny shot a quick glance to her left, and saw an older man in uniform gesturing to the Duke. Some sort of hand signal. She looked back to the Duke, saw that his eyes were hooded now, allowing no expression at all.

But the Duchess hadn't seen Wellington's look, and continued with her teasing questions. "Out of duty, Arthur?"

Again the man answered with a grunt more than actual agreement.

The Duchess seemed to notice Valentine for the first time, and directed her next words to him. "I doubt if even Bonaparte could draw men to him by *duty*."

"The gentleman does seem to have his fair share of fiercely loyal followers," Valentine pointed out quietly.

Wellington laughed then, winking at Valentine. "Oh, Boney's not a gentleman."

"Arthur!" the Duchess exclaimed as Fanny bit her bottom lip, trying not to laugh. Why, the man was nothing but a tease. "What an Englishman you are."

The Duke sobered, and Fanny again saw that same intense yet faraway look in his eyes that she'd glimpsed moments earlier. "On the field of battle his hat is worth fifty thousand men—but he is not a gentleman. Isn't that right, Valentine? You've seen him just this past week."

Fanny looked quickly to Valentine, her mouth slightly agape. "You've *seen* him? This past week?"

"Ha," the Duchess said, her fan moving even faster. "He probably dined with him, young lady. Did you dine with him, Valentine? Tell him amusing stories even as you counted the heads of his army and peeked at his battle maps?"

Valentine bowed to the woman. "You overestimate my powers, madam. There were too many heads to count. But I did do as you requested, and pocketed a silver spoon with the man's crest on it after we'd dined. Lovely thing. I'll have it sent round to you in the morning."

"How glibly you fib!" The Duchess scolded, tapping his arm with her closed fan. "I adore you."

The Duke threw back his head and laughed, then motioned for Valentine to step closer. "Tell me, my grand spy, have you by chance noticed that there is a delightfully beautiful young woman standing beside you, as yet not introduced to me?"

Valentine quickly made the introductions and Fanny dropped into what she hoped was at least a presentable curtsey.

"Enchanted, my dear," the Duke said, then

frowned. "Becket? I have a Becket, don't I, Valentine?"

"Miss Becket's brother, your grace," Valentine reminded him. "The pretty one," he added, winking at Fanny.

"Ah! Yes, I remember. And there he is, over there. Fairly surrounded by our ladies, isn't he?"

The Duchess turned to look at Rian. "Oh, yes, a well set-up young man, Arthur. This year, soldiers are the fashion."

"But not war, madam. War is never in fashion," Wellington told her. "Still, where would society be without my boys?"

"Your boys?" Valentine quipped. "You mean, the scum of the earth, don't you?"

"Only you, Valentine, would dare to contradict your Field Marshal. Now, excuse us, ladies, just for a moment. I have something to say to this man, and wouldn't wish to bore you with trivialities. Even you, my dear," he said, bowing to the Duchess, "who are the best of my generals. This ball was an inspiration, and I thank you."

Fanny watched as the Duke put his arm through Valentine's and took him off, wondering what they had to say to each other that hadn't been said before they'd walked through the doors and into the ballroom. She smiled at the Duchess, not having the faintest idea as to what to say to the great lady, and looked around the room, for the first time noticing that there now seemed to be small knots of officers standing together, talking together in earnest.

"Do you think—" she said, turning to ask the Duchess, only to see a small child tugging on the lady's skirts.

"Mama! Iggy has promised to bring me a cuirassier's helmet to use as a sewing basket. One without blood, of course."

The Duchess smiled down at her daughter, and then addressed the blushing soldier who was standing behind the child. "Good for you, Sarah! And one for me, young man—*with* the blood."

Fanny nearly jumped as a deeper voice came from behind her and she turned to see two men standing there, their uniforms denoting their rank, although their demeanor had already made their importance obvious.

"Where do you plan to stick your Frenchman, Hay?" one asked imperiously of the young soldier.

The Duchess pulled her daughter close against her skirts. "Oh, now, now, Sir William, Sir Thomas, don't you two go teasing the boy. Don't answer him, Iggy."

But the young man simply raised his chin and declared cheekily, "I thought under the right armpit, sir."

The child clapped her hands in glee. "See? He has it all planned!"

"Ah," the second man said. "Under the armpit, is it? When you meet a cuirassier beam to beam, you'll be lucky to escape with your life, much less his helmet. Boy, you'll learn the art of fighting from the French."

"But we're better, sir," Fanny said before she could stop herself. "They'll run from us."

The man lifted a quizzing glass to his eye, and then turned that grossly magnified eye on Fanny. "Well, look here. Another pretty face for us, to take our minds from the trials ahead, your grace? How clever of you. Do you grow them up in your back garden? And what's your name…hmm?"

Fanny exhaled in relief as Valentine slid his arm around the man's shoulder. "General Sir Thomas Picton, may I present to you Miss Fanny Becket, sister to our newest aide-de-camp, Lieutenant Rian Becket. Now, Tommy, go away, you and Ponsonby, too, before I box both your ears. Go talk to the Duke, why don't you? He's in the anteroom."

The general looked as if he was about to protest, but when Valentine raised one eyebrow he merely nodded, and he and Sir William bowed to the ladies and headed for the anteroom.

"Your grace, charming Miss Sarah," Valentine then said, bowing to the ladies, "if you'll excuse us?"

"What's wrong, what's happening? You sent those men to Wellington, didn't you? What do you know, what did he tell you?" Fanny asked quickly as, his hand behind her elbow, Valentine smartly steered her across the floor, signaling to Rian as he went. Within the space of three heartbeats, they were all outside in the meager garden, and Valentine was looking at them both without expression.

He said what he had to say. "The Duke had ordered troops in position at Quatre Bras to move to Mons."

Rian nodded furiously. "Yes, I know that, sir. And?"

"And our good Prince of Orange's own Quartermaster-General disobeyed that order and instead sent another brigade to reinforce Quatre Bras and the crossroads."

"My God," Rian said, clearly shocked by this news. "Why?"

"Who knows," Valentine said, his smile thin, remembering a quiet conversation he'd had earlier with that same Quartermaster-General. "Just thank God he did, because Marshal Grouchy is on the move, going out to engage the Prussians before they can join with us. Mons is not in their sights—but Ligny and Quatre Bras are. Bonaparte clearly wants to divide our troops, keep himself between us and Blücher. It's brilliant, actually. The Duke is even now ordering everyone back there, and all his commanders and aides to headquarters, ready to move at his command. Your Thirteenth, for one, will get its first fight tomorrow, Lieutenant. Most definitely."

Fanny reached for Rian's hand and squeezed it with her own, mentally saying a quick prayer for Sergeant-Major Hart.

"We're to leave now?" Rian asked. "Tonight?"

"Tonight. We'll be hearing the drums and trumpets at any moment," Valentine said. "Get yourself back to headquarters as quickly as possible. I'll give you a moment to say your farewells."

Fanny watched him walk to the far side of the garden, his hands clasped behind his back, and then launched herself into Rian's arms, squeezing him tightly. "Oh, Rian, be careful. Please be careful. Remember Papa's lessons. Remember to rest Jupiter when you can. Remember what Jacko said about fighting and don't be polite about it, don't be fancy—just *win*. Fight as meanly as you have to. Remember—"

"Shh, Fanny-panny," he told her, stroking her back, feeling her body's slight tremors. "I'll be fine. I want this, Fanny. I've wanted this for so long." He kissed her hair, and then pushed her gently away from him. He opened two buttons of his tunic and reached inside, coming out with a single folded sheet of paper. "Here, take this."

Fanny looked at the paper as if it might attack her. "What…what is it?"

"My will, Fanny. Charles said I should write one. Everybody does. In case."

She looked up at him in absolute terror even as she quickly pushed her hands behind her back. "In case— Rian, no!"

"For God's sake, Fanny, don't be such a female," he told her, his attention already more on the flurry of activity, the hasty leave-takings going on a few steps away, inside the ballroom. "We'll laugh about such maudlin silliness, and then burn the thing together when I get back but, for now, just take it. And do what his lordship said, go to Wiggins if things look dire, get yourself and her ladyship out of Brussels, all the way back to the coast." He shoved the will within an inch of her nose. "Promise me, Fanny."

Fanny took the paper, crushing it tight in her hand, her gaze still intent on Rian's face. Her bottom lip trembled, so she clamped it between her teeth until it steadied. "Don't leave me, Rian. Don't ever leave me alone. I…I wouldn't know what to do without you."

"You won't be without me, Fanny-panny. I promise. We'll dine together tomorrow night or the next, and I'll tell you grand lies and silly stories about how I routed Boney all by myself."

She sniffed, blinked. "And I'll pretend to believe them, every one of them."

Rian crushed her against him, holding on tight, as she held on tight, and then set her from him. He smiled at her one last time, and then abruptly turned away, ran back into the ballroom, to where a chubby young Lieutenant was waiting to clasp him around the shoulders as they both made for the doorway.

Fanny watched him go, her hands pressed tight against her mouth, her eyes closing when she felt Valentine's hands on her shoulders.

"Good girl," he said, giving her shoulders a quick squeeze.

The sob she'd been holding back escaped her and she turned into Valentine's arms, pressing herself close against him, her arms tight around his waist as if he were an anchor she could hold on to in a world gone mad.

Valentine held her, let her cry, wondering why it had never bothered him that no one had ever feared for him, cried for him. Wondering why a part of him wished Fanny's tears now were for him.

"Fanny," he said as her sobs lessened, "I have to go now, too. Let me take you back to Lucille."

She looked up at him, her tear-wet eyes shining in the light from the few torches in the garden. "Where? Where will you be? With the Duke?"

He forced a smile to his face. "Me? I imagine I'll be riding higgledy-piggledy from here to there and back again, carrying messages, making suggestions, dodging French patrols. This won't be a matter of hours, Fanny, as we're only trying now to counter Bonaparte's first move. It will be days, but not weeks, as our chess game plays out. We won't let Bonaparte escape us again, I promise you. I feel certain that one large battle will decide the outcome for all of Europe."

She lay her hands on his forearms as he lightly cupped her waist. "Will you…will you be able to ride into Brussels, do you think? To tell us how the battle is going?"

"No, sweetings, I don't think so. But you'll know. We've already discussed this. Stay close to the windows, and if you begin to see half the city passing by in the direction of the coast, take Lucille and go to Wiggins. Rian needs to know you'll do that. *I* need to know that."

Her fingers tightened on his sleeves as the sound of trumpets calling the troops came to them on the night air. "Please be careful, Brede."

He smiled again. "Because you'll worry for me?"

A small smile played at the corners of her own mouth. "Not even a little bit. But Wiggins would be devastated if anything happened to you."

"True. I have to think of the man's loyal heart, don't I?"

Fanny nodded, trying hard to think of something witty to say, something that would keep her from saying anything more serious. But it was no use. The trumpets were sounding; what sounded like a thousand drums had begun to beat out the call to arms. The noisy clatter of horse hooves against the cobbles, wheels bumping along the streets, invaded the small walled garden. She could hear women crying inside the ballroom.

Still holding on to his forearms to balance herself, Fanny went up on tiptoe and pressed her lips against Valentine's mouth in a quick kiss, then just as quickly retreated. "Godspeed, Brede."

He crushed her against him, his mouth coming down to capture hers, needing to take the taste of her, the feel of her, with him into battle. When her arms slipped up and around his neck he slanted his mouth against hers again, invading her softness, feeding on her innocence, needing for her to remember this kiss. Needing her to remember him.

He left her then, and Fanny stood very still, trying to tell herself that she was his Miss Pitney, any available young woman at all. That he really felt nothing for her, and would realize that the moment the battle was won.

And that thought made her sad. Incredibly sad.

She pulled herself up, shoulders straight, and reentered the ballroom, then stopped, amazed, as she saw couples still dancing a Scottish reel, heard the music that played on even as several women stood crying on the sides on the room and even more scarlet-jacketed soldiers took hasty leave of their hostess, who hugged each and every man before allowing him through the doorway.

Miss Pitney came tripping down the dance, her fingers held lightly by a young man in ridiculously overdone evening dress, and Fanny stepped onto the floor, stopping just in front of the woman, blocking her progress.

"Your pardon?" the redhead said haughtily. "You're in my way."

"And you're a silly, heartless, brainless twit," Fanny bit out tightly. "For some reason I no longer understand, I thought you should know that."

Fanny then turned on her heel, located Lady Whalley standing near the door, happily giving out kisses and encouraging words to each scarlet-jacketed man leaving the ballroom, and dragged her out into the night by her elbow.

CHAPTER ELEVEN

FANNY, EXHAUSTED IN BOTH mind and body, slept fully clothed on the uncomfortable settee in the small drawing room of Lady Whalley's slim town house. The drawing room was two floors lower, closer to the street. Ridiculously, irrationally, closer to Rian and Brede.

Not that Fanny had slept more than a few hours since coming back from Lady Richmond's ball. Nor had she eaten. Such mundane, everyday things were so alien to her, when all her concentration was centered on what was happening a good ten miles away.

She had already left the house several times, to mingle with others on the streets, hoping for bits of gossip, snippets of news, and then attempted to winnow the grain from the chaff so that she had a clearer picture of what was going on to the south of Brussels.

Word of Bonaparte's victory at Ligny had served to set off a panic barely mitigated by news of at least a reasonable draw at Quatre-Bras. But there had been no further reports of any substance in at least twelve hours, and many were fearing the worst. The werewolf, the tyrant, the Emperor—he was within striking distance.

Frances had packed all of their clothing and had taken on the role of cook after they'd risen yesterday to find the kitchen fire out, half their larder shelves empty and the cook nowhere to be found.

People were leaving Brussels as quickly as their servants could pack up their bags and arrange transport. Already, three people had knocked on Lady Whalley's door, offering exorbitant amounts for her brother's coach and horses.

Wiggins slept now in the small carriage house, armed to the teeth with pistols, knives and an ancient blunderbuss he'd unearthed somewhere, protecting that coach and those horses, including her own Molly.

These terrible, fickle people. So ready to laugh and dance, so eager to be a part of history—so reluctant to put themselves in personal danger. Fanny loathed them all.

The noise outside the town house never seemed to cease now. The rattle of wheels on the cobblestones, the shouts of angry people pushing and shoving and demanding the respect they believed due their fine clothes and high social stations. All of them running; rats deserting what they'd decided had to be Wellington's sinking ship. And, all the time, the incessant rain, falling on all of them.

Fanny turned her head into one of the pillows and pulled the blanket higher over her head. Whether it was her own fears, or the constant angry and nervous noises penetrating her brain, her sleep became disturbed enough to open her to dreams.

To the dream that had first begun when Rian left Becket Hall well over a month ago...

She could never see herself as she was now in the dream, but she knew she was looking out of her eyes, as if she, the grown Fanny, was standing somewhere straight behind the much younger Fanny. A part of her younger self, the adult watching the child, but strictly in the role of an observer, unable to control or change anything that was happening, that would happen.

The young Fanny was wearing a pretty striped dress cut from material left over from the glorious, striped gown fashioned for the beautiful, kind Isabella. She wasn't supposed to be wearing the dress; it was her very best one, and to be saved for special times. Like when her new papa returned from the sea.

She'd never had a papa, and he fascinated her. All big and strong, and with such a kind smile. He would rub her head and call her his Irish Moonlight because of her nearly white-blond hair and grass green eyes, and she'd giggle. Because that was silly, Rian had said so. Moonlight wasn't green.

He was coming home soon. Fanny had heard him promise as much as he'd hugged them all good-bye, saving a special hug for the beautiful Isabella, a last kiss on the forehead for the infant, Callie. He'd come back soon, and then they'd all leave together, sail off to a beautiful castle in some faraway place. And they'd all be very happy.

So *soon* might even be today, and that's why Fanny had put on her prettiest dress. That's what she'd told Rian, who'd only laughed at her and run off to play with the other boys, first taunting her that she couldn't play with them. Not in that dress.

Which was why Fanny was on the beach by herself a few hours later, dancing in and out of the small wavelets that softly kissed against the sand. She was careful to hold up her skirts as she stood with her bare feet submerged in the clear water that sparkled almost blue-white in the sunlight.

The older Fanny watched her younger self play, longing to tap her on the shoulder, warn her. *Run away. Run away.*

The young Fanny was singing a song, some silly thing she and Rian had made up about Jacko's nose—*"thar she blows!"* She was dancing toward the water, retreating again, not having thought about her mama for whole days now, learning to forget, to move on, as only young children are blessedly able to do.

She was charging a shore bird that began to beat its wings and escape skyward when she saw the ships. Three of them. She clapped her hands in glee, and looked back across the wide, deep beach. Toward the house, the trees. Looking for Rian. Longing to taunt *him,* because she'd been right.

No, no! Count them! Papa had two ships. Two, not three! Fanny tried to warn her younger self. *It's Beales. Beales! Beales had three! Count them!*

Rian was nowhere to be seen, so the young Fanny turned back to watch as anchors were dropped into the water and longboats were lowered. She put a hand up to shade her eyes in the bright sun and looked for her papa in one of the first boats. But he wasn't there. No tall, handsome Chance, with his long blond hair blowing around his face in the breeze. No fierce Jacko and his booming voice. No silly Billy, who had made her a pretty wooden top and taught her how to spin it.

Young Fanny tipped her head to one side, wondering, where was her papa?

Look at them! Look at them! See the pistols hanging around their necks! See their terrible smiles! See, Fanny. See!

"Fanny!"

The little girl wheeled around on the sand at the

sound of Rian's voice, to see him running toward her, his shoulder-length black curls flying behind him as he ran, his face as white as the sands. "To me, Fanny! Run to me!"

She lifted her skirts and began to run. Not because she was afraid, but because Rian was afraid. He met up with her with such force that he nearly knocked her down, and then quickly picked her up, tucking her beneath his arm as if she were a sack of meal. And then running. Running.

Up on the veranda of the house the beautiful Isabella was shouting down to them all. "Run! Into the trees! Hide! Run, everyone! Run!"

Fanny spared a moment from watching herself, to look up at Isabella, standing so bravely on the veranda, Odette beside her, holding Callie. Isabella kissed the child, traced the Sign of the Holy Cross on her little forehead just like Fanny's mama used to do, and then pushed Odette away, shooed her away, down the winding staircase.

A small section of the roof of the huge house exploded, wood flying everywhere, as one of the ships began firing grapeshot. A veritable broadside, directed high and across the wide beach. There were more explosions. A tall palm not ten yards from them snapped in half, its top falling to the ground with a mighty crash. Sand kicked up around them, rained down on them.

"Run! Run!" Isabella urged yet again.

Odette waved Rian and his burden and at least another dozen children ahead of her. They all vanished into the lush vegetation as dozens of the island's men and women, the young, the heavy with child, the ancient, all armed with pistols and knives and metal-tipped pikes, ran toward the beach, toward the danger.

Isabella also stood her ground, her fingers wrapped tightly around the wooden balustrade—dear God, she was as young as the now grown Fanny was now—her beautiful young face locked in an expression of daring, defiance.

So brave. So doomed.

The dream shifted, and Fanny was now with her younger self and the others, hidden in the secret cave deep in the interior of the island. Night had come and then gone, and the shots and the screams had finally stopped. No one had passed by their hiding place in several hours, beating at the undergrowth, calling for Odette to come out, come out and she would be spared. It hadn't been easy, keeping the youngest ones quiet, and Fanny had even bitten Rian's hand, drawn blood, trying to be free of his tight grip. But Rian hadn't yelled, even as she'd bitten deep.

The dreaming Fanny tasted Rian's blood in her mouth, moaned piteously in her sleep.

Courtland, at thirteen, the oldest of the children in the cave, handed the sleeping Callie to Odette and left them, returning an endless time later. His thin cheeks were tearstained, but his eyes were dry. There was blood on his clothing, blood stained his hands and bare feet. He was no longer thirteen. What he had seen had made him a man. A stone-faced, stoic, sad man, so much older than his years.

"The curse persists, I can see nothing. Tell me. Isabella lives?" Odette asked him. "You saw her?"

He gathered up the sleeping Callie once more, the blood on his hands smearing the infant's white lawn gown. "I saw her. No one and nothing lives. No one and nothing."

Odette sank to her knees and began keening like a wild animal in pain.

"I will be the one who tells him," Courtland said. It was, in fact, Fanny thought, probably only the third or fourth time she'd heard Court speak since she and Rian had come to the island. His voice was rusty, as if he rarely used it. He'd never played, like the other children. He'd stayed with Isabella, always, Isabella and her now motherless infant. Fanny had thought him silly, but now they—Rian, Spencer, the other younger boys—all looked to him for guidance. "He'll need to see the babe is all right. Stay here. We'll come for you."

Fanny watched all of this unfolding in front of

her as it had done so many years ago, unable to stop watching, even when her younger self fell asleep in Rian's thin arms, still crying that she was hungry, and that her pretty dress was ruined.

And then her papa was there. Tall, strong. Giving orders quietly, knowing they'd be obeyed without question. Fanny watched her younger self scrambling up onto Rian's shoulders, all of them moving forward, moving back through the trees in a long, silent line. Nobody spoke. Even Callie, the youngest of them all, did not cry.

Rian tried to keep Fanny's head pressed into his neck, but she fought to see. The bodies. Hacked into pieces. Burned. Bits and pieces of bodies hanging from the ruined veranda. Old Harry, who used to tell them all silly stories, just sitting on the sand. Except that his head was in his lap. Wasn't that silly! Why didn't he put it back on?

Everywhere, blood. Everywhere, bodies. Even the goats were dead, their bellies ripped open. The chickens, the cows. Fanny had liked the cows.

No birds sang. Everything was quiet, save for the rough sobs of grown men as they knelt over broken bodies.

"Fanny, don't look!"

But Fanny looked, saw with her young, uncomprehending eyes. Saw the markings on the white wall above the veranda. Squiggles, all red and dripping.

"Rian, what's that?" she asked, tugging one arm free and pointing to the house.

But Rian just kept moving with the others. Toward the longboats. Toward the two damaged ships lying at anchor in the natural harbor.

The older Fanny watched herself go. Watched the younger Rian carry her away, to safety. Then she looked back at the house, seeing the squiggles, painted there in blood, and knew them for what they were. Words. A warning.

You lose. No mercy, no quarter. Until it's mine.

"He won't stop," Fanny mumbled brokenly into the pillow as, in her dream, she watched the two ships at last limp out to sea, the big white house, all of the buildings, down to the last chicken coop, now ablaze behind them, sending black smoke high into the bright blue sky. "He'll never stop. But why? Why…"

The grown Fanny stood alone on the sands now, death spread out all around her, watching the world burn, watching the ships disappear over the horizon.

But she was still there. Left behind. Forgotten. Still in danger.

Fanny always woke up at this point, frantically calling Rian's name. Left with her fear, never knowing what would happen next, watching the young Rian sail away with her younger self.

She tried to burrow back into the dream. Continue the dream. Find Rian again, somehow catch up to the ships, and safety. Because Edmund Beales was coming back, and she needed Rian's protection. Needed him to hide her, keep her safe, just as he'd always kept her safe.

The young Fanny was safe. Cuddled up on the ship with Rian's arms around her.

But what about now? What about her *now*? How could he sail off like that, leaving her to fend for herself? How could he leave her alone?

It was time to wake up. She would always wake now, crying, alone. Why couldn't she wake up?

"Fanny."

She caught her breath in a sob, still locked inside the dream. He hadn't left her alone here on the beach. He'd come back for her. But where? Where was he? She turned fully around on the beach, looking for him, straining to see him.

There! Stepping out from the trees. There he was, cast in the red glow from the burning house. He'd stayed!

She ran. Picked up her skirts, her pretty striped, colored skirts, and raced toward him, laughing, crying, feeling safe at last. Rian wouldn't leave her. He'd never leave her, child or man. How could she have been so silly?

"Rian! Rian, here I am! Rian, I—"

He stepped completely into the sunshine, the hem of his dirty gray greatcoat swirling about his high-top riding boots, the long white scarf hanging loose around his neck, his tawny hair unruly, falling down over his cheeks, an unlit cheroot stuck in the corner of his mouth. His eyes were hooded, yet intense. He took the cheroot from his mouth. "Hello, Fanny-panny."

Fanny stood stock-still, her heart pounding painfully in her chest. "Rian?" she asked, breathless. "Where's Rian?"

"Unavoidably detained, I'm afraid. He sent me in his place. But you knew that, Fanny. You're not a child anymore. You're neither of you children anymore."

"No! No, that's not right! It's Rian, you should be Rian."

Brede replaced the cheroot and spoke while holding the thing between his straight white teeth. "Ah, but any port in a storm, hmm?"

"No! That's not the way it is. It's not! Rian understands. We're both seeing the world outside of Becket Hall and…I never knew you existed and… and Rian, he just smiles and says—but we're all in danger now, you, as well. You shouldn't be here. Where's Rian? *Rian! Rian, where are you?*"

"Thanking his lucky stars he's miles away, and can't hear you screeching for him like some banshee, I'd suspect. My stars, Fanny—you'd wake the dead."

Fanny struggled to be free of the blanket and sat up to see Lady Whalley standing there, her nightcap

askew, her dressing gown misbuttoned. "What…
I— Lucie?"

"Not Princess Caroline, that's definite," Lucie
said, subsiding into the facing couch. "I've been
poking you until my finger hurts. My stars, you
gave me a fright. Screaming like that. But you slept
well enough before your nightmare, I imagine. It's
past ten of the clock. Beastly early for me, but who
can sleep with all that racket outside? Especially
now that the rain has stopped."

Fanny rubbed at her eyes and pushed her fingers
through her hair, got to her feet. She walked over to
the window overlooking the street and pushed back
the velvet draperies. The streets were still clogged
with farm wagons and fine carriages, curricles and
people on foot, all of them heading out of the city.

"You're right, Lucie, the rain has stopped. Soon
they'll be able to fight again, won't they?"

"I suppose so," Lucie said, fighting a yawn.
"Wiggins will be pounding on the door at any moment, ordering us to leave, just as he's done every
morning since—what day is it? I keep counting everything from the night of Lady Richmond's ball."

Fanny closed her eyes, tried to think, wishing the
memory of her nightmare would leave her. Her
nights and days had all seemed to blur together.
"The…the ball was Saturday night, and that was
two, no three days ago now. So today is Tuesday?"

"Yes, yes, it must be Tuesday. The eighteenth. Oh, and it's June, my dear, in case you've forgotten that, as well."

Fanny let the drapery fall back into place as she turned to Lucie, feeling suddenly cold. "It's…it's my birthday." *And Rian's, chosen by Papa for the day he found us.* "I didn't realize…"

"Well, isn't that nice? Your birthday, and our day of victory. Now, what do you say you be a good girl and toddle off upstairs for a bath and fresh clothing, hmm? That gown looks as though you've slept in it and—my stars, you did, didn't you? You suppose we'll hear cannon soon? Would that be a good thing, do you suppose? Wiggins told me that once the rain has stopped, and the sun has dried the ground somewhat, the fighting will begin. Fanny? Fanny, where are you going?"

But Fanny just kept heading for the staircase. It was her birthday. Rian's birthday. The day they'd always shared. But not today. Oh, God, not today…

CHAPTER TWELVE

LADY RICHMOND'S BALL seemed so long ago, and yet it had only been three days since Valentine had kissed Fanny goodbye. Three days, and more than a few officers were still wandering headquarters in the evening dress and thin black leather shoes they'd worn to the ball. There'd been no time to return to their rented houses, to don their uniforms, and no time since the battle of Quatre Bras to ride back down the road to Brussels. Not when Bonaparte was still calling the tune.

The English army was now concentrated near the village of Waterloo; Uxbridge, Hill, Picton, Orange…all of them in place now on the highest ground available to them, and at the ready, with Blücher and the Prussians also solidly in position. The Allied forces greatly outnumbered the French, but when Napoleon Bonaparte led his army, such a paltry thing as mere numbers couldn't be counted upon to make the two sides equal in strength.

Valentine felt his nerves stretching taut as he

stood on the hill with Wellington, waiting for the sun to climb higher into the sky, dry out the ground. The silence was deafening, so quiet Valentine was sure he could hear more than one hundred thousand hearts beating, waiting to live or die.

And then the English line began singing, only a few voices at first, but the song quickly spreading from mouth to mouth, until the air was blasted with the rather crude verse mocking Bonaparte.

"Shall I shut them up, sir?" someone asked Wellington, and Valentine waited to hear the man's answer.

"No, no, indulge it, sir. Anything that wastes time is good. Indulge it. Normally I don't like cheering, but there's always a time to cut cards with the Devil."

"You see Boney as the Devil?" Valentine asked him curiously.

"If he is, Valentine, then today we send him back to his Hell, eh? I want only that he is less patient than I and makes his move first. I'd rather counter his action than initiate my own."

Shortly before noon, Bonaparte obliged the Field Marshal by beginning the battle with salvos from his massed artillery, followed quickly by an assault on the Allies right flank.

Wellington clapped Valentine heavily on the back, so that he staggered forward. "Well, that opens the ball."

Valentine nodded, regaining his footing. "Yes, your grace. And now we dance?"

"Yes," the Duke said as a soldier brought their mounts to them, "now we dance. Be a good fellow and take a message to Picton for me."

"My pleasure, your grace…."

Valentine labored for the Duke's pleasure for all the hours of the long, bloody afternoon and early evening, carrying messages, orders, bringing back reports on casualties, on troop strength. Blücher had been and continued to be amazing, the grizzled old soldier surviving having his horse shot out from beneath him, waving his sword in the air and shouting, "Raise high the black flags, my children. No prisoners. No pity. I will shoot any man I see with pity in him."

His children. What mighty fighters. Bit by bit, area by area, front by front, the French lines were splintering, falling back, and Valentine eased his tired mount in alongside Wellington's, believing he was about to share with the man the sight of Bonaparte's *Grande Armée* in full retreat. Final retreat…final victory. By God, no more after this!

The Duke had put himself in danger a dozen times, perhaps two dozen, but now he had retired to the area in front of his headquarters, still sitting proudly on his charger, where every man who looked up could see him, know he was rejoicing in what could only be their greatest victory.

Uxbridge was beside him, looking almost dapper, unscratched, although the horse beneath him was his ninth of the day, as eight others had been shot out from beneath him. The man, it would seem, led a charmed life.

"They'll break now, won't they?"

Valentine swiveled in the saddle, his heart thumping painfully in his chest as he saw Fanny, in full uniform, sitting astride her mare, her gaze solidly on the scene unfolding below them. "Christ's teeth, what are you doing here?"

Fanny kept her eyes straight ahead. "Shh, Brede, don't make a fuss. Did you really think I could remain safe in Brussels when the fighting was taking place less than ten miles down the road? And I've only just arrived, waiting down that road until a cartload of wounded came by, cheering, swearing victory would soon be ours. And they were right, weren't they? Have you seen Rian?"

Valentine nudged at Shadow's flanks, pushing the horse into Fanny's mare, turning both animals, taking them some distance behind Wellington and Uxbridge. "I'd put you over my knee, if I thought it would do any good, damn you."

"Oh, stop," Fanny said, turning Molly so that she once more faced the battle. "Look, it's almost over. They'll raise the white flag at any— Oh!"

Valentine tore his gaze from Fanny and looked

down the hill for the first time, at the battlefield strewn with bodies of both men and horses, to see that Bonaparte was making one last, possibly brilliant move. A desperate move, committing his best soldiers, the undefeated veterans he'd been holding in reserve, straight at the British line. "Sweet Jesus."

"By God," he heard Wellington tell Uxbridge in some awe, "that man does war honor. Uxbridge, give the order. The whole line will advance."

"In which direction, your grace?"

The Duke never took his steady gaze from the battlefield. "Why, straight ahead, to be sure."

"Stay here," Valentine ordered curtly to Fanny, and urged his mount forward once more. "Orders, your grace?"

"Indeed, yes, Valentine," the man said as calmly as if he was ordering tea and cakes. "Have the Guardsmen go head-on. Full volleys. No stopping until the French line is broken. It's now, Valentine. Now is our moment for the ages."

Sparing only a moment to glare at Fanny, Valentine was off to forward the order, praying she wouldn't do anything too entirely stupid until he returned.

Fanny watched Valentine go, then closed her eyes tight the moment he and his mount disappeared down the side of the hill, fading into the blue smoke rising from the line of cannon he rode behind, his filthy gray cloak flapping in the swirling wind caused by the fury of the battle below them, his head low over the horse's neck, just as she'd told Rian to do.

She'd pretended so well, she thought, not flinching at her first sight of the vast battlefield, of all the bodies sprawled everywhere, the screams of wounded men and horses, the shouted orders, the sharp crack of artillery volleys. She hadn't realized there were so many people in the entire world, let alone enough soldiers to make up the dead who had bled enough that there were small streams and pools of red running through the grass and mud.

The battlefield was the island, multiplied a thousand times, two thousand times. Bodies, everywhere. Blood, everywhere. This is what Rian had mostly protected her from, covering her eyes and running her out of the trees and across the sands to the ships. This was the sort of terrible memory he had tried to keep from searing into her young brain.

So that she only remembered now, in her nightmares.

But he'd always known. He'd been older, old enough to remember. And yet he had sought out a war. Why? What was the difference between men and women, that men would seek this sort of terribleness out, even revel in it? She didn't understand, couldn't understand.

For more than two hours Fanny sat with her back

against a tree trunk, turned away from the sight of the battlefield, Molly standing beside her, nibbling at the tall, green grass. She did her best to block her ears to the shouts, the screams, the sound of cannon hurling deadly grapeshot, the blare of trumpets, the relentless beat of the drums, the sharp rifle volleys.

She smelled the gunpowder, could even taste the expended powder in the air, believed she could smell the blood and gore. She trembled, couldn't stop her body from shaking almost uncontrollably, even as she wrapped her arms tightly around her bent knees; even her teeth chattered. She flinched, again and again, when nearby explosions shattered the air, shook the ground beneath her. The sheer randomness of the death those explosions dealt brought frustrated screams against the unfairness of war up from her belly, so that she mashed her closed mouth against her knees, refusing to let them out.

But she would will herself nowhere else.

She'd ridden Molly down the streets of Brussels, straining against the tide of wagons and carriages going in the opposite direction, fleeing the city. Past families dragging their hastily gathered possessions in any cart or barrow they could find. Wiggins had come for them, but Fanny had slipped out the kitchen door in her uniform even as the servant had pounded on the front door, Brede's carriage in the street, Molly tied behind it. In a moment she was astride the mare, in two moments, she was hidden from view by the crowd.

Let Lucie run; she'd be no help to anyone anyway. But Fanny couldn't run, wouldn't run. Her life lay ten miles down the road, on the battlefield.

She'd passed wagonloads of the wounded being transported along the roadway, slowing Molly to peer into each wagon, looking for Rian, looking for Brede, not sure if she wanted to see them or not. To be in one of the wagons meant they were out of the fight, but to not see them there didn't mean they were still alive.

Pushing Molly into a gallop, she'd approached the battle from the rear, shouted, "Message for the Field Marshal!" to anyone who looked eager to question her presence, but only two did. Everyone was too busy concentrating on staying alive.

When she'd seen Brede, seen his ugly gray greatcoat, his rangy gray stallion, she hadn't hesitated, even though Brede was at the very crest of the hill with Wellington and Uxbridge, all three of them boldly exposed to enemy fire. And, from that vantage point, she had looked down at the wide fields, the massive, rolling farmland turned battlefield, and felt bile rising in the back of her throat.

Not that she let Brede know how frightened she was, how horrified...

Eventually she realized that, mixed with the

gunfire and the sharp sound of metal against metal as swords clashed in the distance, she had begun to hear scattered cheers. English cheers she could hear because cannon fire no longer rhythmically boomed from the ridges, raining death below.

"We broke them!" someone was shouting, running past her, pumping his arms into the air. "We broke their lines! They're in retreat!"

Fanny got up from her hiding place and trotted toward the edge of the hill, to the place where Wellington and Uxbridge, after riding at the head of the troops these last fateful hours, were once more side-by-side on their mounts. Their presence, she realized—daringly out in the open, unprotected—had been a rallying point for the soldiers throughout the long day.

The two were speaking to each other, pointing, gesturing toward a distant hill, when the eerie whistle of grapeshot had Fanny instinctively diving toward the ground. She lay with her face in the dirt, her heart pounding, barely able to breathe as small explosions kicked up the dirt and grass around her.

She looked to her left, her cheek still in the mud. Wellington and Uxbridge hadn't moved, hadn't cravenly grabbed for the ground as she had done. Feeling stupid, cowardly, Fanny scrambled to her feet.

"My God, sir," she heard Lord Uxbridge say with a deadly calm, "I've lost my leg."

Fanny stood blinking at the two men as she wiped clots of mud from her face, both of them still sitting tall atop their grand chargers. The Duke of Wellington stood in the stirrups and leaned across toward Uxbridge. "By God, sir," he said, just as calmly, "so you have."

Fanny pressed her hands tightly over her mouth, fearful she would be guilty of an insane, hysterical giggle. How absurd! A pleasant exchange—*I've lost my leg. Yes, you have.*

But then the clock in Fanny's head, that had stopped when she'd thrown herself against the ground, began to beat on, and she watched as soldiers raced to Lord Uxbridge, catching him as he began to slide from the saddle. Taking care to hold tight to his leg that did, indeed, seem ready to fall off, they carried him away just as Valentine appeared, gracefully hopping down from the saddle to take her by the shoulders, block her vision of the gravely wounded Uxbridge.

"I...someone said it was over," she said, looking at the buttons on his sweat-soaked shirt, fingering the second one from the top, needing to see something ordinary, touch something she understood. She understood a button, its purpose. She didn't understand war or its purpose. "Oh, God, Brede. *Why?*"

He pulled her close against him, held her tight. "I don't know, Fanny. I stopped asking that particular question many years ago. But we've got him on the run now." He turned her around, pointed in the same direction the Field Marshal and Lord Uxbridge had been pointing as she had approached them. "Can you see him, Fanny? That infamous hat, that damned green coat. Look hard, Fanny, see a man who knows that, with this one decisive battle, his world is over."

Fanny strained to find Bonaparte in the small knot of soldiers in the distance even as Valentine handed her a spyglass.

"Don't look too high, Fanny, there's a reason they call him the Little Corporal."

She pressed the glass to her eye just as a slight, stooped-shouldered man in a heavy green wool coat that fell past his knees halted in his progress across a grassy field. He clasped his hands behind his back and then turned, glared down at the battle-field, his face nearly gray, his bloodless mouth moving slowly as he said something to the gaudily decorated soldier beside him. Then he nodded a single time, turned, and pulled himself up into a plain black coach, the door closing behind him even as the driver cracked his whip above the heads of the team. Within moments, the coach had disappeared below the rim of the hill.

Fanny lowered the glass, confused. That was the great Napoleon Bonaparte, Emperor of France, hopeful conqueror of the entire world? He looked so small, so ordinary; even ill. "Where will he go now?"

"To Paris," Valentine said quietly, his jaw tight. "To say his farewells to his ghosts, I suppose. When we lock him away this time, Fanny, it will be in a much stouter cage."

She looked up into Valentine's face, his tired eyes. She'd wondered how this so strong, enigmatic man might look in an unguarded moment. And now she knew. He looked incredibly sad, and terribly human.

"So many good men, all of them gone, Fanny. It's as Wellington says. Next to a battle lost, the saddest thing is a battle won. Damn Bonaparte for not staying where we put him, and damn us for not keeping him there."

"Will we chase him now? Will you and Rian chase him?"

Valentine shook his head. "The French are in disarray. Wellington's assigning others, thank God, to urge any stragglers on their way. It's over, Fanny, reduced to a rout now that Bonaparte has left the field. His *Grande Armeé* is defeated for the last time. Strange, isn't it? Ney told the French king he'd deliver Bonaparte to him in a cage when he deserted his Emperor for a space. And it's probably Ney's incompetence against Blücher at Ligny, letting him escape, that provided that cage. Not that the Allies won't hang Ney in any event, if they catch him."

"I hope we hang them all," Fanny said, meaning every word. She looked down on the battlefield, saw women and even children walking among the dead and wounded, sometimes stopping, falling to their knees, dropping their heads into their hands, weeping. Riderless horses wandered aimlessly, others writhed on the ground in pain. Occasional sharp gunshots made her flinch, as the horses were put out of their misery. Thousands. So many thousands of men, seemingly cast down on the expansive battlefield like broken toys dropped from a child's careless hand. "I'm just so glad it's over. Can we go back to Brussels now? Please? Just as soon as we find Rian."

Valentine tore his own gaze from the gruesome tableau spread out below them. "You haven't seen him?"

Fanny's fatigue disappeared as her heart skipped a beat. "Seen him? No. Not yet."

Valentine slipped an arm around her shoulders and led her over to the main tent. "He'll be in here, with the other aides," he told her, throwing back the flap and ushering her inside the dimness ahead of him.

But Rian wasn't there.

"Lieutenant Battenly," Valentine called out, seeing the chubby, red-cheeked aide who had been with Rian the night of Lady Richmond's ball. "Lieutenant Becket—where is he, if you please?"

Charles Battenly got slowly to his feet, cradling his left arm, which was contained in a rude sling. "We've won, haven't we, sir? Isn't it grand? But Lieutenant Becket? I haven't seen him, sir, not since I stupidly fell off my horse and got pushed in here, out of the way. He'd gone to take a message to the Prince of Orange, but…he hasn't returned? That was…but I saw him ride off hours ago, my lord. He should be—by God, sir!"

Fanny was already halfway out of the tent, running for Molly, Valentine hard on her heels. He watched as she levered herself neatly up and into the saddle, then mounted Shadow and pointed to the West. She shouldn't go with him, he knew that, just as he knew she'd follow him unless he ordered her tied to the nearest tree.

They moved on, following the ridges, slowly heading down into the area approaching Reille.

There had been no real fighting in the quadrant they were approaching, not for several hours, which was a good thing, as the Prince of Orange had been wounded and taken from the field. Rian should have returned to headquarters long since. Not that he was about to share his thoughts with Fanny. "Stay behind me," he ordered sharply. "There could be French stragglers. Desperate men who'd kill for our horses."

The clouds were back, bringing a murky dusk with them, and so their progress was necessarily slow. They didn't speak, didn't dare disturb the unnatural silence that slipped over the countryside once they were less than a half mile from the main battlefield.

Brede would hold up one gloved hand from time to time, motioning for Fanny to remain where she was as he dismounted and searched inside deserted houses, barns, small cow sheds. But nothing. There was no sign of Rian Becket.

As he'd climb back into the saddle Fanny would look at him, her eyes wide with fright, her lips clamped tightly between her teeth. And he'd shake his head. And they'd move on.

Perhaps Rian had been injured and taken up into one of the wagons heading back toward Brussels. That was one hopeful answer. But there were other, less hopeful possibilities. So they rode on, following the route that would keep a courier safely behind the concealing hills and ridges as he raced orders to the generals and carried information back to Wellington.

And then, at last, Molly's ears pricked and she gave a soft ruffling sound in her throat.

"Molly senses Jupiter somewhere," she told Valentine, bringing her mount up beside his. Her heart was pounding so hard in her own ears that she didn't know if she was whispering or shouting. "Somewhere close."

Valentine nodded, a finger to his lips, silently

cursing the rapidly falling darkness. The mare sensed something, that much was definite. But whether it was Rian's horse or some French stragglers, he couldn't know. He raised his hand again, warning her to remain where she was, and moved on cautiously, toward the cow shed, whose outline he could see about fifty feet ahead of them.

Fanny was having none of it. She was positive Rian was nearby, probably wounded. Prudently hiding, impatiently waiting for someone to come find him. She put her heels sharply into Molly's sides and shot forward, heading straight for the cow shed, dismounting only ten feet away and then running around to the open front of the shed even as Brede, a pistol in each hand, tried to catch up to her.

"Rian? Rian, it's me. Fanny. Where are you?"

And nothing. No one answered her.

Valentine took her arm and roughly pushed her behind him. Then the two of them slowly advanced into the almost complete darkness, stepping cautiously over the straw-strewn mud floor until he cursed shortly under his breath and moved to his left, to check on a shape he could still distinguish in that darkness.

Fanny had seen it, too, and collapsed to her knees on the straw beside the fallen horse. "Jupiter. Oh, Jupiter," she said quietly, putting out a hand to touch the horse's cheek.

Jupiter's visible eye rolled wildly and the horse struggled to rise, only to fall back against the ground.

Valentine was also kneeling beside the horse now, running an assessing gaze over the animal's side. "Shot. Gut shot," he said shortly. "There's nothing we can do except put the poor thing out of its pain."

"Oh, God, Brede," Fanny said, leaning forward until her forehead was pressed against the bay's cheek. "Where's Rian? He'd never leave Jupiter like this. He wouldn't. Not willingly."

Valentine got to his feet and searched the remainder of the small three-sided cow shed. He found a saber, most probably Rian's own, and kept his back to Fanny as he kicked straw over it, concealing the weapon, the bloody weapon, from her view.

He'd removed Rian Becket from the 13th, thinking he'd be safer on Wellington's staff. Had he instead sent the eager young man to his death?

Valentine slipped one pistol back inside his great-coat pocket and cocked the other one. "Go outside, Fanny, and hold on to the horse's bridles. We can't have them running off when they hear the shot."

"No, wait! Maybe we can do something," she begged, looking up at him, her eyes wet with tears. "Maybe Rian went for help and…and…"

Valentine knelt beside the horse's head. He couldn't make this easier for her, but he'd be damned if he'd have her here to see what he must do. "Now, Fanny. Rian would have done the same as we're doing, if he could have."

"I know. Oh, God, I know…." She pressed a kiss against Jupiter's cheek, and then used the backs of her hands to wipe at her wet cheeks as she stood up, stumbled out of the cow shed. She took hold of the two bridles and stepped between the horses, speaking softly to them both in the crushing silence that seemed to bear down on her from every direction.

Waited for the sound of the shot.

"It's all right, my pretty ones. Nothing to worry about, nothing to fear. Nothing to—" She flinched at the sharp report of the pistol, holding tight as both horses pulled up their heads. "*Shh.* Nothing to worry… Oh, God, Rian, where are you?"

Valentine emerged from the cow shed, the now empty pistol still in his hand. He was tired. So incredibly tired. "Are you all right, Fanny?"

"I will be, when we find Rian," she told him, handing him the reins to his mount. "He can't be far, can he?"

Valentine put his hands on her shoulders, holding her in place. "Fanny, we'll never find him anymore tonight. It's too dark, and there could still be some French in the area, doing their best to avoid our soldiers, and that shot may have alerted them to our presence. We'll have enough trouble trying to make it back to our main encampment."

"Headquarters? But…but Rian's out here some-where. His horse gone. Possibly even wounded. I'm not going back to any encampment. You can," she said, her upper lip curling. "If you're afraid of the dark. If I can't move on, then I'm staying here until morning."

"Fanny, for the love of God, use your head. Rian's not here. His horse has been shot out from under him, not in the field, but most probably right here, inside that damn shed behind us. What does that tell you?"

"Nothing," she said, her chin trembling. "It tells me nothing. Why should it tell me anything?"

Valentine turned his head away for a moment, took a deep breath and then let it out slowly. Turned to look at her once more. "He was being followed. Chased. He rode his horse into the cow shed to hide, wait out of sight until whoever was out there passed him by. That was good, solid thinking. But they didn't pass him by, Fanny. They found him. Inside the shed, trapped in a corner like a mouse. They fired on him. That's how Jupiter was shot. A wound like that, into his underbelly? For whatever reason, Jupiter was already down when he was shot."

"Then…then where is Rian?" Fanny asked, her chest rising and falling rapidly as she tried to control her breathing, her racing heartbeat. "If he was cor-nered, if Jupiter was shot, then where's Rian? Where's his…where's his body?"

"I don't know, sweetings. I don't know. They took him, for some reason. Maybe to use as a shield or a hostage until they were free of our lines. It's madness now, all up and down the countryside. The French running, us chasing them. But after that, Fanny, once clear of here, they'd have no use for him anymore, would they? His sword is in the shed. I hid it from you until I could think of something to do, something to say that might explain what happened. But there's nothing to do, Fanny, and nothing else to say. There's blood on the sword. Whoever they were, Rian fought them. But…but he didn't win. If he had, he'd have put Jupiter out of his pain, and he'd still have his sword. You know that and I know that. I'm so sorry."

"No," Fanny said quietly, then drew in a ragged breath and began pounding her fists against Valentine's chest. "No…no…*no!* You're wrong! You're wrong! Damn you, Brede, *you're wrong!*" She collapsed against his strength. "Please…please say you're wrong. Please…"

Valentine held her as her entire body trembled with her sobs, but then pressed her face close against his chest as he thought he heard movement in the trees and dense bushes surrounding the cow shed. The report of the pistol. Fanny's anguished cries. They had roused something…or somebody. Why in *hell* had he let her come along with him?

He roughly pushed her toward the cow shed even as he grabbed the reins of both horses and pulled them after him, into the darkness of the shed. He might be repeating Rian's mistake, but the cow shed offered the only real protection in the area.

Fanny didn't fight him. In truth, she didn't do much of anything. She was too shocked, too caught up in her grief, to even realize what Valentine had done, or what his actions meant. She just took herself to the far end of the shed, away from the body of Rian's horse, and sat down, her back to the corner, and curled into herself, both physically and mentally.

Valentine loosely tied the horses to the center post of the shed, praying they wouldn't spook at the sight of the dead bay or the smell of fresh blood. He pulled the still-loaded pistol from beneath his cloak even as he rooted in the straw for Rian's sword.

Then he went down on his knees in front of Fanny and lifted her chin with his hand. "Stay here," he whispered, then squeezed at her chin until the resultant pain forced her to look up at him, acknowledge him. "Fanny, sweetings, pay attention. Start counting. Slowly—one...two...three. If I'm not back by the time you reach five hundred, or if you hear shots, get on your horse here, inside the shed, and then set her at a full gallop back the way we came. Leave Shadow here—but you go. *Fanny*," he repeated in a fierce undertone. "Do you understand me?"

She blinked up at him. "Rian's dead, Brede," she told him. "Why didn't I know? Why didn't I sense it?"

"Enough, Fanny," he told her shortly, giving her chin another sharp squeeze. "Time to think about yourself. Do you want to die here?"

She gave a sharp shake of her head, freeing her face from his painful grasp. Why couldn't he just leave her alone? "I don't care…."

"No? Well, I by damn *do* care where and when I die, and it won't be here, and it won't be now."

How she hated him. "How can you be so heartless?"

Valentine leaned in closer to her. He had to rouse her, even if that meant rousing her anger. "My heart doesn't enter into what I do, Fanny. I *survive,* and that's enough."

She closed her eyes against the intensity of his gaze. "It's not enough for me, Brede. And it shouldn't be enough for you."

Valentine's head snapped back as if she'd slapped him. He picked up Rian's sword and moved silently toward the open end of the cow shed. He stopped, listened and then stepped out into the night. He did not look back at Fanny.

His back to the shed, he moved to his right, pushing into the chest-high brush and trees, planning to circle the structure, once, then again a good ten paces deeper into the brush. Then once more, securing a perimeter a solid thirty feet around where Fanny sat in the corner of the shed. One way or another, nothing could be allowed to remain alive inside that perimeter.

Whoever was out there couldn't possibly see in the dark any better than he could. Besides, he and Fanny had mounts, and whoever was out here with him was on foot, or else either Shadow or Molly would have sensed the other animals, even with the smell of Jupiter's blood in their nostrils. A clear thirty yards would protect them as they rode out of the cow shed and back the way they'd come.

Fanny should have counted to at least one hundred and fifty by now. He still hadn't seen anyone, heard anything, but he knew better than to dismiss the uncomfortable feeling that someone else was out here with him in the dark.

He was halfway into his third circle when he tripped over Rian Becket's boot, crashing to the ground, his head not two feet away from the boy's handsome face.

"My lord…" Rian said, his voice weak as he lay awkwardly propped against a tree trunk. "Pardon me for…for not rising."

Valentine pushed himself into a sitting position, running his gaze over Rian's body. "Where?"

"My hip. Jupiter went down with me landing beneath him. Something…something's probably broken inside somewhere, I think." Rian grimaced. "My leg, too, but that's not as bad. And then this…"

"Christ," Valentine said as Rian struggled to raise his left arm. Back in the cow shed, Fanny was still counting. "What happened?"

"I…I rode straight into them. They came at me from both sides, grabbing for Jupiter's bridle. Never saw them coming. Four…maybe five of them, on foot. Jupiter reared—clipped one of them with his hooves, and we were off."

"Easy, Rian. We'll talk later. Once we're clear of here."

"Oh, I don't think so, sir." Rian smiled, his teeth showing white in the pale moonlight revealed when one of the clouds scudded farther across the night sky. "They were on foot, so I figured we'd outrun them. Jupiter must have…must have stepped in a hole. We got up but…couldn't leave Jupiter, could I? Not that I could go far with this hip. Hurt like the devil for a while. There was nothing for it but to… Saw the cow shed, figured it would give good protection. But it was like…as if they were hunting me. Must have wanted Jupiter, don't you think? They… they overpowered me." He stopped, took several shaky breaths. "Jupiter? He's all right? I heard a pistol shot. Woke me up, actually."

"Your horse is fine," Valentine lied smoothly, swiveling about on his haunches, peering intently into the brush that surrounded them. "How the hell did you get out here?"

"It wasn't my idea, I assure you," Rian told him, lying back against the tree trunk once more, clearly losing his grip on what small strength he had left to him. "They overpowered me. I said that, yes? Dragged me out of the cow shed, dragged me away along with their dead—two dead, my lord. I have at least that to take with me to hell. I'm afraid…I'm afraid I passed out then. Woke…woke only when I heard the pistol. They're gone? I suppose the shot scared them away and they dropped me like…like so much unwanted baggage."

They'd left him here? So they knew where he was, out here in the dark. But Valentine couldn't know where they were, how far they'd retreated at the sound of his pistol shot. He put a finger to his lips. Listened. Wondered where Fanny was in her count. "Four or five, you said. And two dead? That leaves two or three. But we're not going to wait around here in case they come back, merely in order to count noses, are we, Lieutenant? I've got to get you and Fanny out of here."

"Fanny? Sweet Jesus—you brought her out here?" Rian struggled once more to rise, but his injuries were too much for him and he fell back once more. "You stupid bastard."

Valentine smiled slightly. "I agree completely.

And, much as I'd like to stay here and talk about how well *you* were able to keep her where she should be, I think it's time we were on our way. I'll get Shadow, bring him here. You can't ride, not with those wounds, but I can tie you to the saddle."

"No," Rian said, shaking his head. "I'm done. We both know it. Look at me, for God's sake. I'd only slow you down, and for no purpose. Just…just take Fanny and get out of here."

"I can't do that, Becket," Valentine told him quickly. "Fanny's back there, half out of her mind, believing you dead."

"I *am* dead, at least most of me is, and the rest will soon follow. Have some compassion, man. I don't even hurt anymore. We both know what that means. Don't…don't make her see me like this…remember me like this. Take her away from here."

Valentine opened his mouth to protest, but whatever he was going to say was silenced by the sound of rifle shot that, he noticed with half his brain, came only a split second after the dirt a few yards away was kicked up by the impact of the ball. Someone had fired in the direction of their voices, which made whoever it was too damn close.

"They're back. I wonder why." Rian reached out his right hand. "Your pistol, man. Give it to me. At…at least I may get one of them…slow them down. Give it to me, and go. Get Fanny and go."

Valentine thought with his head, not his heart. Staying alive counted on him thinking with his head. But now there was Fanny. He had to get her to safety. That was paramount. Whoever was out there would see her for a woman with only a cursory glance. What they might do to her wasn't to be imagined. He could hope that the sound of the rifle shot had shaken Fanny from her misery, and that she'd ride off on her own, as he'd instructed. But he already felt that to be a futile hope. She wouldn't leave, not until she was forced to do so.

What she'd do to him, if she ever learned that he had left her brother here to die, to most probably be hacked to pieces now that he couldn't be used as a hostage or shield, didn't bear thinking about at all.

To stay here, try to guard Rian and still protect Fanny, thirty yards away from him, really wasn't possible. Not with a sword and a single pistol. Not when he couldn't even see the enemy.

His thoughts took only seconds, but they seemed like hours; wasted time, when he already knew what he had to do. He was a survivor. He stayed alive because he had long ago made it a point to stay alive. He should already be gone. If he stayed, they'd all be dead, Fanny worse than dead. If he left, Rian would die within moments. He'd die anyway, most probably. His injuries were that numerous, and that grave.

But if he left now, ran away, Fanny might survive. She'd live, and he'd never be able to look her in the eyes again, knowing what he'd done.

"They haven't fired again, so they may be out of powder. I can circle around to the north…come up behind them," he said, keeping low, shifting his gaze left and right, for the Frenchmen must be on the move by now, trying to outflank him.

"No time. Would you, for Christ's sake, *go*."

There was a rustle in the tall brush, over to Valentine's left. If there were two, if there were three, they had doubtless moved off singly, spreading themselves out, just so they could close in on their quarry. That's what he'd do. One of them could even now be inching toward the cow shed. They'd want the horses, definitely. He knew he'd go for the horses.

There was no decision to make, not really. Rian couldn't be readily moved, and Fanny couldn't be allowed to stay.

Valentine cocked the pistol, fairly certain Rian didn't have the strength to do so, and handed it to him. "Godspeed, Lieutenant Becket."

Rian took the pistol, looked at it. "I wonder. Should I use this on the Frogs, or on myself. Hmm? No, I'm too much the coward for that, and I think I'd like to take another one of them with me. Promise me. Promise me you'll take care of Fanny. That you'll…you'll make her forget me. She…she has to forget me."

Valentine didn't understand what Rian was saying to him. Forget him, her own brother? Why? But there was no more time for conversation. "I'll take care of her, Rian, for as long she needs me. You have my solemn word on that."

Rian smiled wanly. "I've just cursed you, my lord, haven't I? But there's worse fates than Fanny, I imagine. Wait."

Valentine was already off his knees, standing in a low crouch, ready to run. "I can still take you. On my back."

"No," Rian said, shaking his head. "Just…just this. Did we win? Did we send those bastards all to hell?"

Valentine smiled grimly. "Oh, we did that, my friend. We most certainly did do that."

Rian closed his eyes, seemingly satisfied. "Good. Wish I'd seen it. Now, get her out of here."

Valentine took off low, keeping himself small against the surrounding brush and thin tree trunks, the saber transferred to his left hand as he pulled out the stiletto he felt more comfortable with, the knife that had served him well in the past.

The pale moonlight served more to cast confusing shadows than it did to reveal the area higher on the hill, in front of the cow shed. All he could do was risk it, dash into the shed as quickly as possible, weapons at the ready, and hope to God that Fanny was still there, still safe.

When he crashed into the shed she was still sitting in the corner. She had her arms folded on her bent knees, her head resting on her forearms. She looked up, surprised, but said nothing. Stayed where she was.

Valentine grabbed her arm, ruthlessly yanking her to her feet, and nearly threw her up into the saddle, pushing her head down over Molly's neck before mounting Shadow and grabbing the mare's bridle. "Keep low so you're not knocked off as we go through the doorway," was all he said to her, then did the same as he kicked Shadow forward.

The two horses burst from the cow shed, Shadow's muscular shoulder coming into abrupt contact with a dark figure holding a rifle in both hands.

"Merde!"

Valentine saw the man's face for a moment, less than a moment, only two feet in front of him in the moonlight. He knew he'd see that face in his nightmares. The hatred, the animal cunning in those pale gray eyes. Thank the stars that the rifle was obviously unloaded and that the man had chosen to swing it like a club, and not advance with bayonet attached. He'd also remember, puzzle over it, that the Frenchman was not a soldier, not in uniform.

And then the attacker was on his back in the dirt

and Shadow and Molly were straining to fly across the dark, unknown landscape.

Molly stumbled slightly just as a rifle shot split the night, and Fanny cried out, began to fall toward Valentine. He caught her, cursing the scarlet of her uniform, the startling white of her braces, the flash of brightly polished brass on her buckles that had made her the obvious target.

As Molly caught her stride once more, Valentine lifted Fanny by the crosspoint of her braces and threw her unceremoniously across his saddle, all the while using his booted feet to urge Shadow into a full gallop now that they'd gained the ridge.

Behind them came the sound of another shot, this time the sharp report of a pistol. If there were a God, Rian had done as he promised, greatly increasing his sister's chances of escaping the area.

If she weren't already dead…

Molly followed just behind the stallion, and Valentine cursed and prayed and cursed again, all the way back across the ridge, all the way past the posted sentries, not stopping until he reached the area where the surgeons were busily cutting off arms and legs, stacking them like cordwood beside the tents.

CHAPTER THIRTEEN

FANNY SAT IN THE SMALL walled garden behind Lady Whalley's rented town house in Brussels, her back straight, her hands folded in her lap, the bandage around her head reduced just that morning to a thick white patch covering her right ear and cheek.

She barely noticed the change. She'd not complained of pain, not once, nor had she asked if the bullet that had grazed the side of her head would leave a scar. Physical pain meant nothing to her, a scar less than nothing.

She ate, if someone put food in front of her. She slept, sometimes for twelve or more hours at a time. Asleep, she was safe. No memories, no absurd fears, no empty future.

She'd barely heard Lucie tell her that Bonaparte had abdicated just four days after the leaving the battlefield, or that the Allies were now, a week later, already in Paris. Because none of that meant anything to her.

Lady Whalley's maid, Frances, dressed her and

undressed her, tended to her bandage, took her out into the sunny garden in the afternoons for some healing air.

Fanny lived. Fanny breathed. She ate and she slept.

But that was all she did. All she'd allow herself to do.

She hadn't spoken, not so much as a word, in eight days.

In the afternoon of the ninth day, Lady Whalley decided that eight days was more than enough of *that!*

Her brother was driving her to distraction, for one thing. Visiting every day ever since he'd returned from wherever he'd run off to, wearing a hole in the carpet in the small drawing room—not that it was Lucille's carpet, so that really didn't matter. What mattered was that Valentine had become an absolute *bear.* Why, he hadn't even shaved in days, and one could only hope he'd changed his linen.

Honestly, the dramatics of the man! Bringing Fanny to her, declaring first that he thanked God she was there to help him, then cursing her for remaining in Brussels when he'd given *distinct* orders that she should leave.

As she'd told him she was made of sterner stuff than that! Run away? Ridiculous. She'd never had a qualm, had been certain the Iron Duke would put Boney to the rout.

That she'd spent several hours of that fateful June day cowering in the dank basement, Wiggins standing at the ready at the head of the stairs with a blunderbuss— Well, her brother didn't have to know everything.

She certainly didn't know everything, did she? Rian Becket, like so many others, was dead, poor pretty thing. That she knew. Fanny had been shot doing Lord only knew what; she knew that, as well. But Valentine had merely ridden out not ten minutes after depositing the unconscious Fanny with her with orders to keep the girl alive or suffer the consequences, and not returned for six long days. She had no explanation for Valentine's bizarre behavior.

The way he was constantly pacing her carpets now? Lucie wished he had stayed away longer. Perhaps a month or more would have sufficed.

And it wasn't as if he came to actually *visit* with Fanny. He never asked to see her, but only wanted to hear how she was doing, if she'd spoken yet, if she'd cried, if she'd— Well, if he wanted to know all of that all he had to do was step into the garden and find out for himself.

But he wouldn't. Really, for an intelligent man, and she'd always thought him at least intelligent, her brother was behaving like a near lunatic. Which was what she'd told him in no uncertain terms not two hours earlier. She'd sent him packing back to his own town house with a flea in his ear, demanding he not show his face again until he was washed and dressed better than some ragman, and then presented himself to Fanny because she, Lucie, wasn't going to be flogged anymore with his horrid mood.

Now, feeling rather full of her new power, it was only left to Lucie to shake some sense into Fanny Becket, rouse her from the depths of despair that were understandable, but not to be indulged any longer without the possibility of causing permanent harm. That's what Frances had said at least, and since having Fanny up and about once more suited Lucie's plans, she was more than willing to lend her maid's opinion credence in the matter.

After all, everyone was leaving Brussels now, and those who remained were certainly not jolly sorts at the moment; holed up in their rented houses, tending their own wounded. Everyone else was in London, celebrating their grand victory. That Lucie was still moldering here was past comprehension!

Acknowledging herself to be a bad, horribly shallow person—and what else had she been reared to be, after all?—Lucie took herself out into the garden, determination in her every step.

"Fanny? Oh, look, what a beautiful day! My stars, one would think nothing had ever— Well, we won't speak of that, will we? I certainly hadn't planned to speak of that. No, not at all. How are you, my dear? Valentine came calling again, to ask about you. I think he's smitten, to tell you the truth, although with Valentine it's difficult to tell. He plays his cards very close to his vest. But he's either smitten or he's gone stupid, and I never thought Valentine stupid."

Lucie sat down beside Fanny on the stone bench, wishing she'd told Frances to search up a pillow for her, as the stone might snag her gown, which would be a pity. "You know what I'd like, Fanny? I'd like you to blink, my dear. Always staring like that? My stars, it's disconcerting."

Fanny turned her head to the woman. Blinked. Turned away again, clearly dismissing her.

"Oh, that's quite enough!" Lucie said sharply, getting to her feet once more. "What happened was terrible. Such a lovely young man. So many lovely young men. Poor Uxbridge, his leg gone. My stars, he's ordered it buried here, you know— the leg, you understand—and plans to have a monument erected. *That's* what we British do. We lift our chins, and we carry on! We do not *wallow.*"

Fanny looked up at the woman dispassionately. "Go away, Lucie."

"Ah! She speaks! Well, that is above all things wonderful. I'd worried the bullet had struck you dumb, and that would be a pity. I know I'd go mad if I couldn't speak. Valentine would doubtless order a monument erected to his delight in my lost voice—but no, I won't be silly. I didn't come out here to be silly, although I'm not very good at being comforting, am I?"

No, Fanny thought, she wasn't good at being comforting. But Lucie had roused her, speaking of Valentine. So she asked the question she didn't really want to hear answered. "Did...did Brede find him?"

Lucie frowned. "Find whom, my dear? Oh! So *that's* what he was doing, was it? My stars, I never thought of that. He was out looking for your brother's— Uh, no. No, I don't think so. He didn't mention that to me."

She sat down once more, took one of Fanny's hands in hers. "But it was imperative that the bodies be buried, my dear, as quickly as possible. It's this heat, you understand? Wiggins has been helping, poor man. Thousands and thousands dead. Mass graves for most of them, I'm afraid."

Fanny winced, unable to control her anguished expression at the thought of Rian's body being dragged to an open pit, then tossed into it and hastily covered with dirt.

Lucie patted Fanny's hand. "But we'll put up a monument, won't we? If Uxbridge can have one for his silly leg, then we can— Fanny don't look at me that way. I'm so sorry. I'm not doing this well, am I? I've had no practice in such things. Even when my late husband died, I didn't know what to say. I actually giggled during the services, I was that nervous. Quite embarrassing. His harridan of a mother hasn't spoken to me since. Although that's no great loss to me, I can tell you that."

Fanny got to her feet. "I have to go home, I suppose, even without his body," she said, coming to a decision after so many days of not being able to think at all. "I don't want to, but I have to tell them about Rian."

Behind her, Valentine politely cleared his throat. "I wrote to them myself, Fanny, several days ago. To Jack, actually, so that he could choose his own way to inform your family. Sergeant-Major Hart was injured, only slightly, and I convinced him to personally deliver the letter to Romney Marsh. I arranged transport for him."

Fanny looked around to see Valentine standing about six feet away from her. He was dressed in black, in fine town clothes, and he looked tired, thinner. Older. She wanted to throw herself into his arms and insist that he hold her, just hold her tight. But she only nodded, to acknowledge that she'd heard him. "Sergeant-Major Hart. A good man. Thank you, Brede."

Valentine stepped closer. The sight of her bandage still put his stomach in knots. The bullet had grazed the side of her head, rendering her unconscious. A relatively minor wound, as wounds went, but accompanied by so much blood that he had been certain she was dead when he'd reached the encampment and pulled her from the saddle. If Molly hadn't stumbled when she had, the bullet could have proved fatal.

"He told me you'd offered him a home at Becket Hall. As he decided he'd seen his last battle, he accepted. How are you, Fanny? How's your wound? Do you have headaches?"

She shook her head, avoided looking at him. "Not for days," she said, raising a hand to touch the bandage. "I don't remember being shot. Do you suppose Rian didn't remember, either? Before he died? I can't bear... I can't bear to think of him hurting."

"Then don't, Fanny. It does no good. Lucille?"

His sister got to her feet, twisting her fingers together in front of her. "Yes, yes. I must go instruct Frances to pack, mustn't I? We will be leaving now, won't we, Valentine? Now that Fanny's so much— Well, she's talking, isn't she? That would be a good thing."

"Lucille."

"Yes, yes, I'm going," she said, lifting her skirts as she stepped around him. "You could at least *attempt* to be civil, you know. A simple thank-you to your sister who— Oh, my stars! Don't *glower* like that!"

Valentine waited until his sister had disappeared into the house, then sat down next to Fanny. "I tried, sweetings. But I couldn't find him. I'm so sorry."

Fanny bit her bottom lip between her teeth. Nodded, to show that she'd heard, she'd understood. "We'll never know what happened to him, will we?"

"No, I don't think we will," Valentine said, longing to tell her the truth. How he'd found Rian. How he'd left him. How he'd gone back to the cow shed at first light, but Rian's body hadn't been there. Hadn't been anywhere. How he'd ridden south, chasing the retreating French, searching, searching. And all the time trying to make sense of what Rian had told him, make sense of the light-eyed man he'd seen for that one, taut second before Shadow had knocked the Frenchman to the ground.

Fanny turned forward once more, looking across the gardens, seeing nothing, feeling only the deep, constant dull ache that was Rian's loss.

Valentine sat quietly beside her, remembering his conversation with Sergeant-Major Hart. He'd told Valentine that he had been approached the morning of the battle already known as the Battle of Waterloo, that a well-dressed Englishman had come into the camp, asking for the whereabouts of Lieutenant Rian Becket.

Hart had informed the man that Rian was serving as a junior aide to Wellington, and the man had thanked him and gone off again. "Seemed queer to me, my lord. Like the fellow had been searchin' everywheres for the Lieutenant," Hart had told Valentine. "But then I thought it might be someone from his family, come huntin' up Miss Becket to take her off home with them. Did they find her, my lord?"

Valentine had answered vaguely, then gone off to sit alone, think some more. But he hadn't been able to come up with any answers. According to Wiggins, no Beckets had shown up at his door, looking for Fanny. Not in these past eight days. If someone had come to Brussels, surely it would be Jack Eastwood himself, and Jack hadn't contacted him.

So who had spoken to the Sergeant-Major? Who were the men—not soldiers—who had followed Rian, because Rian had even said he felt as if they had been chasing him? And, most important of all— where was Rian Becket's body? The burial parties had not been so far flung, searching out bodies so far from the battlefield. Not at first, at least, and Valentine had ridden out that very next morning, to collect the body so it could be transported home for burial.

"We'll leave tomorrow, Fanny, now that you're

fit to travel," he said at last. "My yacht is moored at Ostend, and we'll sail straight to Dover."

She shook her head. "Not Dover. Becket Hall is on the Channel, with its own small harbor. We can go directly there. We're to the west of Dymchurch, and I'll be able to point out where we… Oh, God. I can't go home. I just can't. Not yet."

"Fanny, your family needs to see you, know you're all right."

She turned to him, took his hands in hers, not even realizing she'd done so. How could she put into words the irrational fear she'd felt explode from the recesses of her mind ever since seeing all those broken bodies lying on the battlefield—all of the horror bursting out of her nightmare and into reality? She couldn't, could she?

So she'd say what she could say. "Rian's there. Everywhere I look, he'll be there. I can't go home. Not yet. I can't face not seeing anything there but his ghost. Don't you understand that, Brede?"

Promise me. Promise me you'll take care of Fanny. That you'll make her forget me. She has to forget me.

"Sweetings, be reasonable. You have to face the truth some time. He's gone. One day the pain will fade and your memories will be happy ones." Valentine cursed himself silently as he heard the ridiculous platitudes echo inside his head. Stupid, stupid! If only he could tell her the truth. That her brother had died a hero, saving her…saving Valentine, as well.

But he couldn't say that. No more than he could tell her that Rian had made him promise to take care of her…make her forget him. Forget her own brother. Why? Why would Becket have said that? Valentine couldn't sleep, trying to reason out why Rian had said such a strange thing.

Fanny kept tight hold on his hands and allowed the silence to grow as she worked up the courage to put her wild plan into motion. Maybe she'd think more clearly once her head didn't hurt so much, but for now, she only knew one way to stay clear of Becket Hall until she could beat down her nearly overwhelming sense of dread. And there was only one person who could help her do that.

How she longed to just cease living, permanently flee from this crushing fear. But Rian wouldn't have allowed her to do that. His ghost would mock her as she rode the marsh, as she sat on a rock and stared out over the Channel. Better to be where he couldn't see her….

She withdrew her hands at last to unbutton the three top buttons of her morning gown and reach inside the bodice, coming out with a paper folded several times over. She handed it to Valentine. "Read this, please."

Valentine took the paper, warm from its contact

with Fanny's skin, unfolded it, quickly recognizing it for what it was. Rian Becket's will.

The document was far from customary. But, then, Rian had been a young man, and probably not familiar with the high-flown language of such documents.

Valentine scanned the single sheet quickly, passing over the disposition of Becket's horse, Jupiter, and his favorite swords, and his collection of toy soldiers, which had been gifted to a William Henry Becket.

"William Becket?" he asked, pausing for a moment.

"Our brother Spencer's son," Fanny said quietly. "He's little more than a baby, and Rian wants him to play at war."

Valentine nodded, read on. Read through to the end. Carefully folded the page and handed it back to Fanny. Without saying a word.

"Rian said…he said we'd read it together when he got back. Laugh over it," Fanny told him, slipping the page back into her bodice. "Do you think it's funny, Brede?"

"He knew I had put myself in position as your temporary guardian," Valentine told her. *Promise me. Promise me you'll take care of Fanny.* "I was… honored to do so."

Fanny looked at him, her eyes stinging with unshed tears. She wasn't being fair to the man, but her need was great, beating down her better instincts. "Not your ward, Brede. You read what he wrote. Rian...Rian *gave* me to you. Like I was his to give."

Yes. Valentine wondered about that, as he already wondered about so much else. *Make her forget me. She has to forget me.*

"It's a moot point, Fanny," he said at last. "You have a father, you have a family. You'll soon be with them again."

She shook her head again. "I can't go back there, Brede. Not yet. He's not there, yet he'll be everywhere I look." She looked up at the blue sky, praying for Valentine's understanding, his compassion. "What am I going to do?"

"As you have a family, adoption is out of the question. So I suppose you could marry me."

The words were out of Valentine's mouth before he could draw them back. He hadn't meant to say them. He'd thought them, over and over these past eight days. Thought them, wished them, believed them. But he'd never imagined he'd ever say them. Even if Rian had asked him to take care of her, gained his solemn word that he would.

What had Rian said, joked? *I've just cursed you, my lord, haven't I? But there's worse fates than Fanny, I imagine.*

And the boy had been right. There could be worse fates. Like living with Fanny and never tell ing her the truth about her brother, how he had died. Living together, living a lie.

Fanny hadn't spoken since he'd blurted out his ridiculous suggestion.

"Fanny, I— Please, forget I said that. The last thing I should be doing is pressuring you. Not now. Let me take you home and—"

"Yes," Fanny said, cutting him off before he could take back the words, words she'd prayed to hear, but not for the reason she'd given him. "That would be a solution, wouldn't it? Rian admired you very much. He… I suppose he'd like that."

Rian again. What did her brother have to do with where his sister wed?

But before Valentine could find his tongue, Fanny was speaking again. Not that she'd look at him. "We'd go to your home, of course. Nowhere near Romney Marsh. Somewhere safe. Somewhere where I'd never have to even think about…about bad things happening again."

"Bad things, Fanny? Bad things happen at Becket Hall?" He didn't understand, and he was more intrigued than ever. Who were these Beckets? What sort of family had his friend Jack Eastwood married into? "Fanny? Is there…is there some sort of *problem* at Becket Hall, with your family? Is that why you ran away?"

She blinked, pushed back her shoulders, Valentine thought, as if snapping herself to attention at a command only she heard.

"No, of course not. I shouldn't have said that. I…I'm tired, and would like to return to my room. But we're settled on this now, Brede? We'll marry?"

She started to rise, but he gently pulled her back down beside him. "I believe I have enough consequence to arrange for a vicar by tomorrow morning, before we leave for Ostend. If you really want it."

Fanny closed her eyes, fighting back the tears she hadn't shed in eight long days and nights. Rian would want this, wouldn't he? He'd want her to feel safe. And there'd been the dream, that strange dream, with Valentine standing in Rian's place. Protecting her, allowing her to feel safe again. Maybe she didn't really understand what she was doing, what was driving her, leading her to Valentine. Odette would, but Odette wasn't here, was she? Just as Rian wasn't here. She had to protect herself. "I think that would make Rian happy."

Valentine didn't understand. Damn Rian. What did he care about a dead man's happiness? Yet he did. He owed the man that much, and more.

But now was not the time for questions, was it? Especially now, when he was getting just what he wanted. Did that make him selfish? And if it did, he'd deal with his guilt at another time.

He helped his now affianced bride to her feet,

bent to kiss the bandage on her cheek. "Rian would want *you* to be happy, Fanny."

"I know. Thank you, Brede. I don't want to be a burden."

"You won't be," he told her, walking her to the door to the back of the town house. "If my sister is to be believed, I'll be your burden."

At last she smiled. Only a small smile, but it was there, and Valentine dared to believe he could one day make her smile again. Be happy again.

"I'll just always make sure to keep you well fed," she told him, then disappeared up the steep servant stairs, leaving him to shrug his shoulders at Frances, who was bobbing a curtsey at him even as she held out a plate of warm cherry tarts.

He shook his head and left the kitchen....

CHAPTER FOURTEEN

THEY'D BEEN MARRIED for six hours, and Fanny had
pointedly avoided Valentine for all of them, pleading the headache and spending the entire crossing
belowdecks.

She'd hugged Lucille goodbye on the Dover
docks, Wiggins traveling with Lady Whalley and
her maid in order to hire a coach that would safely
deliver them to the Brede mansion in Portland
Square in the fine style to which her brother's
fortune had accustomed her.

Valentine had been glad to see her go, nearly as
pleased as his sister was to wave her farewells.
Knowing Lucille, news of his impetuous marriage
would be dinner table conversation all over Mayfair
by the following evening, with Lucille the center of
attention. She'd been positively giddy at the prospect.

And Fanny had been glad to see her go. Not that
she didn't enjoy Lucie, because she did. The woman
could be quite amusing in her silly, selfish way. But
Fanny wanted to be alone with Valentine. Her hus-

band. She might try not to be happy that they were wed, attempt to concentrate only on her very real grief, but she couldn't ignore the man beside her. She hadn't been able to ignore anything about him ever since they'd first met.

"Lady wife," Valentine said, extending his arm to Fanny as Lucille, chattering nineteen to the dozen with a friend she'd spied on the docks, walked away without so much as a final wave goodbye. "We can stay here in Dover, dine and return to the *Pegasus* tomorrow morning."

Fanny looked up at him, attempting to gauge his mood. He'd called her his lady wife. Was he mocking her? Already regretting his decision?

"Or?" she asked as she slipped her arm through his, hoping he'd give her another option, as she wasn't enamored of the idea of spending the night—her wedding night—at a Dover inn. As for the rest of it, she knew she was a bride, and what her groom would expect of her. She had weighed all of that when she'd decided on this course of action, and decided it was a small price to pay for her selfish safety.

A very small price, as she enjoyed Valentine's kisses. Enjoyed them, longed for more, just as she longed for his smile, his touch. That was also selfish of her. She was a terrible person, with her beloved Rian dying even as her heart had been pulling her in two directions at once. Oh, her head ached. Her heart ached....

"Or we could continue directly on to Brede Manor, passing the night on the water. I would like to get the horses offloaded as quickly as possible. The *Pegasus* wasn't really designed to carry horses."

Fanny nodded, thinking of Molly and Shadow tied to the rear deck outside of the cabin, tucked inside a rude construction meant for Shadow alone and now forced to accommodate both horses.

"I think we should push on, if you don't mind." Then she smiled as a ridiculous thought struck her. She had absolutely no idea where they were going. "Where, precisely, is Brede Manor?"

"Not all that far from where you tell me Becket Hall is located, actually. Your home is on the coast, but Brede Manor is about a half dozen miles inland from Hastings, in East Sussex."

That close? Fanny tripped over the plank leading up onto the yacht, catching at his arm so that she didn't fall. "But...but you said you thought only sheep lived in Romney Marsh."

"And I stand by my ignorant statement, having never traveled there. Brighton, London—those, lamentably, are my more familiar haunts. But earlier I took the opportunity to consult one of the maps belowdecks, and it turns out that, as the crow flies, Dymchurch itself is on the coast and probably less than forty miles from Brede Manor, considerably more if we sailed there, hugging the coastline. And yet the whole of Romney Marsh could be on another continent for all the attention I've paid it, I'm afraid. Even my maps, admittedly a few years old, seem very vague in their drawings of the Marsh coastline."

Fanny knew that, at least. Wasn't that one of the reasons her papa had chosen Romney Marsh in the first place? It's ever-changing shoreline, its—to most Englishmen—monotonous scenery, its lack of inhabitants, the commonly held belief of most Englishmen that the approximately one hundred square miles of the Marsh was worthless except for its wool and hops? And the goods brought across the Channel by the wild, uncivilized local smugglers, of course.

"Less than forty miles? I thought…I thought you lived in the North, or possibly in the West, or—we'll be sailing past Becket Hall on our way to your estate, won't we?"

"Yes, I would suppose so, although we won't be sailing too close to the coastline, not at night," Valentine said, not unaware that her complexion had gone quite pale. "Have you reconsidered? Would you like the *Pegasus* to put in there? I would feel much more comfortable apprising your family of our marriage in person, rather than via a letter."

"No!" Fanny put her hand to her mouth, as if she could take back her quick response, or at least phrase it differently, keep the panic out of her voice. Her family would be full of questions—incisive questions for which she currently had no logical answers. "That is, I really would like to go to your estate for...for a few weeks? Until my wound is healed?"

"Your wound. Of course," Valentine said, not understanding, but willing to agree to anything she wanted, if it would bring the color back into her cheeks. She'd been so brave, even fearless. Her obvious fright now, her seeming emotional frailty, tore at his heart. "I spoke with Lucille's maid, and she assured me the scar, if there is one, won't be too terrible. Is that what's worrying you? That the sight of your bandage will upset your family?"

Fanny shrugged, then turned to stand with her palms pressed on the rail as the *Pegasus* lifted anchor and set out into the Channel once more. "I don't mind if there's a scar. Do you?" She looked up at him. "Would it disgust you, if I was scarred?"

He lifted her hand to his lips, looking at her intently as he pressed his mouth against her sweet-smelling skin. "It would have destroyed me entirely if you had succumbed to your wound. Anything less than that is cause for rejoicing."

"Thank you, that was very prettily said." Fanny lowered her chin, hiding her eyes from him even as her stomach did a small flip inside her. She'd been amazed to feel attraction for him when Rian was still alive. Surprised to know she could react the way she had when Valentine had kissed her, as she had been so certain of her love for Rian. But what had seemed interesting, intriguing, perhaps even eye-opening, when Rian was alive, now seemed like a betrayal of his memory.

Brede felt the first spit of rain and turned Fanny away from the rail. "Time to go below again, I'm afraid. Are you hungry?"

"I suppose," she told him, and then quickly realized that she was starving. She'd thought she'd never really want to eat again, never feel the need. But the sea air had worked its miracle, and she was actually hungry for the first time since she'd awakened in her chamber in Lucille's town house, her ear and cheek seemingly on fire, and remembered that Rian was dead.

Valentine escorted her down the few steps to the main saloon and carefully untied the bonnet she'd been wearing, easing it off her head without touching the bandage that still covered her right ear and cheek. "Why don't you go lie down for a bit, and I'll wake you when the food arrives. We've a considerable galley for the size of the yacht."

Fanny smiled weakly. "Built to your specifications, I'm sure. You should never be allowed to go hungry."

"Or?" Valentine asked, raising one eyebrow.

"Or you turn into an ogre," Fanny told him, slipping off her light cloak. "Wiggins didn't precisely say so, but I'm convinced I'm correct. I remember the first night you brought Rian and me to your—" She looked down at her toes.

He put his hands on her shoulders. "Do you blame me, Fanny? If I'd left him where he was, his chances would have been no better. Perhaps worse."

"I know," she said, keeping her head down. "He was so happy, Brede. Finally doing what he'd always wanted to do. If we could have seen only a few days into the future…"

"He did his duty, Fanny, and he did it well. He's a hero." And he, Valentine told himself, was a bastard of the worst sort. He knew he should tell her the truth. Except then she'd hate him, and with good reason. He felt he could stand anything, even living with the lie, as long as she didn't hate him.

She finally looked up at him, saw her own pain reflected in his usually unreadable eyes. She raised a hand to his cheek, pressed her palm against his skin. He was, truly, a wonderful man. "Oh, Brede, how do you stand me? I'm wallowing in pity for myself, for what I've lost, and not giving a thought to you. It's our…our wedding day. I'm so sorry."

Valentine covered her hand with his own. "You're mourning your brother, Fanny. I understand that. You're still recovering from your wound. I understand that, as well." He smiled slightly. "No matter how *hungry* I might be for my new bride, I promise not to turn into an ogre, ask anything more than you're willing to give."

Fanny's eyes clouded as she considered his words, his seeming affection for her. She had been curiously attracted to him from the first, even Rian had seen it, pointed out to her that now they moved in a wider world. But what did she really know of love? She hadn't realized, hadn't thought that Valentine could actually— Oh, God, she was such a silly, selfish idiot, a child masquerading as a woman. She'd made a better soldier than she did a wife…and she had made a terrible soldier! "But everyone…everyone was kissing the ladies."

He'd probably spend the rest of his life trying to understand the workings of her mind. "I beg your pardon?"

She rolled her eyes, wishing she hadn't said anything. "At the ball. Rian was chatting up Miss Pitney. Everyone was chatting up someone, he told me. Flirting with someone. Kisses before fighting. But the kisses? They didn't really mean anything, did they? It was…it was just the moment. The not knowing what would happen next, if anyone would survive…"

Valentine's mouth curved slightly in a small smile. "And that's what you thought it was that drove me to kiss you, Fanny? The moment?"

She felt her spine stiffen. "You said so yourself, remember? That it was *necessary*. That some things seem rational at the time. *At the time,* Brede. You said all of that, and even more."

"Do you have to remember everything I say, and then flog me with it?" he asked her, lifting her hand from his cheek in order to press a kiss into her palm.

Her heart, the one she thought dead inside her, gave a small skip. "But you meant what you said, didn't you? Rian didn't say as much to Miss Pitney, I'm sure of that. But he did admit as much to me. So I thought…I felt I could only assume that you, like Rian, were only…"

"Shh, sweetings. Don't think. Not so much, and not about this. I assure you, I wouldn't have asked you to marry me if I didn't want you as my wife." He fought for some levity. "Again, it also might have been the sight of you in those trousers. Among your other attractions."

"So," she said, wishing she could sew her lips shut and stop saying everything she thought at the moment she thought it. "So it wasn't my idea? You didn't marry me because I all but asked you?"

"You did?" Valentine shook his head. "Clearly, my memory doesn't match yours. I don't remember you proposing to me. I'm fairly certain such a thing wouldn't have slipped my mind."

"But I did," she protested, wanting to make herself clear on at least that one point. "At the very least, I said that Rian *gave* me to you in his will. You may not have realized that if I hadn't pointed it out to you."

"Oh, I doubt that, sweetings. His words were very clear, quite succinct." *Nearly as succinct as they were as the poor boy lay dying against a tree.*

Some devil pushed Fanny into saying more. "But if I wasn't so afraid to go home, I wouldn't have—"

"Wouldn't have agreed to marry me," Valentine finished for her. Something else was going on here, he felt sure. Something he had seen a hint of yesterday, but not understood. "How flattering, I'm sure. But why, Fanny? Why this fear of going home? I know what you said, that Rian's ghost would be everywhere you looked. But that's not so terrible, because he loved you, and you loved him. Rian isn't really the reason, is he? Or at least not all of it."

Fanny bit her lips between her teeth, fearful that if she said anything else she'd then say everything…everything no one outside the Becket family was ever to be allowed to know. About the island. About the return of that monster, Edmund Beales. About living in fear this past year or more, knowing their enemy could appear at any moment to repeat what had happened on the island so many years ago. About her nightmare…and Valentine's presence in it.

Her papa and the others tried to keep the truth from her, but she'd known. The world was drawing closer to their long-time sanctuary at Becket Hall, and when the two worlds collided everything she knew and loved would be changed. Already everything was changing. Rian had died. More might die. And she didn't want to witness those deaths. She couldn't. Not again.

Rian wouldn't be there this time, to pick her up, run with her. Hide her and protect her. So she'd found herself another protector. Brede. Only he didn't know that, did he?

Shame on her. Shame on her for being a coward, for wanting to hide, to be safe. And she felt safe, when Brede held her. Safe. Protected. But did a man, a husband, want to be thought of as a sanctuary? Fanny doubted that.

"Fanny? You don't look well, sweetings. Is it the headache again?"

She blinked herself to attention. "No, I— Yes, I suppose so. I should probably lie down?"

"Yes, I think someone might have suggested that, earlier. Myself, I believe," Valentine said, guiding her across the small saloon to the sleeping quarters where she had spent most of the hours since their marriage. He pushed open the slatted door and held it open for her as she passed by him. He saw the bed he'd had installed when the *Pegasus* was built, feeling fairly certain he would not be invited to share that bed later, with Fanny. "I'll knock when our dinner is ready."

Fanny took hold of the edge of the door as Valentine went to pull it shut. "Brede?"

Stupidly, his heart skipped a beat, as if she might just be inviting him to join her on the bed. And wouldn't that be a mistake that could haunt him to the grave! No, he couldn't bed her, not even if she might think she wished it. Not until he told her how he had left Rian to die.

But, once he told her, she'd never let him near her again.

"Yes, sweetings?" he asked, wishing she didn't look so vulnerable.

"Perhaps…perhaps later we could…we could talk?"

He bowed to her slightly. "As much and for as long as you might please. May I inquire as to the subject you have in mind?"

Fanny had come a decision. The Duke of Wellington had trusted Valentine. More important to Fanny, Rian had trusted him. When Ethan had married Morgan, when Elly had wed Jack, those men had been brought into the family, told its secrets. Julia and Mariah, married to her brothers, were equally trusted.

Her papa might not be here to make his final judgment, but Fanny felt fairly certain he would agree that Valentine not be kept at arm's length. She owed Valentine that much. She owed him the truth. About her family; about their pasts, as well as their precarious present.

And about her selfish reasons for marrying him. For, however much she might care for him, she had tricked him into marriage. For all the wrong reasons.

Besides, she'd never been a very good liar. She could tell a fib, but she always got found out by anyone who simply waited long enough for her pesky conscience to push her into a confession. If she'd been a more steadfast liar, she wouldn't have spent so much time during her younger years peeling carrots in the kitchens, or counting the flowers in the canopy hanging over her bed.

"What shall we talk about? I don't know, Brede. But I suppose I'll think of something," she said, smiling wanly, and then shut the door.

CHAPTER FIFTEEN

THE RAIN CONTINUED as darkness fell over the water, forcing Valentine's captain to steer the *Pegasus* by compass alone. But although the rain had been considerable for a time, the Channel remained relatively calm, allowing the steward to use the stove in the galley, presenting Valentine and Fanny with a simple but delicious meal of roasted quail and small, browned potatoes, turnips and carrots in a fine sauce.

Fanny ate as if she'd been starved for a week, and Valentine delighted in this return of her appetite. He sat back in his chair, his glass of wine aloft, and admired the way she daintily yet efficiently laid waste to the meal. She had changed into the gown she'd worn the night of Lady Richmond's ball, and the candlelight glowed almost golden against the creamy skin of her chest and arms, that same flattering light turning her hair nearly silver.

Had she any idea how unusual she was, how very beautiful she was? That wide, lush mouth. Those devastating tip-tilted green eyes? Her tall, slim, body; yet rounded in all the right places. She'd believed it possible to pass as a soldier? With that graceful carriage, that proud tilt to her cleanly sculpted chin? He'd known her for a female in a heartbeat, and with the next heartbeat he'd felt himself begin to fall victim to her unaffected charms.

Then she'd shown him her daring, her backbone, her utter fearlessness, and he'd passed beyond merely wanting her. He admired her courage. And she stood in absolutely no awe of his supposed consequence. She'd stood toe-to-toe with him, dared to taunt him, dared to disobey him. Dared to laugh at him…make *him* laugh.

He took a sip of his wine. Yes, she was young. Centuries younger than himself, as he'd felt old for almost all of his life. Carrying the burden of his father's unreasonable expectations, his constant criticisms, and then escaping to the Peninsula, only realizing too late that his father's carelessly inflicted wounds meant nothing once he was put up against the brutal realities of war.

When Bonaparte had escaped Elba, Valentine had been reluctant to join Wellington once more. After so many years, he was tired of fighting. Tired of the once exhilarating risks he'd taken to gather information for the Duke, tired of battlefields, weary unto death of the carnage that never seemed to stop.

And then there was Fanny, exploding into his world and turning all his preconceived notions about his capacity to feel normal human emotions on their heads. Completely unexpected, wonderfully unique, extraordinarily challenging. He'd felt instantly younger, revived and most definitely interested.

He wanted that eager young woman back. Biting, spitting, impulsive, even mocking. He wanted to see her fire again, needed to feel its warmth.

Her brother was dead, and she was in mourning. That was understandable, allowable. But it was more than Rian's death, Valentine believed. Sorrow he expected to see in her eyes…but not fear. Not fear of him, her new husband, he felt sure of that. Fear of going home, fear of her family? Yes, that seemed to be the problem.

But why? Why?

Fanny at last laid down her fork, patted at her mouth with her serviette and then smiled at Valentine. "I'm sorry. I hadn't realized I was so hungry." She shot a quick look to the silver domes covering a pair of plates still residing on the tray that had been carried into the room. "What do you suppose is under those covers?"

"I don't know. I'll ring for the steward to clear these plates and serve us, shall I?"

She rolled her eyes, a bit of the old Fanny back

again. "Oh, nonsense, Brede. We're not more than five feet away from the tray." She got to her feet, picking up his empty plate, as well as her own and carried both over to the tray as he watched in amusement, returning with the uncovered plates where sliced peaches in burnt-sugar sauce lay carefully displayed. "Do you know that Lucie rings the bell for Frances when she wants her pillows rearranged behind her? I find that ridiculous."

Valentine watched her work, amused. "And told her so, I'm sure."

Fanny sat down, lifted her spoon after pushing a slice of peach onto it with her finger. She popped the slice into her mouth, and then licked at her sugary fingertip. "She thinks I'm a barbarian. She also explained that she is doing good works, employing people otherwise left to starve in gutters. I just think she's indulged, and lazy."

"And you told her that, as well."

Fanny grinned, her first real smile in too long. "I think so, yes. And now she's my sister-in-law, and she's probably hoping we're rarely in company. But I really do like her."

"Most people do. I'm the Ogre, remember?"

She looked across the table at him, sitting there looking so formal in his evening clothes, his hair combed back straight from his brow. She realized that she missed the hideous gray greatcoat, the opened collar at his neck, how he clamped a cheroot in the corner of his mouth between his teeth, the way his hair seemed to naturally part at the center, allowing the long straight locks to tumble down around his face. Like a small boy at play, and delighted to be dirty.

"You're not an ogre. Most times," she amended. "You're just rather…formidable, that's all. Look at you now—all starch and arrogance. Why, I should be trembling in my shoes, just being here alone with you. But I've seen you otherwise, remember?"

Valentine shifted uncomfortably in his chair. It was a strange feeling, being uncomfortable in his own skin. But he was; Fanny had that power over him. "You've seen me other than arrogant? And when was that?"

Fanny held up one finger as she chewed on the last slice of peach. "The day you took me to Lucie's. I had no bonnet, so you didn't wear your hat. You were being kind."

"Kindness, my dear, had nothing to do with it," he said, relaxing somewhat. "I was daring the world to point to you and your obvious fashion faux pas, and snigger—for to insult you would be to insult me, as well. There are not many who would choose to do that. In point of fact, not that I remained in town to satisfy my curiosity, I imagine that there were at least a half dozen young sprigs of fashion daring the sidewalks of Brussels sans bonnets and curly brimmed beavers after our appearance. Now, how is that for arrogance?"

Fanny giggled. "I stand corrected. Morgan said that London Society is silly, and if meeting Lucie didn't wholly convince me, you have just now proved her point. Are you going to eat your peaches? Because if you aren't—"

Valentine slid the plate across the table. "Here you go. Indulge yourself, even as I step outside into the rain to smoke my cheroot."

"You don't have to do that, Brede. I like the smell of a cheroot. I even puffed on one the once, but I have to tell you, the aroma is one thing and the effect is another. I had to lie very still on my bed for hours, until the room stopped spinning. Rian kept threatening to jump up and down on the mattress so that I'd be sick, and I— *Oh.*"

So much for lighthearted banter. Rian's ghost, mercifully absent during dinner, was now back in residence. "Fanny? Are you all right?"

She put down her spoon, took a deep breath. "I…I suppose it's going to be like this, isn't it? I can forget, even for an hour or more, but then I remember again. I don't know which is worse. Forgetting for a few moments, or remembering again." She looked up at Valentine, who had gotten to his feet. "How do people live like this? It hurts so much."

"The pain has to begin to fade at some point, Fanny. Otherwise, how could anyone go on? Let me ring to have this table taken away, and then I'll leave you alone for a while as I check on the horses and smoke my cheroot, as I make it a point to never smoke in here. The threat of fire, you understand."

"No," Fanny said quickly, jumping to her feet, suddenly loathe to be alone, even for a moment. "Wait, please, and I'll go outside with you. I…I'd like some air."

"Fanny, it's still raining."

"I know," she said, heading for the other room to fetch her hooded cloak. "I don't melt."

She returned to the main saloon, the cloak around her shoulders, and Valentine stepped forward to lift the hood up and over her head. "We can't let that bandage get wet."

"I suppose not, although I'd rather be rid of it, if you must know. Odette always says that soap and water and good clean air are the world's best physicians."

"Odette? And who would that be?"

Fanny tied the strings of her cloak before answering. She'd thought of several ways to broach the subject of Becket Hall, but she hadn't considered Odette as an avenue with which to begin her explanations. Still, the door had seemingly been opened, so she might as well barge in any way she could.

"Odette is a Voodoo priestess Papa brought with us when we came to live at Becket Hall. A *real* Voodoo priestess. Cross her, Brede, and learn to live the remainder of your life croaking like a toad."

"Then I'm forewarned," Valentine said in genuine amusement as he donned his old gray greatcoat, pulling a black knitted seaman's cap from one of the pockets and pulling it down over his head. "And you brought this Odette with you, you said. Then you haven't always lived in England?"

Fanny was still thinking about Odette, and wondered yet again what that woman would say if she knew about Fanny's fears. Perhaps she'd say Fanny had been given the gift of seeing the future and her fear was a true premonition of disaster. Or she might say that her nightmares were a sign that bad *loa* were bedeviling her. Or perhaps she'd just call her a silly, selfish girl….

"Pardon me? Oh, no, we haven't always lived at Becket Hall. And I must say, Brede, you'll start no new London fashions looking like that," Fanny added cheekily as he opened the door to the short hall and half-dozen steps leading to the deck. She brushed past him, pleasantly surprised by the clean smell of warm, rain-washed sea air that greeted her.

The rain was little more than a drizzling mist now, and she lifted her face to it for a moment, as she'd always liked to walk at the shoreline when it rained. She and Rian would come back to the hall, soaked, and Papa would say they looked like drowned rats, and Rian would— No. She wouldn't allow herself to think about that right now. She'd begun a much-needed explanation, a confession, and she had to finish it. That her face, and Valentine's, would be in shadow, hiding their expressions, could only be a blessing.

She walked first to the temporary wooden enclosure to look in at Molly, and Valentine stood close behind her.

"The slight roll of the yacht soothes them somewhat," he told her as he put a match to his cheroot, "but they'll be happy when we dock at Hastings."

"We'll ride them to Brede Manor?" Fanny asked him as they walked over to the rail.

"If you wish, certainly."

Fanny frowned, her unpredictable, mercurial mood plunging yet again. "No, I can't do that. I'd have to wear the uniform again—and I can't do that, either. Never again."

Valentine spoke quickly, to reassure her. "We'll find you a proper sidesaddle in Hastings. I've a coach waiting there for me these past months, at a stable near the docks. But it will do Shadow good to have a gallop rather than to be tied behind the coach all the way home."

"Thank you, Brede. I'd like a gallop, myself." She turned around, pressed her hips against the rail, to see that she'd been right—the tip of his cheroot glowed red, but she could barely make out his features in the darkness. "Brede, there's something I need to tell you."

"Yes, I rather thought there might be," he told her, taking his cue from her and standing beside her, his back also to the rail. "It's about your family, isn't it?"

She nodded, began again with Odette. "Papa brought Odette with us from the islands. From our own island, actually, very near to Haiti…"

Valentine remained silent for the next quarter hour, smoking his cheroot as Fanny recounted life on the island, life as Geoffrey Baskin and his family and those of his crews and their families had known it. She spoke quickly, but she left nothing out of the telling.

She told him how, over the years, she and five others had come to live on the island as Geoffrey's adopted children.

She told him that Geoffrey had married his Isabella, who had borne him his only natural child.

How Geoffrey Baskin and his partner, Edmund Beales, had sailed so successfully as privateers, Geoffrey on the Black Ghost, her brother Chance and their friend Jacko eventually captaining the *Silver Ghost,* and Edmund and his crews on their own ships.

How Edmund had so cruelly betrayed Geoffrey when Geoffrey had announced he was leaving the islands, leaving "the life."

How the eighth and last Baskin child had been added to the family on the same day that Edmund had landed his own crew on the island and killed Isabella and every other man, woman and child who hadn't been quick enough to escape the terror he'd brought with him.

How Geoffrey had survived a terrible betrayal at sea, his ships limping back to the island, to be met with the devastation Beales left behind him.

How Geoffrey had gathered up any survivors and taken them all across the Atlantic, to the mansion he had earlier ordered built for his wife, turning all their backs to the sea and the life they'd led, longing only to hide, to be safe. To nurse their wounds of both body and heart.

She told him how they'd all taken the name of Becket, and how they might have wanted to live quietly, but years later had been drawn into helping the local inhabitants when their smuggling runs were put in danger by the appearance of a violent group of men called the Red Men Gang.

How her brother Courtland and the others had taken turns riding out as the *Black Ghost* in order to protect the local smugglers, and ended with Valentine's friend Jack playing a large part in unmasking the Red Men Gang's leaders…only to discover that the man those leaders had worked for was none other than Edmund Beales, long considered dead.

How they had just last year learned that Edmund Beales was much more than a smuggler, that his ambitions ran to controlling the destinies of entire countries, and that he had seemingly thrown in his lot with Napoleon Bonaparte…

"You see, Beales was using his Red Men Gang to smuggle gold to France, to ingratiate himself with Bonaparte," Fanny told Valentine as he remained silent, forced to acknowledge that Fanny Becket was much, much more than the beautiful young girl he had desired, then married. "That ended, of course, when the Red Men were exposed, but we might have been exposed, as well, to Beales. He…he could come back. He could find us. We have no where to go, not again, even though Papa has ordered another ship built, to take us all away if need be."

Valentine tossed the remainder of the cheroot into the sea. His mind was reeling, even as the trained soldier in him not only had taken in her every word, but had also dissected every fact, listed questions in his mind. He'd begin with the one most troublesome to him personally. "You'd go back to the islands? I could have taken you home, never to see you again."

Fanny had felt herself becoming more and more upset as she neared the end of her story. Most of what she'd told him was the story she had learned by rote and had rather recited for Valentine. It was her nightmare that truly frightened her now. The past haunted her, yes. But the future terrified her.

"No. Never there, I'm sure. We could never go back there. You know, I never really remembered more than bits and snatches of that last day. Most of what I think I know was only told to me. I always knew that it was Rian who had saved me, kept me safe. But when Rian left to take up his commission, I began...I began having these dreams about that day. These nightmares..."

Valentine took her hands in his. "*Shh,* sweetings. You're trembling. I want to hear everything you feel comfortable telling me, but that's enough for now."

She shook her head violently. "No, I have to say this, Brede. I have to tell you what I remember— what I saw in my nightmare. I could see Rian running with me tucked under his arm. I could feel his hand clamped tightly over my mouth as we hid in a cave, so I wouldn't cry out, so we wouldn't be discovered in our hiding place. I...I remember biting him, actually drawing blood. Rian still has...had the scar on his palm. And then...later, I could see him running with me toward the ships once Papa had found us. I...I could even see the dress I wore that day. All of it."

She turned, looked up at his face in the darkness, her expression bleak. "I can still *taste* the memories, Brede, even taste Rian's blood. I was standing next to the Duke of Wellington, but all I could see or hear or taste was that last day on the island. It was so very horrible. I was so horribly afraid. I hid behind a tree, willing myself not to scream, and I shook, for hours…."

"When the island was attacked. How old were you, Fanny?" Valentine asked, still reeling from what she'd told him, trying to take it all in, wondering how in hell he could comfort her.

"Three, I think. That's what Papa and Odette decided was a good age for me when we first came to the island. Rian was closer to nine. We…we shared the same birthday, growing up. That's how we settled on birthdays—we used the day that Papa first found us. It was our birthday, Brede, the day of the battle. Now I'll have that birthday alone, won't I? How will I face it?"

She took a shaky breath, pushed on with her explanation. "Rian stayed with me on the ship. He told me that I wouldn't let him go, not for a moment, day or night. I followed him like a faithful puppy, I suppose, the whole time we were growing up, and drove him near to distraction more times than I can count. But I always feel safe when I'm with…when I was with Rian."

"He saved you, he took care of you," Valentine said, nodding. He was beginning to understand at least that much. She and Rian had shared a terrible yet special bond from the time they were children. Any other questions he had could wait until he saw Jack, who would certainly give him more details about this Edmund Beales person and his grandiose plans.

"Yes. Rian took care of me. He was mine, and I was his. And now he's gone." She pulled her hands free of Valentine's and wrapped her arms around her waist, squeezed her eyes shut. "It's silly, I suppose. No, I don't suppose. I *know* it's silly. I'm a grown woman now, not a child. Nightmares are just nightmares. But Edmund Beales is still out there somewhere, and even with Papa and the others, I don't...I don't know how to feel safe anymore...."

Valentine stepped in front of her, gently pulled her into his embrace. "You'll be safe with me, Fanny. I promise you. You'll always be safe with me."

Fanny caught her breath on a sob and nestled closer into him, rubbing her uninjured cheek against the damp wool of his greatcoat, slipping her arms inside the cloth so that she could hold tight to his waist even as his arms closed over her back. She shut her eyes, feeling his strength, craving his protection....

CHAPTER SIXTEEN

VALENTINE WASN'T SURE how long the two of them stood that way beside the rail, but eventually he realized that it was raining harder again. He leaned down, gently lifted Fanny into his arms and carried her back down the steps to the main saloon.

His mind was still reeling from all she'd told him, the secrets she'd allowed him. He felt humbled. He now had the power to destroy her family, and she'd given him that power because she trusted him never to use it.

And he wouldn't. But that didn't mean he wasn't going to confront Jack Eastwood with what he now knew, to have his old friend fill in any information Fanny may have neglected to tell him, or possibly did not know existed.

Because Fanny was his now, and he also knew how to protect what was his own.

He carried her through the main saloon and softly kicked open the door to the stateroom, not putting her down until they were beside the bed.

She kept her palms against his chest, looked up into his eyes. He saw the question in them, but no fear. Had telling him about her fears helped to banish them? He could only hope that was true.

"It's getting very late, sweetings," he told her as he untied her cloak and eased the hood away from her bandage, then removed the cloak and tossed it in the general direction of the doorway. His great-coat and knitted hat, both beyond damp, followed. "Time for you to sleep."

Fanny's stomach clenched at the thought of being alone here in the stateroom. Talking about her past had all but guaranteed that she'd dream of that past, and any dream about the island had to turn into a nightmare. If that made her a foolish female afraid of bogeymen, then so be it. "But…where will you sleep?"

"I can make do in the main saloon. I've had worse accommodations."

She could hear her heart rapidly beating in her ears. "But that's silly. It's an enormous bed. We can both sleep in here. Can't we?"

"Fanny," Valentine said, hoping she'd see reason. "That's probably not a good idea. You're still recovering from your wound, and you've had a…a full day."

She grazed her fingertips across his chest. "Is it

what I told you? You're appalled with all of us, aren't you?"

He shook his head. "By your family? Not a bit. After all, how can a spy be appalled by a privateer, a smuggler? And I wouldn't want anyone climbing too far up the Clement family tree, to tell you the truth. We're all descended from sometimes nefarious ancestors, most especially those who somehow managed to wrest a title from one of our kings, let alone hold on to it for several centuries. I am angry, incensed actually, at this Edmund Beales and what he did to all of you."

"I'm terrified that he'll find us," Fanny told him, a shiver running down her spine just at the sound of the man's name. "We were safe, for so many years, but everything's been different since last summer. Papa ordering the ship, my brother Chance visiting so much more frequently, closeting himself with Papa and Jacko and my other brothers for hours and hours. I wasn't allowed to ride Molly on the Marsh anymore unless someone accompanied me. And then Bonaparte escaped from Elba, and Rian was so angry he said more than he should to me, let slip that Edmund Beales might have aided in that escape."

"But Bonaparte's been defeated, Fanny. This man Beales may have lost all his power along with that defeat."

"Or he'll have more time now to search us out,"

Fanny said, for she'd had considerable time to consider bogeymen. "We're well protected at Becket Hall, Brede, I know that. But we're also very isolated, with the Channel to our backs."

"In other words, attack could come by land or sea. Or both," Valentine mused aloud. Yes, he'd have to take Fanny home soon, see Becket Hall and her interesting Papa, speak with Jack. Strangely, he felt his blood running faster, intrigued by the prospect of facing and outwitting this Edmund Beales. "That's enough for tonight, sweetings. We'll speak about all of this another time, when you're feeling stronger. For now, I only want to thank you for trusting me enough to tell me about your family."

Fanny lowered her head, ashamed. "I married you so you'd take me away, Brede, protect me. You know that now, don't you?"

He smiled slightly. "Yes, you saw me as your port in a storm, didn't you?"

She raised her head sharply, her cheeks pale. "You…you said that in my dream."

"I was in your dream? I'm flattered. Now, ask me if I really think that, if I'm sorry I married you."

She shook her head. She didn't want to hear his answer.

"Did it ever occur to you, Fanny, that you might be my port in a storm?"

"But…but that's ridiculous. How could I possibly help you?"

He stroked her cheek with the back of his hand. "For one, you remind me I'm alive. I can't consider that a bad thing. Even if you do bedevil the life out of me more often than not."

She felt her strength returning, and with it, the thrill of bantering with this infuriating, fascinating, kind and very appealing man. "Oh, I do not. I— Well, I probably do, don't I?" she said, a smile tugging at the corners of her mouth.

"You don't listen," he pointed out. "You seem to think that orders are merely guides to point out ways to misbehave."

She nodded. "Now you sound like Sergeant-Major Hart."

"He's very fond of you."

"I don't know why. I caused him nothing but trouble."

"While making my life a veritable picnic with your sweet obedience," Valentine teased, and pressed a kiss against her forehead. Then he sobered. "Time for sleep, Fanny. There will be other nights."

Fanny plucked at the buttons of his shirt. "I…I don't want to be alone *this* night, Brede. Stay with me. Please."

"Fanny, for the love of heaven, don't you realize that—"

She didn't *realize* anything. She wanted, needed, to be held. To feel alive. To avoid the nightmares. Before he could point out any flaws or potential problems in hopes they would dissuade her, she put her hands on his shoulders and went up on tiptoe, pressing her mouth to his.

Valentine knew it was wrong, on so many levels, but that didn't keep his arms from finding their way around Fanny's back as she inexpertly ground her lips against his.

"Again, please," he said when she broke the kiss, mimicking what she had said to him in what seemed like a lifetime ago. "But this time...like this."

He put the pad of his thumb to her chin, lightly pulling down her bottom lip, and then took her mouth with his own slightly open mouth. Gently at first, slanting first this way, then that...tugging provocatively on her bottom lip with his teeth, then sealing himself more tightly to her, his tongue sliding into her sweet mouth. She tasted of sugared peaches, she tasted of youth, of life, and all he wanted to do was to feed on her.

He drew slightly away from her, giving her a chance to say no, to turn away. But she only grabbed his face in both her hands and pulled him back to her.

This time it was she who nipped at him, boldly mimicked what he'd done with his tongue, the student eager to impress her tutor with what she had learned.

Like a man sliding under the surface of the water for the third time, Valentine gave himself up to his fate, drowning happily in Fanny's kiss, scooping her up only to deposit her on the burgundy satin coverlet, then follow her down.

Fanny reveled in the warm weight of his body along her length, caught between the pleasure of his hands on her and a feeling that she was safe. Nothing could hurt her, as long as Valentine was with her. Not the demons of the past or those looming over the future. She didn't have to think; she couldn't think. She could only feel, experience. Learn.

Her fingers went to his shirtfront and she loosed the buttons, slipped her hands inside to touch Valentine's warmth, his strength. Pressed her palm against him, felt his heart beating fast. For her? Or was this simply *necessary* for him, as it was for her? A man like Valentine, he must have demons of his own.

He knew so much; she knew so little. But where he went, she eagerly followed.

While the beat of a heavy rain pounded unheard on the roof of the stateroom, as the yacht began rolling slightly in a sea growing rough, Valentine continued to learn of her, even as he tutored her. Their clothing had disappeared, sliding off the smooth, slippery satin to the floor. Fanny's silvery-blond hair splayed out on the burgundy satin, her back arched as he kissed her exposed jawline, trailed his lips down her to awaken new desires as he took her nipple into his mouth, suckled gently. Filled himself with the taste of her, dragged his tongue over her until her body responded, as her breathing quickened and she moaned low in her throat.

She grew passive, accepting what he was doing, each new and unexpected way he touched her, concentrated on her body's response to his ministrations rather than initiating any of her own.

She didn't know what to think, so she merely ceased thinking. She *felt*. She gave herself over to him, her limbs feeling almost liquid, a heat growing deep in her belly, turning her boneless. Pliant. Accepting.

And then eager. He'd slipped his hand between her legs, touching her so intimately, eliciting a response so devastating, that Fanny could no longer just lie there, accepting. She had to move, just as he moved his fingers. She had to touch, so she clasped on to his back as best she could, her fingertips curving into his skin, holding on, because she felt herself spinning out of control.

Valentine could feel her growing heat, her sweet arousal; he sensed her confusion. He couldn't spare her the pain, but he knew it was best to get past it as quickly as possible.

So young, so sweet, so trusting. He didn't want to hurt her. God knew she'd been hurt enough. Why was it that women had to feel the pain before the pleasure? Perhaps his own pain, knowing he was about to hurt her, was no less hurtful, but was only a different pain.

He settled himself between her legs, whispering against her ear as she held on tight. "Do you want me to stop, sweetings? I could stop now. Just hold you."

She turned her head slightly, looked into his eyes in the near darkness. "You'd do that?" she asked him quietly.

Jesus God, he would. He, a man who had always taken his pleasure where he found it. "You've only to ask."

"But I won't do that," she told him, reaching up her hands to push her fingers through his nearly chin-length hair, that had fallen forward onto his face, turning him from the redoubtable Earl of Brede into the man who had risked his own life to help her find Rian. The faintly nervous man who had kissed her in the gardens, who had asked her to be his wife only because he was concerned for her, perhaps felt some sort of duty toward her. A good man. An honorable man. An unselfish man.

"Then God help us both, sweetings, because there's no going back now."

He eased himself against her, pushed past the barrier that separated them, and slid deeply inside her, catching her soft cry with his mouth. Held her tightly against him for long moments…then began to move.

Fanny clung to him with all her strength, matching his movements with her own, until her limbs turned liquid again, the tension inside her coiled tighter, and then tighter still. Until she felt a warm flush all over her body and the urgency turned to unexpected glory.

Valentine let go of the tightly held reins on his own desire and gained his own release, holding Fanny tightly, for to let her go would be to lose everything he'd only this moment realized he'd never had before, had been looking for all of his life.

Without another word, he kissed her mouth, her cheeks, her closed eyes. He helped her slide beneath the covers and then turned her back to him, pulling her close against his body, his arm across her waist, holding her tight.

He would hold her now, let her find sleep. Words could only ruin what had just happened between them. Besides, he wasn't sure what *had* happened. He only knew that where once he had been so sure of himself, sure of his life, he now looked toward the future with a mix of anticipation and fear. He'd never had someone in his life like this before, someone he felt fairly certain at last gave meaning to that life.

Fanny lay beside him, fighting sleep, her eyes slowly closing as she clung to the delicious but fading feeling of complete and utter pleasure. Valentine had been correct—what they'd done had been necessary. Needed, by them both.

It was only as she slipped into sleep, the sound of the steady rain on the roof soothing her, that she remembered that she had no right to be so happy, to feel so suddenly secure, safe, even loved. "Oh, Rian…" she breathed softly into the dark, begging his forgiveness.

It was then, and only then, hearing Fanny breathe her brother's name on a sigh, that Valentine realized something he should have realized the instant she'd told him that Ainsley Becket had taken her in, had taken Rian in, as well.

Rian Becket hadn't been Fanny's brother by blood. They hadn't really been brother and sister.

Make her forget me. She has to forget me.

Finally, those words made sense.

Fanny had loved her brother…who was not her brother by blood. And he, Valentine Clement, the once honorable Earl of Brede, had left that brother to die alone…and then bedded the grieving sister as she reached out for comfort.

Because he'd wanted to. Because he could.

Valentine slid out from beneath the covers, picking up his clothing and taking it with him to the main saloon. He dressed quickly, his mouth set in a tight line, and then pulled the stopper on a crystal decanter, poured himself a generous measure of brandy and headed up on deck. To raise a glass to the bloody stupid fool he was.

CHAPTER SEVENTEEN

FANNY AWOKE TO FIND herself alone, sunlight streaming in through the small round window across from
the bottom of the bed. *Porthole.* She was fairly certain
it was called a porthole. She'd really never paid much
attention to anything the least bit nautical, preferring
to ride her mare, practice shooting and fencing with
Rian. She certainly had no interest in the day-to-day
running of Becket Hall, and if Valentine had to
depend on her to manage his household, they'd both
probably starve to death within a fortnight.

Still, she was reasonably sure the window was
called a porthole.

She knew definitely that she was alone in the
stateroom, which was why she'd rather consider
portholes than Valentine's absence.

Not that she was in any crushing rush to see him
again, after what had happened between them last
night. She'd had a vague idea of what transpired between men and women; she wasn't a baby, she
wasn't a fool.

But she'd had no idea how *intense* an experience it could be. How unsettlingly personal. Intimate. She'd encouraged Valentine, and then first accepted his caresses before eagerly seeking them out. And then, stupidly, she'd fallen asleep.

Was he disappointed in her? They'd done what married people do on their wedding nights. Morgan had been more than happy to share that fact with her long ago, but even Morgan's frank speech hadn't adequately prepared Fanny for the reality.

What possibly could?

Fanny's thoughts kept running round and round in her head, making little sense, she knew, as she washed in tepid water and quickly dressed herself in one of the three gowns she possessed.

There was a round clock tacked to the wall inside a heavy brass-and-glass case, but she didn't really need to look at it to know that the sun had been up for a good while. Her empty belly told her that. She was sure she had slept through breakfast, and could only hope that there were more peaches onboard the *Pegasus*.

There was nothing else to do, and as thinking about what she'd say, how she'd feel, when she first saw Valentine wasn't helping her courage at all, she knew she could no longer delay the inevitable. After all, unless Valentine had jumped overboard during the night, it wasn't as if she could avoid seeing him.

Fanny opened the door to the main saloon, then climbed up onto the deck, to see the object of her apprehension and curiosity standing at the rail, with his back turned to her.

She was still shocked to see him looking so much the London gentleman. He looked so formal in his finely tailored clothing. He was so many different men, and she didn't really know any of them. He was nothing she'd ever seen before, nothing she'd ever imagined or experienced. And he fascinated her, in so many ways.

Difficult to believe she'd dug her fingernails into his strong, bare back. Difficult to believe he had kissed her, touched her so intimately. Not so difficult to believe that she'd never tire of looking at him, never tire of his face, his voice, his touch.

She didn't say anything. She just stood there, drinking in the sight of him, the absolute wonder of him. The Earl of Brede. *Hers.* If she went to him, put her arms around him, would he kiss her? Or would he tell her that such things were best left for the nighttime? She didn't know. If she followed her instincts, she'd go to him, step into his arms. There was no more wonderful place to be; held by him, safe inside his embrace.

Valentine sensed her presence. How could he not? She was in his blood now; his heart beat for her, God curse him. "Good morning, Fanny," he said without turning around. He was so tired, weary unto death. Empty of everything save his shame. So he'd take his usual refuge in sarcasm, his cutting tongue that had always well served to keep people at a distance. He was, he knew, the worst of cowards.

"Uh…yes, good morning. I overslept, didn't I?"

"That, I would imagine, depends on your usual habits, with which, I might point out, I am not accustomed. My sister, for instance, would believe rising from her bed before noon to be a crime bordering on sacrilege."

Her nervousness fled, and Fanny raised her eyebrows at she stared at Valentine's back. My, wasn't he being starchy this morning. Maybe it was the clothes? He always seemed easier in his skin when he was dressed like a rat catcher. Or perhaps he'd waited for her to come up on deck before he broke his own fast. She ought to get him something to eat, so he didn't feel the need to bite *her* head off!

Then Fanny felt her temper begin to rise. If he had a problem with her, why didn't he just come right out and say so? Fanny loathed anything less than a direct approach, direct action. Then again, weren't those just the things that had gotten her into so much trouble over the years?

Perhaps she should take a page from Valentine's book, and be more subtle.

"You slept well?" she asked him, determinedly staying where she was, trying again to have him turn around, to *look* at her at least, for pity's sake. For she also was unaccustomed to being ignored.

"As well as could be expected, yes."

She waited…mentally counted *one, two, three*… "Yes, I also slept well, thank you for asking."

Finally, he turned to face her. She nearly put her hands to her mouth in shock, seeing the expression on his face. Or, rather, the complete lack of expression on his face. He wasn't looking at her. He was looking *through* her. Dear God, she was young, inexperienced, yes. But had she been that much of a disappointment to him?

"Brede?"

"Come here, Fanny, if you please. We're nearing the point where your assistance is necessary."

"My assistance? I don't understand," she said, but nonetheless joined him as he stood at the rail, once more looking toward the shoreline less than a mile away.

He didn't say anything else, waiting for her to realize exactly what she was looking at, while schooling himself not to look at her. He was an idiot. He was behaving like an unmitigated ass. But, Lord help him, he couldn't seem to stop himself.

Fanny was silent for a few minutes, leaning on the rail, and then stood up straight. "We're close to land, aren't we? How pretty. But shouldn't—shouldn't land be to the opposite side of the *Pegasus?*"

"Off our starboard side, yes, that would be correct. If we were still on route to Hastings. Which we're not. You were still asleep when I ordered the *Pegasus* turned about some time after midnight."

Fanny ran her tongue around the inside of her mouth, trying to manufacture enough spit in order to swallow. "Why?"

"Because I'm taking you home. To Becket Hall. We'd sailed almost as far as Dungeness, but are on our way back toward Dymchurch, hugging the coastline. Becket Hall is somewhere in between, correct? Directly on the Channel, you said, below Dymchurch, somewhere in the Marsh?"

"But I don't want—"

He cut her off. "Please, wife. Disabuse yourself of any thought that what you *want* enters into this decision. We're married and, thanks to my actions of last night, that can't be changed. But I am at last doing the right thing. I'm taking you home."

Fanny didn't know what to do, what to say. "And…leaving me there?"

"Perhaps, at least for a while. It's for the best." He couldn't look at her. Refused to look at her. "You and Rian, your constant companion. You weren't related by blood."

Fanny looked up at him sharply, as his words

sounded like some sort of accusation. "Yes. I told you all of that. And?"

At last he did turn to her, saw and did his damndest to ignore the confusion, the hurt, in her lovely green eyes. "And, madam wife, it would seem that you also talk in your sleep."

"I do? I did?" Fanny felt her entire body grow cold. "What…what did I say? I don't understand, Brede. What could I have possibly said?"

He ignored the question as he looked toward the shoreline once more, lifted the spyglass to his eye. The landscape had been changing gradually. Flattening, displaying a ragged, uneven shoreline. He'd seen stunted trees, a low horizon, an expanse of what he felt sure was an offshoot of the infamous, treacherous, Romney Sands. A smattering of miniscule villages he would be hard-pressed to put names to, no more than a few rough houses and shingle beaches lined with crude longboats.

He'd been watching, searching the shoreline, since dawn.

But now there was something else visible, situated in the center of an area seemingly scooped out of the shore by a giant hand, surrounded on three sides by the low vastness of the Marsh. A large manor house, four stories high if he included the attics; sprawling, with a stone terrace that ran the length of the building. Sunlight winked back from at least three dozen large windows; several levels of steep roof were dotted with massive chimneys.

Looking more closely, he noticed that none of the windows were on the lowest level of the house, and that no trees or shrubberies offered any sort of cover to anyone who was to come within two hundred feet of that house from at least the three directions he could see. He imagined the fourth was equally bare. There were two stone stairways leading up to the terrace, but anyone coming up to the house via those steps would be exposed at all times.

It didn't take a particularly vivid imagination to picture sturdy wooden shutters inside each of those windows, ready to be shut tight against any enemy, be it storms coming off the Channel, or assault of another sort.

An impressive sight. It wasn't a castle. It didn't boast a moat or a keep. But it was nonetheless a thoughtfully designed and positioned stone fortress, cleverly disguised as a country residence.

Beyond it, following a slight rise, lay a small, neat village consisting of one long street and a few alleyways. He squinted through the spyglass, amazed to see what he believed to be a carved mermaid, a wooden figurehead, probably once attached to a ship's bow, standing at the Channel-side entrance to the village.

There were two sloops and a frigate—fine ships—

anchored in the natural harbor, as well as longboats pulled up on the beach. Valentine would wager his eyeteeth that there were cannon aboard those innocent-looking sloops, even if he couldn't see them.

At last Valentine smiled, but without amusement. "I suppose I didn't need you at all, did I? Or, as the ancient proverb put it so well, 'Home is home, be it never so homely,' hmm?"

"Oh, God," Fanny whispered, holding the rail tight with both hands, so that she wouldn't fall to her knees. *Home.* The way she remembered it. The way she had stupidly feared seeing it again. Now all she wanted was to be off this yacht, safe inside her old bedchamber, so that she could think what to do next, how to fix whatever had been so brutally broken between Valentine and herself. "What did I say? Tell me what I said."

"Nothing you hadn't said before, wife. You made it clear to me often enough that you loved your brother. You followed him all the way to Brussels, didn't you? The misunderstanding is mine, Fanny, and the blame is likewise mine. I seduced a vulnerable, grieving young woman, and should most probably be flogged, if not summarily taken out and shot. Now, if you'll excuse me, I need to speak to the captain."

Fanny put out her hand to stop him, but quickly realized it would do no good. Anything she said would be suspect, taken as a betrayal of Rian and her feelings for him. Taken as selfish lies meant to ingratiate herself with Valentine. With her husband. If he considered himself guilty of some crime or sin, that did not place her in the role of the innocent.

With a last look at his departing back, she turned once more to the railing, and didn't move again until the *Pegasus* had dropped anchor beside the *Respite*.

Her family had gathered on the terrace, standing together, watching the progress of the *Pegasus,* but Ainsley Becket was already waiting on the shore, Jack Eastwood beside him. A longboat was already in the water, being rowed out to the yacht, as even a smaller vessel like the *Pegasus* had to be anchored a good hundred yards from the shallow waters along the shore.

"They're wearing black armbands. They know about Rian," Fanny said as Valentine stood beside her at the rail. She didn't care if he stood beside her, or if he simply tossed her into the longboat when it pulled aside, and then ordered the anchor lifted and disappeared back into the Channel.

Because she now felt numb. She felt nothing at all. She didn't think she could ever feel anything again.

But Fanny was wrong. The moment she stepped onshore, the moment Ainsley Becket put his hands on her shoulders, looked into her eyes, at the bandage on her face, she felt an unbearable pain rip through her, taking her breath with its intensity. "Oh, Papa…I'm so sorry," she managed, and then fell into his arms, sobbing.

Valentine watched as the tall, impressively handsome man with the penetrating blue gaze nodded to him as if to say *later, I'll deal with you,* and then turned, his arm around Fanny's shoulders as he held her close to his side, guided her across the shingle and sand toward Becket Hall.

"You brought her home," Jack said, extending his right hand to Valentine. "How badly was she injured? And how, Valentine? How the hell did she manage to get herself shot? Have you brought Rian's body home for burial? Your note was brief, and the Sergeant-Major didn't have many answers for us."

"Later, Jack." Valentine tilted his head toward the village. "Is there a taproom anywhere close by, old friend?"

Jack frowned. "There is. *The Last Voyage.* But I think you'll be wanted, up at the house."

"Then they can damn well wait for me. Right now, Jack, I feel a crushing need to get myself very, very drunk."

Jack's frown disappeared and he smiled slightly. "Fanny can do that to a person, I suppose. She meant well, Valentine. She was the younger, but she always seemed to put herself in the role of Rian's protector."

"Yes, among other things," Valentine said, starting for the village, only to have Jack take hold of his arm.

"Later, friend. Ainsley will want to talk to you as soon as he's turned Fanny over to the women. He's been haunting the shoreline for this last week, prowling it, actually, watching the horizon, waiting for Fanny, for more news on Rian. I don't think he's slept, the poor bastard. He's such a strong man. Intelligent. Decisive. It's unsettling, seeing him vulnerable, hurting. But he's still very much in charge, Valentine. Don't think he isn't. Ainsley Becket makes our Iron Duke look like a babe in arms when it comes to keeping a steady hand on the reins."

Valentine looked at Jack, who was still the handsome rogue he remembered, for the most part. But now he had a settled look about him, an easy assurance that came from, perhaps, being part of a family. Being married. Being loved. Most definitely a far cry from the wary, sharp-eyed adventurer he'd once been. Maybe Jack had been the smart one, had gotten himself out in time. Waterloo and the tense, dangerous months leading up to that battle had been just one more brick placed on Valentine's shoulders…and one he wished he could have avoided carrying.

"The lord and master of Becket Hall, hmm? The *captain?* And if I don't want to talk to him? Will he have me walk the plank, do you suppose, or will he order me dropped down a well, the way I hear the smugglers do it?"

"So you know. Fanny or Rian told you. Very well, I have no argument with that—God knows you know how to keep your own counsel." Jack dropped his hand. "But who put the stick up your ass? There was a time you'd find the whole subterfuge exciting or, at the least, amusing."

Valentine shook his head, let out a ragged breath. "Forgive me, Jack. I'm not used to having to answer for myself. I'm less used to admitting my failings."

Jack clapped his arm over Valentine's shoulder and turned him toward Becket Hall. "You mean, Rian, don't you? Don't, friend. His death isn't your fault, Valentine. It was war. God knows we both understand that nobody's safe on the battlefield. I only thank you for taking him in hand, helping him live out the dream he'd always longed for. Rian is...he was a splendid young man. A bit of a dreamer, I'll grant you, but he made his own choices. In the end, we all do."

Valentine looked up at Becket Hall as they neared the steps leading to the terrace. "And you chose this place."

Jack grinned. "Let's just say this place, this life, chose me. When you meet Eleanor, you'll understand. It was complete and utter surrender on my part, Valentine. And I couldn't be happier. Now, come on. Let's get this over with, all right?"

"I suppose we may as well. I've seen Becket. Who else is waiting for me in there?"

"Fanny told you about us, correct?"

Valentine nodded. "Eight children. Seven now."

"Yes…seven now," Jack said quietly. "We're still having some trouble, getting used to that. All right. Chance is the oldest, but he's not here. He's helping at the War Office, hoping for some sort of information that might lead him to—"

"Edmund Beales," Valentine supplied for him. "Fanny told me about the island, and what's happened since."

"Fanny? I doubt she knows the half of it, although Rian probably told her some of what's been happening."

"Enough to have her frightened half out of her mind that Edmund Beales will be arriving at any time, to repeat the massacre on the island," Valentine told his friend. "She was afraid to come home, Jack—now that her protector is gone."

Jack stopped walking down the terrace, turning to move to the stone balustrade looking out over the Channel, and Valentine followed him. "Christ. She's still a child, isn't she?"

Valentine leaned his elbows on the balustrade, looked to his left and idly wondered how in hell, lacking a wharf, they were going to get Molly off the yacht. "Not really, I'm afraid. Not anymore, and for more than one reason," he said, lowering his head. "So Chance isn't here. Who is?"

"Court—Courtland. Steady as a rock, Court is. And fiercely loyal. Spencer's still here, that's the last remaining brother. He fought in Canada and America, poor bastard. Marriage has softened him some, but he's got a temper. He put his fist into a wall when the Sergeant-Major showed up to tell us about Rian. Becket Hall is damn near built like a fortress. Spence broke a few knuckles. Mariah— that's his wife—never said a word. She just fetched a bucket of ice from the icehouse and stuck his hand in it. They're quite a pair."

"Sounds as if you've got a fondness for all of them."

"They're my family. We're a hodgepodge, but we all seem to suit each other. Callie's here—she's the youngest, and Mariah and Eleanor, of course. Morgan married Ethan Tanner a few years ago."

"Aylesford? Interesting. And how does the infamous Earl fit in here?"

"Remarkably well. Some of us only play the fool."

"While some of us only fool ourselves," Valentine said quietly, looking out over the water. "All right," he added quickly, before Jack could question his unguarded statement. "Let's get this over with, shall we?"

"Anyone would think I'm marching you to your execution," Jack said, indicating with his arm that they should continue walking toward the French doors near the end of the terrace. "Oh, one more thing. I don't know if Jacko is going to be in Ainsley's study. But if he is, ignore him."

"Fanny mentioned the name. Who is he, again?"

"You know, I'm never sure. He's been with Ainsley from the beginning, I can tell you that. He was probably quite formidable, years ago, but he's gone to fat, and to drink, more now than ever. Still, I wouldn't cross him, or hope to see him coming out of the dark for me. Just a word of warning."

"I'll keep that word in mind. Shall we?" Valentine said, and Jack stepped forward to open one of the French doors.

CHAPTER EIGHTEEN

AINSLEY BECKET stood up behind his desk and walked around it, crossing to Valentine with his right arm extended. "Your lordship, welcome to Becket Hall. I only regret the circumstances."

Valentine took the man's hand, felt the dry, warm, firm grip. "As do I, Mr. Becket. My most sincere condolences on the loss of your son."

He looked around the room. A sandy-haired young man with a short but full beard and steady eyes waited a moment, then also moved forward to offer his hand.

"Courtland?" Valentine asked. "I'm Valentine."

Courtland nodded and stepped back, and a second man, taller, leaner, dark and rather Spanish-looking, slightly inclined his head to him as he stood behind a chair, his hands on the back of it, the right one heavily bandaged. "And you'd be Spencer."

Spencer held up his injured hand. "Forgive me my lack of manners, my lord," he said, and then added, "Valentine. Our brother wrote us about you.

Said he'd mistaken you for some indigent, applying for work as his batman. I always thought Rian was smarter than that."

"He had his reasons," Valentine said, smiling faintly at the memory. "He was a good man, and a brave one. You all have my sincere sympathy."

"Rather have the boy," an older man, stout of body but keen of eye grumbled from his seat on one of the leather couches. He hauled himself to his feet and headed for the doorway. "I'll leave you to it, Cap'n. I've no stomach for hearing what I don't want to hear."

"Very good, Jacko," Ainsley said and they all watched the man leave before Ainsley turned to Valentine once more. "A glass of wine, Valentine?"

"Thank you, sir, yes." Valentine looked at the two Becket brothers, at Jack, and then asked Ainsley, "Is it possible, Mr. Becket, that you and I could speak…alone?"

He watched as Courtland just stood there, expressionless, and Spencer Becket quite obviously bristled. Jack had described them very well. The only thing he'd left out, Valentine was sure, was that they were both obviously intelligent and potentially dangerous men.

Ainsley handed Valentine a fine crystal wineglass half filled with a rich burgundy liquid. "I see no reason to deny your request. Gentlemen?"

Courtland grabbed Spencer's arm and pulled him toward the door, and Jack, with one last curious look at Valentine, followed after them.

"More comfortable now?" Ainsley asked, re-taking his chair behind the large desk and motioning for Valentine to sit down wherever he chose.

"Yes, sir, thank you," Valentine said, pulling a straight-backed chair away from the wall and placing it in front of the desk.

"I'll begin, if you don't mind," Ainsley said, picking up a brass paperweight and balancing it in his palm. "And, to do that, let me apologize for saddling you with the care and welfare of my impetuous daughter."

"My impetuous wife," Valentine corrected, looking levelly into those remarkable blue eyes.

Ainsley didn't blink. Nothing in his posture betrayed his surprise. But then his hand slowly closed around the paperweight. "Indeed."

Valentine raised a hand, rubbed at his forehead. "That was cow-handed of me, wasn't it? Forgive me. But, yes, Fanny is now my wife. Since yesterday morning, in point of fact, and in all ways since last night."

"And it was necessary for you to tell me all of that?"

"Yes, it was, it is. I made a mistake, a terrible mistake. For my own selfish reasons, I took advantage of a young woman in the depths of despair over the loss of her brother. I have no excuse for my actions, none. But they can't be undone."

One corner of Ainsley's mouth rose slightly, his blue eyes twinkling. "My lord Brede, my daughter—none of my daughters—does anything they don't want to do. If Fanny married you, that's what she wanted to do. It remains to you whether she comes to regret her actions."

Valentine couldn't sit still. He drained his wine-glass and placed it on the desktop, then got to his feet. "She loves Rian. She sees me as…as someone to protect her, keep her safe. But she came to Brussels, followed him, because she loved him. Loves him."

Ainsley was quiet for long moments, his chin in his hands as he watched Valentine pace the carpet. "Jack told me you weren't an ass," he said at last. "As I have never had reason to mistrust his judgment, I can only think that you, Valentine, are laboring under some strain. I agree, Fanny loved Rian. He loved her, very much. But don't see bogeymen where they don't exist. You're a man grown. You know there are kinds and levels, even ages of love. You care for her, don't you?"

Valentine stopped pacing to look at Ainsley. "For my sins, yes, I believe I do. But that does not excuse my treatment of her at such a vulnerable time."

Sitting back at his ease, Ainsley said, "I'll leave that to the two of you to sort out, if you don't mind. I have no fears about Fanny, she takes very good care of herself. I might, however, spare a moment or two to worry about you." He got to his feet. "In the meantime, allow me, please, to welcome you to our family."

Valentine held up his hands, stepped back a pace. "Thank you, sir. But I'm not done yet."

Ainsley settled back into his chair. "Go on."

"First, let me say that Fanny told me about… about your family. I pass no judgments and will keep your secrets safe. I would, however, be honored to do what I can about this man, this Edmund Beales, if you should require my assistance in any way. In fact, I insist."

Ainsley raised one eyebrow. "Fanny told you all of that? I admit, I'm surprised to hear it. You rather hold our collective futures in the palm of your hand, don't you?"

Valentine shook his head. "I would never do anything to hurt Fanny. I've already done enough, don't you think?"

"I think it's going to take some time to hear all that *you* think, and to tell you anything else you should know. As for my former partner—"

Valentine sat down once more, using the arms of the chair to pull himself closer to the desk. "I've another confession to make, Mr. Becket, as well as something to say. Something that's been bothering me since I last spoke with Rian."

Ainsley picked up the paperweight once more, keeping his silence.

Valentine rubbed at his mouth, collecting his thoughts, putting them in order, and then began his story.

"The evening of the battle, when Rian didn't return from carrying a message to one of our commanders, Fanny and I went looking for him. Fanny...Fanny thinks we didn't find him, but that's not correct. I did find him."

Ainsley's hand closed tight around the paperweight once more.

"Let me keep this brief, sir, and I promise to fill in the details later if you wish. But, for now, let me give you an idea of the situation as I saw it. Fanny was where I'd put her, inside a cow shed, next to the body of Rian's horse. He wasn't there, and all I could think was that some French soldiers found him and decided to use him as a shield as they made their escape, or even take him, an officer, for ransom. In any case, he was gone, he wasn't there. His sword, however was, and it was bloody. He'd engaged the enemy, put up a fight. But where was he? I went out into the dark, to assure myself that no French stragglers were still out there before I could feel it safe to take Fanny back to our encampment. What I found was Rian, propped against a tree trunk, badly injured."

"How badly?" Ainsley asked, his voice tight.

"Very badly, sir. Jupiter had fallen on him, injuring something inside the boy, I think, and he had a bullet wound to his leg. And then there was—but I'll tell you about that in a moment, if I can, because there's something to say first. As we spoke, the French came back, and Rian begged me to give him my pistol, as he felt he was dying and he wanted me—ordered me—to get Fanny to safety."

"She shouldn't have been there."

"I agree, sir. I most heartily agree. But I was left with limited choices, and with Rian telling me there were three or more French who, it seemed, had dragged him from the cow shed, then abandoned him when they heard my pistol shot as I put Jupiter out of his pain. I had one pistol, one shot. I had Rian's sword. I had two horses. And I had Fanny, left unprotected a good thirty yards away, in the cow shed."

"You *left* him there."

"I did," Valentine said, looking straight into Ainsley's eyes. "I cocked the pistol for him and did what he asked me to do. I got Fanny out of there. That's when she was shot, as we rode off. I also heard another pistol shot. I'm sure that was Rian, doing what he wanted to do, which was to take one of the Frenchmen with him, making his sister's escape easier."

At last Ainsley reacted. He dropped his head into his hands. "Sweet Jesus. God. *Sweet Jesus.* They hacked him to pieces, didn't they? That boy, that good, good boy. My beautiful boy…"

Valentine sat forward, put his hands on the edge of the desktop. "Possibly, that's what happened. And possibly not."

Ainsley lifted his head, looked at Valentine, his emotions sharply reined back under his control after his short lapse into fatherly grief. "Explain yourself."

"I went back, early the next morning. Before dawn. I knew I had to bring Rian's body home, here, to his family. But the body wasn't there. I searched the area, thoroughly, in case I'd mistaken his position, but nothing. No sign of him. And no burial parties had been in the area up to that point. So I rode South, chasing the French. For days. There was no sign of him. And there's more."

"I'm having quite enough difficulty with what you've already told me. But continue, please."

"I began to remember things I'd glossed over at the moment. I'd been intent on getting Fanny safely clear of the area, you understand. For these men to capture her, realize she was a female beneath her uniform— Well, Rian was right, I needed to get her gone. But the man my horse collided with as we began our retreat from the cow shed wasn't wearing a French uniform. He wasn't wearing a uniform at all. And then I realized something else. Something I said I'd tell you. Rian had another wound. A wicked, bloody one, to his left forearm. Slashed through to the bone."

"And?"

"And when he lifted his arm, to show me why he felt he was already past saving, I saw the tourniquet. Somebody had tied a tourniquet around Rian's arm to stop the bleeding, and I don't think it was Rian. He'd have no time for that, under attack as he was. I thought about that, thought that whoever had captured him wanted to keep him alive long enough to use him as a shield, if not for ransom. But then I remembered something else Rian had said to me and my conclusions were even more disconcerting."

Valentine stopped for a moment, collected himself. He'd spent so much time wondering about Rian's curious words to him about Fanny, that he'd overlooked something very important.

"Rian said that he'd felt as if the men who were after him had been *hunting* him. Expressly hunting him. One horse would do five men on foot little good, and the battle was already well on the way to being lost for them. So why would they be hunting him? And, even if they abandoned him for a space when they heard my shot, they did come back. Again, sir, *why?*"

"They took him," Ainsley said, his eyelids narrowed, his face a dark cloud of anger and real pain. "They took him because they knew who he was."

Valentine let out a pent-up breath and subsided against the back of the chair, relieved that Ainsley Becket had come to the same conclusion. "Yes, sir. After what Fanny has told me since, I believe they did. The pieces all just seemed to fall into place. Sergeant-Major Hart had already told me that someone had come to the Thirteenth, to ask about Rian's whereabouts, just before the battle. He thought it was one of you, looking for Fanny, but that's not who it was. Someone was expressly hunting Rian. Not to kill him, but to take him. I will go to my grave regretting that I didn't overrule him, try to take him with me."

"You really were left with no other reasonable alternative at the time," Ainsley told him. "Rian's first and only thought would be to save his sister. His injuries were grievous, clearly."

"I can't imagine him surviving them for very long, no, sir. He'd lost a considerable amount of blood. If Jupiter hadn't gone down, if Fanny hadn't been with me—maybe, possibly, I could have gotten him past those men and back to headquarters, inflicting severe pain when I moved him. I can't say he would have survived his injuries even if I'd gotten him to the surgeons, however. I doubt it. His death would only have been delayed, especially in the heat of Brussels. We've often lost more men to heat and infection than we have on the battlefield. I thought I wouldn't have been doing him any great favor, even if I thought I could manage the logistics of the thing. At least that's what I keep trying to tell myself. But I am certain that Rian isn't alive now. Not as a prisoner."

"Enough. You made a decision. You made a choice between a gravely injured Rian and Fanny. If it helps you at all, Valentine, I believe I would have come to the same conclusion. I've been forced to make similar decisions more than I care to remember, and I don't envy you the sleepless nights you'll spend second-guessing yourself. But we have to put it behind us."

"Because of this man. This Edmund Beales."

Ainsley nodded. "He's getting closer. I don't know how, but he is. I have to send someone to Chance immediately, insist he leaves London, returns to his family. Possibly even brings them here. Morgan, as well."

"You've quite the fortress here, sir."

Ainsley nodded absently, his mind busy. "I had hoped for a home, some peace. A future for my crew, my children."

He blinked, clearing his mind, and looked at Valentine. "Beales must know something. Obviously, not yet enough. He's also been quite busy, we believe, with his own pursuits, so perhaps he's *saving* us until a time of his choosing. But, whatever is happening, if they tortured Rian, if he lived long enough to give them any hint of where we are, *who* we are, then we're rapidly running out of time. Romney Marsh consists of about one hundred square, sparsely populated miles of England itself, and we're in the most remote part of those hundred square miles. We're sheltered, our people are loyal to us, but we aren't invisible."

"He'd still be so much your enemy? After all this time?"

"No less than he's mine, if for different reasons. Now, if there's nothing else, please excuse me as I— Fanny."

Valentine leapt up from his chair and turned to face the door to the hallway, to see her standing there, her eyes wide, her complexion as white as chalk.

"Fanny," Ainsley said gently, "come over here to me, my dear. What did you hear, hmm? What did you— Fanny!"

But she was gone.

"Christ! What did she hear? Where would she go? Where would she run to? Quickly, man."

"Sit down, Valentine," Ainsley told him. "Give her some time by herself."

"But if she heard me say that I might have been able to bring Rian back if she hadn't been with me—"

"Yes, I understand that. I'm afraid there's enough pain for all of us in this, enough blame for all of us to share. For now, let her be, let her grieve. Jack will be in the main drawing room, with the others. Just turn to your right as you leave here and follow the hallway. Tell him I suggested you and Court and Spence visit *The Last Voyage.* Choose a dark corner and tell them what you've told me, please. It's enough I'll have to deal with Jacko."

Valentine didn't want to repeat his story. He wanted to find Fanny, hold her, tell her nothing had been her fault. But he realized Ainsley Becket was probably right. He'd needed time alone himself once he'd finally put all the pieces together, God knew. Valentine didn't much care for taking orders. But this was Ainsley Becket's house, and Fanny was his daughter.

"Oh, and one thing more," Ainsley said as Valentine headed for the open doorway. "Sit as far as possible from Spencer while you're first doing the telling. I don't think Mariah would appreciate it if the boy broke his other hand on your head."

"Sir, I—"

Ainsley shook his head slowly. "No. Going over what has happened, time and again, aids nobody. We move on from here. That's what we must do, what we've always done. We survive."

Valentine looked to the open doorway one more time, his chest tight. "Survive. Yes, I used to think that would be enough. To survive. But it isn't, sir. It really isn't. Not anymore."

"No, and it never was," Ainsley told him, walking to the French doors, to look out over the Channel. "But, sometimes, my new friend, it's all we have…."

CHAPTER NINETEEN

VALENTINE'S MEETING with Jack and the Becket brothers hadn't gone especially well, but at least it had been mercifully brief and relatively bloodless. He'd left them where they sat, Jack making small motions with his head, encouraging him to leave, and he'd walked down past the mermaid figurehead, having decided to row out to the *Pegasus* to check on the horses.

But the yacht wasn't anchored in the small harbor. He stood, his hands jammed on his hips, considering the possible ramifications of this development, until he heard a voice behind him.

"Sent your captain off to near Littlestone-on Sea, milord, where there's deeper water and a dock. It was either that or a winch, and we didn't much feel like haulin' that out for a couple of horses. Sent Jacob Whiting, too, to ride the mare and bring your stallion back here with him."

Valentine turned about, to see what could only

be a wizened old seadog, right down to his bandy legs and skinny shanks. "And my yacht?"

"Told your man to shoo it off home. Don't need such a silly thing here, do we now? Can't even mount a single decent gun on it, can you? I'm Billy, by the bye. An' I know you. You're the one what left our Rian to die."

Valentine's stomach knotted. "Yes, that would be me. But I didn't see you in the tavern, Billy. Were you perhaps hiding beneath the table?"

Billy's grinned, showing a new, rather raw gap squarely in his bottom jaw, where another of his teeth had recently lost the battle to the tooth drawer. "Nobody ever sees me. That's m'talent. Hit you good, didn't he? And you didn't so much as blink, or hit him back, neither, him with only one good hand." Billy poked his tongue at the new gap, then ran it around his lips, smiled again. "Don't be doin' that with Jacko. He'd just hit you again, twice as hard. Then he'd start in with the kickin', once he had you down. That's Jacko, and all you need to know about him."

"The man's twice my age."

"So? He's twice as big, too, grantin' that most of it's round his middle now. One hit, that's only to be expected. But never two. Two, and you're showin' him your soft underbelly, and that's never good."

"I'll remember that, thank you. Are you going to hit me now, too, Billy? A single hit, of course."

"Me? No. Spence did it all, I'm thinkin'. And now he's sorry, like he always is when he goes off his head. That wife of his is goin' to give him what for anyways when she hears about it. They're still there at the *Voyage,* you know, talkin' about things, figurin' you did the right thing. Hurts, though. Rian was a good boy. A dreamer, but a good boy."

"He was a soldier, Billy, and a man—not a good boy. And he died a soldier's death. A hero's death. I'd like you all to remember that."

Billy worked his closed mouth for a few moments, and then spit on the ground. "That he was, that he was. But now we're short a *man.* Bad times coming, and we're down a man."

"No, Billy, you're not."

All the gaps in Billy's mouth showed now, thanks to his wide grin. "All right, then. Suppose that's only fair."

Valentine watched as Billy turned back toward *The Last Voyage.* What strange people. Blunt, fierce, but then a grin and an "All right, then." Clearly, he'd passed some sort of test he hadn't realized he was taking. Billy, whoever he was, had accepted him.

Absently rubbing at his tender right cheekbone, Valentine walked closer to the shoreline and began walking along it, back toward Becket Hall. He needed to see Fanny. Apologize to her, for so many things. Make sure she was all right, that she didn't blame herself for Rian's death.

But what would he say? How could he convince her?

He'd walked about one hundred yards before he looked up, glanced out at the horizon and then turned inland, toward the terrace.

Fanny was sitting up on the balustrade, a light cloak over her shoulders in the cool breeze coming off the Channel, her white-blond hair blowing in that breeze, her feet dangling over the mix of sand and shingle a good twenty feet below her.

She was looking out to sea, her expression impossible to read from this distance.

Should he go to her? She certainly wasn't hiding herself from him, was she?

He didn't wave to her, but just walked to the nearest set of wide stone steps and climbed to the terrace, walked down its length to where Fanny still sat, waiting for him.

He leaned his forearms on the balustrade beside her, clasped his hands in front of him. Looked out at the same horizon Fanny was concentrating on so closely. Said nothing.

"Has anyone fed you?" she said at last.

Valentine whipped his head around to look up at her. "Pardon me?"

She wouldn't look at him. Couldn't look at him. They were cursed, both of them. And Rian had paid the price for what they'd done.

"I said, has anyone fed you? It's a simple question."

"No. No, I haven't eaten. Not since last night, I suppose. It doesn't matter."

"No, I suppose not." Fanny shifted slightly on her perch. "How could you bear to have even touched me?"

"A better question, Fanny. How can I bear not touching you now?"

She turned her body away from him then, lifting her legs up and over the balustrade, dropping her feet to the stone terrace. "It's my fault. It's all my fault. If I hadn't gone to Brussels…if I hadn't gone to the battlefield…if I hadn't raced out after Rian as if he couldn't possibly take care of himself…"

"Fanny, no…" Valentine said, gathering her into his arms. "If Bonaparte hadn't escaped from Elba. If he'd never been born. What happened, happened. Don't do this to yourself, sweetings. It serves no purpose."

She pulled away from him, even as she longed to stay in his arms. "I've ruined two lives, Brede. Rian's, and yours. You'll never be able to forget that you left him there…and I'll never be able to forget the reason you did. Go away, Brede. Please. Go home. There's no reason for you to stay here."

"Fanny—"

"No! Don't say anything else. I loved Rian. I did! And then I married you. He was gone, and I turned to you. I'm willful and I'm selfish and the only thing I can bring you is disaster. It's enough that…that I killed one man."

"Fanny, you didn't *kill* anyone."

She looked at him, her eyes blazing green fire. "If I hadn't been there, Brede. If I hadn't been with you when you found Jupiter, when you found Rian—would you have left him there to die? No, don't answer me. I know you wouldn't have done that. You would have picked…you would have picked him up, brought him back. You would never have left him."

"I might never have found him, if I hadn't been worried about you. That's the only reason I went out there into the bushes, Fanny. To make sure nobody was approaching the cow shed. It was full dark, impossible to continue a search, with some of the enemy still nearby. Alone, I would have simply returned to headquarters and resumed my search in the morning. Rian would have been gone. Or dead where he fell. It would have made no difference."

Fanny looked away from him. Did he have to sound so *rational?*

Valentine pressed his advantage. "And, if you hadn't come to the battlefield, Fanny, I might not even have realized that Rian had gone missing until the next day. But you were there, and when you ran for your horse, to ride out looking for him, I went with you. So stop this, stop it now. Rian's last words to me were about you, having me promise to take care of you."

Her bottom lip began to tremble. "He gave me to you. All…all I could think about was myself, what my life would be like without him. And all he…all he thought about was me, when he should have been thinking about himself. I want him back, Brede. I want him back, so I can tell him how sorry I am. But I can't have that, can I?"

She had her arms wrapped tight around herself, rocked back and forth slightly where she stood, all but keening in grief.

"No, sweetings, you can't."

She lifted her chin. "I'd like you to go, Brede. There's nothing here for you. Rian would understand."

"Fanny, you're my wife now. If I leave here, you're leaving with me. But that's a battle we don't have to fight right now, because I'm not leaving. I've already told your father as much."

"That's…that's not what you wanted this morning. You couldn't wait to leave me here. Could you? What's changed, Brede? I don't understand."

"I suppose it was something your father said to me, earlier. About ages and levels. Something I should have understood on my own. That, and perhaps your brother Spencer knocked some sense into my thick head. You're my wife, Fanny. I'm your husband. We can't either of us change the past, but that doesn't mean we can't find a future."

She shook her head as she began backing away from him. "I don't...I don't think we can do that, Brede. I'm so sorry...."

She ran from him then, just as she'd run from the words she'd overheard in Ainsley's study. She threw open one of the French doors and burst into the drawing room, running past Mariah, Eleanor and Callie, who looked up from their quiet conversation just to see her race toward the foyer and the staircase.

Fanny didn't stop running until she was in her bedchamber. She locked the door and then stood with her back to it, breathing hard, unaware that her cheeks were wet with tears.

"Didn't I teach you better than that, child? No matter how fast or far you run, you've still got all of yourself stuck to you when you stand still again."

"Odette," Fanny said, belatedly wiping at her cheeks as she walked farther into the darkened chamber, as all of the drapes had been closed ever since she'd last been in the room, hiding as she planned her escape to Dover. "I...I don't want to talk right now, please."

Odette, tall and thin, clad in mourning clothes only a few shades darker than her skin, the same unremitting black she'd worn every day since Isabella and the others had died, shook her head at Fanny's answer. She slowly pushed herself up and out of the rocker that had sat in a corner of Fanny's room for as many years as they'd been at Becket Hall, back before the village had been constructed, and many of the crew had slept side-by-side on the floor of the third-floor nursery. She turned around, pushed at one of its arms, set it to rocking.

"You don't remember when you were so sick with the measles, do you, Fanny girl? How I'd sit here with you, rocking, and rocking. You all but burning up in my arms, you were so hot. All my learning, all my fine potions and medicines, and we felt sure we were going to lose you."

"Odette, I—"

The old woman let go of the chair, to shuffle across the floor in her worn carpet slippers, one long, gnarled finger wagging. "You hush, girl. I'm still talking. Worried about your eyes, as well as your little heart, we did. Kept this room all dark, night and day. Rian sat with me, watching over you. Never left, even when we told him he could get the spots, too. He didn't care. You were sick, and he wouldn't leave you. Only a boy, but loyal. Loving."

"I was too young. I don't remember," Fanny said,

taking hold of a bedpost and hiking herself up onto the coverlet.

"Didn't matter to him, what happened to him. Not as long as you were all right. Never did matter to him."

"Did Rian get sick, Odette?"

She shook her head. "No, child. You didn't make him sick. And you didn't make him dead. Sometimes things don't happen and sometimes they do. We can't stop the bad things sometimes, Fanny. Not you, not me, not anybody. We can't know. We don't see the bad things coming at us. They just come."

Fanny felt the first stirrings of shame, came outside of her own grief and hurt to feel a new compassion for her long-ago nanny. "You mean, the island, Odette, don't you? What happened there."

Odette nodded. "For so many years I kept telling myself, Odette, you should have known. You should have looked at Edmund Beales and *seen* him, really *seen* him. Him, and Loringa both."

Fanny had been wiping at her wet cheeks with the backs of her hands. But she stopped, looked at Odette. "Who?"

The old woman smiled, showing a mouthful of still strong, white teeth. "Think you know everything, don't you, child? But you don't, do you? Loringa. My sister. My twin. The other side of my coin. It was she so many years ago, rousing the *baka*, casting a spell over me, to keep me blind to the danger. Let me see how much you remember of what I taught you. Tell me about twins."

Fanny sniffled, forgetting that she'd wanted to be alone, to just lie in the dark, and concentrated on what she remembered. Odette had something to say to her. She was easing into whatever that was, as she was wont to do, but it had to be something important, or else Odette would not be here. Odette would not be so kind to her, but only tell her to stop being a baby, stop sulking, feeling sorry for herself.

"In the world of Voodoo, twins are the *marassa,*" she recited by rote. "Powerful, exceptional, privileged. They can be as strong as *loas.* They belong to different nations, and have different names. The Nago *marassa,* the Ibo *marassa,* the Congo *marassa,* the— I don't remember."

"The Dahomey. We are Dahomey," Odette said proudly. "Dahomey *marassa.* Dahomey *hungan.* Priestesses. More powerful than most. For good or evil. Opposite sides of the same coin. For us, for every good there is an evil, for every left there is a right, for every up a down."

Fanny nodded, remembering more of her lessons. They'd all learned in their childhood that to ask Odette to speak of the Voodoo was to keep her from remembering that sometimes they'd been bad children she'd planned to scold for one transgression or another. But, although she'd told Fanny about twins, she hadn't told her that she, Odette, was herself a twin. And now she was fairly certain why Odette hadn't said anything.

"She hates you, this Loringa, doesn't she. Don't twins often hate?"

"Often, yes, when they are children, and know no better. They can inflict great harm on each other. But as I grew, as I learned the depth and height of my powers, I told myself to follow the sun. So I followed your papa."

Now Fanny understood. "But Loringa, your sister. She followed the dark, didn't she, Odette?"

"Beales. She followed Beales. She follows Beales. For years, I could not feel her. But I feel her now. Deep in my bones, I feel her."

"And that's what you want to tell me, Odette? That you feel your sister? Coming closer?" Fanny unconsciously reached for the *gad,* the alligator tooth she had pinned inside the bodice of her gown.

"Closer, but not yet near. I am the stronger one, as when we were children. I can keep her muddled now that I know what she is about, keep her away. But not forever. And so I told your papa. So I am also telling you. I feel your fear, child, and that fear is inside you for good reason. I hold that fear in respect. It is a gift to you from the good *loa,* to remind you to be careful. The day will come, it is already on its way. But I also know this, am sure of this. The day is not here yet, there is time yet to prepare for the day we face our final battle."

Fanny sometimes believed Odette could see everything, that she knew everything. Then, at other times, she thought of her as just Odette, the woman who had loved and scolded them all. Fanny couldn't remember her mother, save for that one single memory of her pushing her down, covering her with her body. Odette had been her mother, as much as she'd ever had one, and at the moment Fanny wanted to believe everything Odette said to her.

But it was hard. So hard.

Odette put her hand on Fanny's shoulder. "And one thing more. When you look at the man, see the man. Be fair to the man. Do not see the fear, plan for the fear. Do not see the past. See the man, look into his eyes, for there you will find your truth. Do you understand me, child? Rian would want that."

Fanny lowered her head, spoke softly. "Rian and I weren't twins. But we were different sides of the same coin, weren't we? From the time we were children. He was the giver, and I was the selfish one who only took. He was the good to my evil."

Odette's sigh was loud, exasperated. "You're as evil as that bedpost, child, and just as thick. Mourn your brother. That is right to do. But do not bury yourself with him, for that is to dishonor his memory."

"Brede said we can't change the past, but we can find a future." She looked at Odette. "But I can't see it. I can feel the fear, and I can't see any other future, not until Edmund Beales is gone forever. I lost Rian to him by my own selfishness, that's what they think, I know they do. I can't lose Brede to him, too. So I'm sending him away."

"He won't thank for that, child."

"I know," Fanny said. Then she reached out to hug Odette around the waist, bury her head against the old woman's soft bosom. "I know."

CHAPTER TWENTY

FANNY STAYED in her bedchamber for the remainder of the day. She cried a little, slept a little, and then decided that—as had been the opinion of her family many times during her youth—she still "wasn't fit to associate with reasonable human beings."

Callie had come knocking on her door earlier, bringing food to her, and Fanny had surprised herself by downing every last bite, then wiping at the last bits of juice with a hunk of fresh bread. It was both a wonderful and horrifying thing; how life went on. The sun still rose and set, bellies still insisted on being fed, younger sisters were still interminable pests….

As the hours dragged by and the sky outside darkened and the sounds inside Becket Hall seemed to go low and hushed, she wondered what Valentine was doing. If he'd eaten. Where he'd sleep. If he'd decided she was right, and he had taken advantage of what she'd so stupidly said and was already on the road to Brede Manor.

She also spent some time thinking about what Odette had said. Odette believed her, believed her nightmare and her fears were real. A gift from the *loa,* the good spirits. How could fear be a gift?

Because her fear was also a warning? Yes, that made sense. Edmund Beales was still their enemy, still bent on destroying all of them. Loringa, Odette feeling aware of her again, was a warning.

Rian had been the most heartbreaking of warnings.

All of her life, for as long as she could remember, Becket Hall and her family had been Fanny's world. Romney Marsh her home. She'd felt safe, sheltered. Cocooned. Blissfully unaware.

A child.

Now she'd seen some of the world. She'd seen a city. She'd seen a battlefield. She'd seen the beauty and the horror. And all she'd wanted, all that she'd thought would heal her, keep her safe, would be to run to Valentine, who would then shield her, protect her.

That's what she felt for him, about him. Wasn't it? This strong man, this worldly man. This man who, when he looked at her, made her long to race into his protective arms.

To hold her.

To kiss her.

To make the world go away.

Her thoughts stopped her as she stood naked in the middle of her bedchamber after washing at the basin, her arms raised as she pulled a white lawn nightgown over her head. She tugged the material down and over her hips, her thoughts echoing in her head. *Hold her. Kiss her.* Revel in the softness that came into his world-weary eyes when he looked at her. Feel her heart flutter in her breast when she looked at him, when he teased her, when he blustered, when he…

Where had Eleanor put him? Which chamber?

No. She couldn't do that.

Make the world go away.

Yes. She could.

Fanny pushed her fingers through her hair, hunted in her wardrobe for the slippers Callie had embroidered for her last Christmas.

Make the world go away.

Slipped her feet into the slippers. Dragged a dressing gown from the wardrobe, shoved her arms into it, tied the satin strings at her neck.

She clapped a hand to her mouth to hold back a startled yelp when someone knocked on her bedchamber door. She turned toward the door, saw a spill of light beneath it. Whoever was there had come bearing a candle, as if unfamiliar with the way in the near dark and needing extra light.

"Who…who's there?"

"Open the door, Fanny."

"Brede," she whispered, her heart skipping a

beat. He'd come to her? Just as she was about to go to him? That wasn't fair. Now he was the better man, not she. Besides, he'd just ordered her to open the door. Who was he to give her orders?

Oh. Her husband.

Well, wasn't that *convenient* for him!

"Go away," she called out loudly enough for him to hear her through the thick wood. "I'll… We'll see each other tomorrow."

"Fanny, open the door. And I won't ask you a third time."

"Good," she said in a firm voice. "Then I won't have to hear from you again tonight."

She thought she heard a low chuckle on the other side of the door. But that couldn't be right. She hadn't said anything the least amusing.

Then she watched, her eyes wide, as the large key in the lock fell onto the floor. She heard another key fumbling in the lock, from the other side of the door. She watched as the latch was depressed. Stood stock-still as the door opened and Valentine walked into the room.

"How…"

"Odette gave it to me, along with directions to your chamber and a warning to begin as I plan to go on, or else be henpecked for all of my life," he said, placing the key in his waistcoat pocket. "She hardly seems to physically fill the role of Cupid, but she seems a pragmatic woman. After all, you and I are married. And I have to sleep somewhere, don't I?"

"Might I suggest the stables, my lord," Fanny said, backing up several steps, even as she longed to run to him.

Odd. He was dressed in his London clothes, but his cravat was hanging untied and he looked…he looked a bit *fuzzy* around the edges. He was part haughty peer, part ruffian tonight. He was a twin, all by himself, two halves of the same whole. Two men, inhabiting the same body, sharing the same soul. Why hadn't she seen that before? Had Odette seen it? Was that another meaning Fanny had been supposed to understand? Two men; but one body, one heart, one soul. One who had often been forced into the dark, one who hoped for the light. Which one of them craved *her?*

Valentine smiled. "The stable, is it? There's five pounds I owe Spence."

Fanny shook herself back to attention, looked at him owlishly. "I beg your pardon? Spence?"

"Yes. After he knocked me down, we decided we rather like each other. He said the stables. I had thought you'd simply tell me to take myself to hell."

"Spence— Spencer *hit* you? Why?"

"Well, there remains a difference of opinion on that," Valentine said, depositing the candle on a nearby able. "Court says it was because Spence is most articulate with his fists, rather than his mouth, but Jack's position is that I simply possess a face many men see and would like to hit."

Fanny stepped closer, to get a better look at Valentine in the dim light. She saw that his cheek was rather red, a bit puffy. Then she looked into his eyes, and narrowed her own at him. So, *that* explained his rather fuzzy look. "Brede—you're *drunk.*"

"Nonsense," he said, walking past her, already slipping off his cravat. "A bit in my altitudes, possibly, but surely not cup-shot. Three parts inebriated, if anything. I'm an earl, my dear. Earls don't condescend to getting *drunk.*"

"I did this to you, didn't I? I reduced you to this—crawling into a bottle."

He turned to face her. "You give yourself too much credit, my dear. I am perfectly capable of lifting a glass on my own."

He began opening the buttons on his waistcoat, ticking off reasons as he did so. "We drank to your brother. We drank to Wellington. To Blücher. To lasting peace. To pretty Uxbridge. And, again, to Rian. Many, many times to Rian. We would have drunk to the Prince Regent, but we don't much care for Fat Florizel, none of us. Oh, and we drank to my marriage. Can't forget that, can I? So here I am… presenting myself to my bride."

"Oh, Brede…"

He stripped out of his jacket and waistcoat, pulled his opened shirt clear of his buckskins and then looked about the dimly lit chamber. "No boot-jack? Pity." He sat himself down on the rocker and held up one booted leg to her. "You'll do the honors, wife?"

"I'll call for someone," Fanny told him, suddenly nervous. Valentine was so elementally male. He'd taken her to bed, yes. But that had been different from the way he was now. He wasn't comforting her now. He was…why, he was almost *taunting* her. *Daring* her with a naughty, little-boy smile on his face.

She was most certainly going to have a stern talk with the interfering Odette tomorrow, and her brothers, as well—and she hoped those brothers, and Jack included, would spend most of the rest of the night hanging their heads over their chamber pots, sick as dogs.

"Call for someone? Nonsense. You're no more than five feet away from me, and perfectly capable," Valentine said, waggling an admonishing finger at her. "Why, wasn't it you, Fanny, who pointed out to me that we're much too lazy, too dependent on others when we could just as easily fend for ourselves?"

"Oh, shut up, Brede," Fanny said. "I don't need to be flogged with my own words. Brace your hands on the arms of the chair."

Valentine rocked back and forth. "Feels like

we're back on the yacht, doesn't it?" His eyes clouded. "Would that we were…."

Fanny shook her head, giving up the fight. The sooner she had gotten his boots off, the sooner she could lead him to her bed, where he'd probably promptly fall asleep. "Keep your leg stuck out, and plant your other foot firmly on the floor," she ordered.

Then she turned her back to him and rather mounted him, as she would a horse, one foot planted on either side of his leg, her back to him.

"Ah, isn't that a lovely sight," Valentine said, not so deep in his cups that he didn't know he was driving his new bride insane. Seemed fair enough…as that's what she'd done to him. "Wiggins's rump doesn't hold a candle to yours, sweetings. But he does wear white gloves when he removes my boots. To avoid smudging the leather, you understand. Do you by chance have a pair of white gloves handy, wife?"

"Hang your smudges. I could cheerfully strangle you at the moment, Brede, *and* my brothers," Fanny growled from between clenched teeth as she put one hand on the heel of his boot, the other beneath the sole, and then began to work the high boot free of his leg. The boot had been well-made, and fit him like a second skin. She couldn't budge it.

"Here we go," Valentine said, lifting his other leg and planting the sole of that boot on her backside.

"You pull, sweetings, and I'll push. Seems fair enough, and much like what we're already doing between us now, at any rate."

"You *are* drunk, aren't you, Brede?" she asked him, daring to turn her head to glare at him. She'd seen her brothers drunk a time or two over the years, but she didn't remember them being quite so articulate at the time, being more prone to hanging on each other's shoulders and singing bawdy songs.

His smile was lopsided, as if he had a cheroot stuck in the corner of his mouth, which he didn't. "I'm beginning to believe so, yes. Whatever I am, it's an exceedingly pleasant feeling."

"How happy I am for you," Fanny snapped as she applied all her strength to pulling off the boot as he pushed against her rump.

Seconds later she held the boot in her hands and the rocker had tipped sharply backward, loudly crashing to the floor. "And even happier now," she added in some satisfaction, watching as Valentine looked up at her, his expression perplexed. And rather comical.

"Unhorsed, by gad," Valentine said. And then he giggled.

Giggled! The Earl of Brede? *Giggling?* He was still somehow sitting in the rocker, but with the rocker now having fallen backward to the floor. His one booted foot and one stockinged foot were both waving high in the air. He was totally helpless, and giggling. Oh, how low she'd brought him!

"Stop that," Fanny ordered, tossing the boot to one side and holding out her hands to him. "Here, for pity's sake, let me help you up before someone comes to check on the noise and sees you like this. Your position lends nothing to your consequence, my lord."

Valentine laughed all the harder.

"Oh, you're impossible," Fanny said, circling behind the overturned rocker and grabbing the top ends of the spindles. She put her back into it, trying to raise the rocker, but it was no use. Not with Valentine lending her absolutely no help whatsoever. "You know something, Brede? I should just leave you here, like a tortoise turned over onto its shell."

At last Valentine sobered—slightly—and maneuvered himself until the rocker tipped onto its side. Slowly, admittedly clumsily, he at last managed to get his feet, and even righted the chair. "Perhaps, wife, we should move to the bed, and try this business of the boots again?"

Fanny considered this suggestion for a moment, and then decided that he probably should get into bed, before he passed out where he stood. She waved him in the general direction of the tester bed, and he sat himself down on it, then laid back, closed his eyes.

"Last time I felt like this," he told her as he gazed up at the canopy, admiring the embroidered roses,

"I wasn't much younger than you are now, Fanny. I seem to recall that, marvelous as I feel now, the feeling won't last. Pity, as I believe I'm rather enjoying the sensation…."

Fanny didn't answer, but just worked hard to remove his other boot, finally succeeding in her third attempt. She then lifted his legs while urging him to shift himself more fully onto the bed.

"Certainly, my dear. Your every wish is my command. I'm sure it is. Now, precisely what did you want me to do?"

"If I asked you to go soak your head in one of the horse troughs, would you do it?" she grumbled, giving his legs one last push.

Valentine pulled himself backward, his head almost reaching the pillows, so that she helped him as best she could, trying to make him more comfortable.

"Lift your head, Brede, so I can slip this— Yes, that's better. I hope you don't get… Well, that you won't be sick. Not because of me. Rian was right, when he'd tease me that I could drive a man to drink. It's very lowering, you know, that you should prove him right, and I hope you're satisfied. I think I'm going to cry."

Valentine reached up a hand and grabbed her shoulder, pulling her down to him. His head had begun to spin, not quite as pleasantly as before. Odd, not feeling in control, in charge; master of his actions. Odd, yet somehow freeing. He felt his heart open, escape the tight leash he'd learned to keep on his feelings. He wasn't sure if he imagined, or actually said the words.

"Women weep, sweetings, while men pour themselves into a bottle. All to forget. Come lie with me, Fanny. Together, we can forget. War, the terribleness of it…all the good men lost for no reason than another man's ambition, another man's greed. Another man's lust for power. No more deaths, Fanny. I'm so damnably weary of all the deaths, all the good friends lost to me. So many dead. Before, at the end of the day, we'd ask who had died. Now we can only ask, sweet Jesus, who is still alive? So many gone…too many. But it's over, this time it's finally over. Lie with me, Fanny, and we'll have no more nightmares…."

"Oh, Brede, I'm so sorry. I didn't realize, I didn't see. You've been carrying the whole world, haven't you?"

Instead of answering, he only closed his eyes, sighed and turned onto his side, his back to her, sliding into sleep.

Fanny looked to the rocker, and to the chaise on the far side of the bedchamber. Looked to Valentine, lying in her bed. And knew where she belonged.

It wasn't only Rian's death or even her childishness that had pushed Valentine to drink tonight. It was *all* the deaths, all the years of war.

He'd looked tired unto death himself, the first time she'd seen him, Fanny remembered now. And all she'd done was to add to the crushing weight already bearing down on him.

He'd reached for her, had seen something in her that he felt he needed, and in return she'd taken from him, selfishly. Now it was time to give something back. He needed her, even as much as she needed him.

She blew out the last of the candles and crawled up beside him, slipping her arm around him to anchor herself in the small space he'd left to her.

Kissed the fevered skin of his neck.

And fell into a dreamless sleep.

CHAPTER TWENTY-ONE

VALENTINE WOKE AT DAWN, years of habit overruling the drink he'd downed the previous evening, and rolled over to see Fanny asleep beside him.

Now, wasn't *that* interesting?

He had a vague recollection of stumbling back across the beach in the dark to Becket Hall from *The Last Voyage* with her brothers and Jack, none of them walking too straight or thinking too clearly.

He remembered the Voodoo priestess pulling him aside and pressing a key into his hand. Vaguely, he could recall being handed a candle, and then finding his way to Fanny's bedchamber.

And something about boots? He chuckled softly. Oh, yes. He remembered now. He'd landed on the floor like a beached whale, hadn't he? What a blow to his immense consequence. The Earl of Brede, helpless on his back, his idiocy displayed in front of his lady wife.

He looked up at the flowers embroidered on the canopy. He didn't remember those. Indeed, he couldn't seem to remember anything beyond being dumped to the floor by a rogue rocking chair intent on maiming him.

So how had he gotten into her bed?

His poor, sweet Fanny. He must have shocked her down to her toes, seeing him so badly cup-shot. Well, he'd at least spare her the sight of his sorry self this morning.

He eased himself upright, his stockinged feet hanging over the side of the bed, and waited until the room stopped spinning. Which it did, one moment before someone started beating at his temples with a pair of hammers.

And something furry clearly had died in his mouth. He moved his tongue from side to side, and decided that, whatever it had been, it was still there. He'd never drink mead again, and he'd shoot the next man who told him the honeyed, homemade brew was a harmless concoction.

Valentine gathered up his boots, his jacket and waistcoat, and felt the weight of the key in his pocket. He might want to keep that, in case she locked him out again, which he wouldn't blame her for doing.

Looking toward the bed one last time, wishing himself back in it, curled up next to Fanny, who looked so malleable at the moment, so innocent and trusting in her virginal nightrail, he padded across the large chamber to the door and stepped into the hallway.

He turned, careful to close the door without the latch making a sound, and then figuratively jumped out of his skin as a raspy female voice whispered from behind him.

"Come with me now. I give you the *traitement* to take the ache from your head."

Valentine turned to look at the Voodoo priestess. "If it's anything like our English way, a hair of the dog that bit me, then I'm afraid I'll have to politely decline, madam," he said, wondering if the woman had stationed herself outside the door all night, waiting for him.

Odette smiled, her teeth blindingly white in her dark face. "No, I did not spend the night pacing here. I heard your eyelids open, and I came to help you. Come, I have made a place ready for you down the end of this hallway, and laid out everything you need."

Valentine followed her. "You heard my— Hell, woman, I thought I was the only one who heard that. Like cymbals crashing inside my head."

Odette chuckled, her shoulders shaking. "You will wash, you will dress and you will drink the liquid in the glass I put beside the basin for you. Drink it all, and then walk in the sunshine on the shore for ten minutes. You do not know how to pray to the Virgin, but the Lord's Prayer, three times, should also work."

"And this will cure me?" Valentine asked, peeking into the room Odette had indicated, to see his *portmanteaus* there, a change of clothing laid out on the bed. Why, she'd even matched his preferred waistcoat to his jacket.

He'd seen many things over the years, met many different sorts of people, been forced to consort with some unique characters during the course of his exploits. But Odette was outside his experience.

"Fanny will cure you, and you, her. That is the way since before time. But, yes, the potion will help rid you of the poisons you put in your body." She touched his arm, holding him in place for a moment.

Valentine didn't know what else he could add to that bit of early-morning profundity. His head still hurt too much for deep thinking. So he merely gave a slight bow of his head and thanked the woman.

"She's very afraid, you know. She's seen things. I did not know she could see things, as even I do not see all things, to my shame. But Mr. Ainsley, he told me it is sometimes that way with the Irish. Still, she cannot see all that I can see, for the good *loas* protect her. You're a good man, Brede, I *do* see that. You are her future. Only give her time to make her peace with her past, even as you make peace with your own. It won't be long. Have patience. Patience, and a firm hand. You've caught her as she moves between the child and the woman. Wait for the woman—for she is winning now."

Valentine opened his mouth to comment on Odette's words, but she had already turned her back on him and was walking away down the hall, shuffling in her worn carpet slippers, singing a song in a mix of French and some other language he didn't understand.

Not, he realized, that he understood much, if anything, about the woman. Odette, the Voodoo priestess. A priestess? He could believe, or he could not believe, and his more skeptical self did not. He'd seen too many tricksters, too many gullible people who had crossed their palms with silver in the hope of hearing what they wanted to hear.

Still, Ainsley Becket kept the woman around, and Valentine doubted that Ainsley did that only in order to hear what he wanted to hear.

So Valentine stepped inside the bedchamber and stripped out of his wrinkled clothing. He washed himself, cleaned his teeth, carefully shaved himself with the razor Odette had left for him—although Wiggins kept to the illusion that his master could not perform such a task on his own—and donned his smallclothes, buckskins, a fresh white shirt.

He tied his own cravat without bothering to look into a mirror as he did so. He donned the clean waistcoat and the dark blue superfine jacket. He used a towel to wipe Fanny's fingerprints from his boots and then pulled them on—another task Wiggins would like to believe beyond him.

And, lastly, he drank the potion, all of it, and headed down the stairs to find the terrace, and the now sunlit beach.

Courtland was already on the terrace, leaning his forearms on the stone balustrade, eating an apple as he looked down onto the beach.

"Best thing for you after a night like we had," he said, turning to Valentine, holding up the apple. "Of course, some would say a thin gruel or a dish of tea strapped with molasses. But I favor apples."

"Odette gave me something to drink," Valentine told him. "I don't know if I should admit to it, but I feel remarkably better."

"Said your prayers to the Virgin?"

"Ah, yes, thank you. I knew there was something I'd forgotten."

"Don't forget them. She'll know." Court turned back to watching the beach. "She always knows."

Valentine walked over to the balustrade, to look down at the beach, wondering what had so captured Courtland's attention. What he saw was Sergeant-Major Hart and another man, all the way down near the water, walking up and down in front of a long line of men.

Men. And boys. Women. Girls. Young, old, fat, slim, tall, short. A smattering of children. All of them standing at least somewhat at attention, and with broomsticks resting on their shoulders.

"I'd better go say those prayers," Valentine said, blinking. "I think I'm suffering an hallucination. Although I am fairly certain that's Sergeant-Major Hart. Who's the other fellow?"

"Oh, that's Clovis. Clovis Meechum. He was once Spence's batman, when he fought in America. They're drilling the troops."

The corners of Valentine's mouth twitched in amusement. "Of course they are. I should have realized as much."

Courtland finished his apple and threw the core in the general direction of the "troops," although it fell far short of them. "The gulls will take care of that," he said, licking at his fingers, and then he motioned for Valentine to follow him to the nearest set of stone steps leading down to the beach. "We were sailors, all of us, and many know nothing else," he explained. "But Spence believes we should prepare for a land battle, as well. He says it's a different sort of discipline needed there."

"And you'd send women out to fight? Children?"

"Whoever wasn't there that day on the island still knows what happened. We've all been fighting the same damnable memories for over seventeen long years. If Beales makes no distinction in who he kills, we can't afford to limit whom all is prepared to fight, now can we?"

"No, I suppose not." Then he remembered something he had asked Fanny. "Have you ever considered leaving here? Simply packing up and going somewhere else?"

Courtland nodded his head. "That's why Ainsley commissioned the frigate, just in case we were forced to leave. But, really, where would we go? We ran once, out of necessity. But we won't run again. If Rian lived long enough, if they found a way to make him tell them where we are, *who* we are? Why run, to be always looking over our shoulders for him, when Beales will eventually come to us?"

"He already knows the name. Becket."

"Yes, we know that now, don't we?" Courtland said, picking up a handful of small stones, to begin tossing them across the beach. "We think that must have happened when Jack and Eleanor went to London in hopes of unmasking the leader of the Red Men Gang. You know about that?"

Valentine nodded, watching the long line of hopeful soldiers milling about, forming themselves up into four distinct lines. "The smuggling gang Beales was using to funnel gold to Bonaparte. Fanny told me some of it, and Ainsley filled in most of the blank spaces for me after dinner last night, before we went to the tavern."

"Good, that makes this easier to explain. One mention of the name wouldn't have meant much to Beales. But then Spence and Mariah took their turn last year, both in Calais and in London, although our participation during the Peace Celebrations was not known to anyone save Wellington. But if, somehow, the name was heard again, involved in an entirely different—well, we'll say *adventure*—it would have piqued Beales's interest."

"And sent him on the hunt."

"Except that suddenly Bonaparte was loose, and Beales would have been fully occupied doing whatever in hell he thinks he's doing on the Continent. He didn't have time for what he'd see as a minor irritant here in England."

"But he does now."

"Yes, he does now. There's still one thing in our favor. We know who he is, but he still probably doesn't know that we're anything *but* Beckets. Spence, Eleanor, Rian, all of us, we were only children seventeen years ago. He wouldn't have recognized them, and most probably doesn't realize who we really are, other than enemies who have put a spoke in the wheel of his grand plans. Spencer was careful not to let everyone remain alive to report back to Beales."

Valentine wasn't so sure about that. Becket was a common enough name, but whoever had hunted Rian had a particular Becket in mind. Still, as Ainsley had pointed out last night, Rian also had been to London; he may have been seen. "So you're hoping Beales could still believe you're…what? Just another gang of smugglers, among so many operating along our coastline from one side to the other? Kent? Sussex? Cornwall? A thousand different places. Even so, that would explain Jack's mission in London, but not Spence's."

"We know. It's all pretty much of a muddle, and we can't really know how much Beales knows, how much he might suppose he knows. What hurts us most is that I stupidly rode out as the Black Ghost a few years ago, when first we began guarding our own local smugglers from the Red Men Gang. If Fanny didn't tell you, Ainsley's ship was the *Black Ghost,* Chance and Jacko's, the *Silver Ghost.* Ainsley himself was called the Black Ghost. It's a mistake that can't be fixed."

Valentine knew the how of it wasn't important, not how Beales had first heard the name Becket. What mattered most to them all now was what they were going to do about the danger Beales presented. "So you're planning a completely defensive maneuver?"

"No. Ainsley's had men all over the Continent ever since we first realized Beales is still alive. So far, we haven't been able to locate so much as a hint of him. We know he was in London using another name, and he's probably used a dozen different names. We'll keep trying, but in the end, it will be him who finds us, as we're the ones staying in one place."

"Your own armed fortress, with flat, open land in front of you, the Channel behind you. Good defensively, unless attack comes from both land and sea, and you're caught in the middle. Still, there'll be no way Beales can physically approach without his presence alerting you. Is there anyone else who can help?"

"We're isolated here, far from being of interest to anybody. Romney Marsh is its own country, even though it's a part of England. And we're our own country inside of it, almost as if we were back on our island. With Bonaparte and the fear of invasion finally gone, there still will be the Waterguard about, more free to look for smugglers. But there will be fewer troops stationed here, which means less protection. A final confrontation here is inevitable. Perhaps even destined."

"So Fanny thinks," Valentine said quietly. "I want to take her, you know, take her away from here, keep her safe. She was only a child when Ainsley and Beales had their falling out. This isn't her fight."

"What happened on the island was considerably more than the result of thieves falling out, Valentine. It was a massacre." Courtland turned to look at him. His short beard covered his lower jaw, but Valentine felt sure that jaw was set as tightly as the man's lips. The man was remembering something, obviously something far from pleasant. Then Courtland nodded his head. "But you're right, of course, and Fanny is your wife now. So you'll take her?"

"I've been absent from my estates ever since word of Bonaparte's escape reached England. There are several matters I probably need to personally attend to, yes, and they will take me away from here for at least one month, possibly two. I can't leave Fanny here during that time, not if I hope to sleep nights. You do understand that, don't you?"

Both men watched as the marching troops began to take on the look of people who at last understood the concept of moving together, as a unit. Even now, they were forming two squares made up of triple rows, the first line going down to one knee as the second row aimed their broomsticks in four separate directions.

"Edmund Beales is a very organized man," Courtland said at last. "He plans, prepares, and only then does he strike. What he did to us so long ago took months of planning, possibly years. Ainsley knows him best, knows how the man thinks. He'll have pieces to pick up, new alliances to form, now that Bonaparte has abdicated. He'll first and foremost protect himself. It isn't like him to rush off halfcocked. He's methodical, and very thorough."

"Thorough in what way?" Valentine asked, trying to better understand their now common enemy.

"Well, we're going to assume Rian didn't live

long enough to tell them anything, even if…even if they tortured him. But Beales, armed only with the name *Becket,* still will search us out, sooner or later. He'll dispatch several of his men to England, to investigate in any area where the Red Men Gang attempted to control the local smugglers. The gang operated in a large area, stretching from Kent to Hampshire, and beyond."

"A considerable area, I grant you. But he'll search the coast first."

"Possibly, but not probably. We've given this a lot of thought, Valentine, in order to prepare for any eventuality. Beales would consider the smugglers themselves to be pawns in a larger game, just as they were to him. He will probably be more inclined to look among those who finance the smuggling efforts, those who distribute the goods once they're off-loaded and moved inland. In other words, he'll be looking for the head, not the body, just as we did when Jack went to London."

Valentine thought about this for a few moments, and then agreed. "There are more than a few peers who've dabbled in free-trading for the considerable profit involved. Peers, and bankers, others. I can even name a few who have blatantly bragged of the fact."

"Which explains why Beales will more prob- ably have his men begin their search in London, and then work outward, toward the coast. They may already have begun. That's why Ainsley has warned Chance to leave London, set someone to manage his estate, and then bring his family here. Once Beales's agents have exhausted themselves searching London for us, they'll begin to look along the coastline, among the smugglers themselves."

"Which is when you'll eventually be discovered."

"Eventually, yes. Valentine, let me assure you that locating anyone within thirty miles of us willing to speak to a stranger will not be an easy task. Beales can't have his men simply stroll into a tavern and inquire if the patrons know of anyone in the area with the name of Becket. Not if those men aren't prepared to be dropped down a dry well, and then stoned from above until they're dead. The local free-traders know that to be found out is to be transported at the least, and hanged in chains at Dover at the most. In addition, we'd like to think they feel loyal to us for our help to them over the years. The moment someone does inquire about us, we'll be told."

Valentine, who had been contemplating the shingle beach at his feet, looked up as Spencer rode by, gave them a jocular salute as he continued to the shoreline, probably to inspect his *troops*. "Everything you've mentioned takes time. Possibly considerable time. Now, tell me what happens once Beales's people have located Becket Hall."

"He'll be surprised, we hope, to discover that Ainsley Becket is actually his former partner, Geoffrey Baskin. That will stop him for a while. He'll fall back, regroup, adjust his plans, consider his enemy. He may want us all dead, but he'll need Ainsley alive, and that will take planning. Beales couldn't have taken us by surprise all those years ago without help. Help, I'm afraid, from some of the people we assumed loyal to us. That may be what he does again—puts a cat among the pigeons as it were. A spy."

"To tell him how many of you there are, the limits of your defenses, the lay of the land, the best way to attack for effect. Your strongest positions, your weakest points. Even ingratiate himself in some way, in hopes of gaining your confidence, and your secrets."

"My congratulations, Valentine. That was almost word-for-word what Jack has already told us."

"A spy is a spy," Valentine told him, his smile wry.

"And a traitor, a traitor," Courtland added. "Considering the danger from both traitors and spies, we looked long and hard at your Sergeant-Major Hart when he first arrived here with news of Rian, Valentine. Long and hard."

"And then accepted him."

"And then accepted him for the good man he is, yes. He seems to feel almost fatherly about Fanny.

Ah, and speaking of my reckless, wayward sister—
there she goes, across the beach."

Valentine turned around to see Fanny, dressed in
a plain black gown that only emphasized her tall
slim figure and white-blond hair as it filled with
light in the sunshine. She walked slowly across the
sands, stopped for a moment and then ran ahead,
straight into Sergeant-Major Hart's open arms. The
two stood on the beach, holding each other tightly.

"Seeking comfort, the both of them," Courtland
said sadly. "Hart is of the opinion that he pointed
those men straight at Rian. We helped him into a
bottle, too, as we did with you, and then Spence and
Clovis took him in hand, gave him something to do."

"Thank you for that. Now *I* need something to
do. My estates can manage without me for a while
longer," Valentine said, watching as Fanny stepped
away from the Sergeant-Major, wiping at her eyes.
"You said Beales may send men Becket-hunting
in London."

But Courtland shook his head. "No, my friend,
not that. Fanny needs you here, and we need her
somewhere she won't be getting into more mischief.
Callie told me Fanny is still blaming herself, as if
she's responsible for what happened to Rian. When
she's done kicking herself from one end of Becket
Hall to the other, she'll begin to convince herself
that Rian is still alive somewhere in France, and she

should take herself off to find him. She may be your wife now, but I know my sister, Valentine, and that moment *will* come."

At this, Valentine whipped his head around to glare at Courtland. "But that's not possible. I saw him, Court. Men with lesser wounds would be dead by now, even with careful care. He'd lost so much blood. Rian was feeling his life slip away even as he spoke with me."

"I know that, Valentine, much as it pains me to say the words. My brother's dead. You know that. Ainsley, Jacko, all of us—in our minds, we know that. Now make Fanny believe it."

Valentine turned back to look at Fanny, saw that she was now holding both of Hart's hands, and was deep in conversation with him. She'd followed Rian to Belgium. She'd followed him onto the battle-field. She was stubborn, brave, determined and, yes, as Courtland had said, reckless.

"Christ," he swore under his breath.

"You wanted to know what you could do, Valentine," Courtland said, putting a hand on his new friend's shoulder. "Do what you first suggested. Take her away from here with you, take her to your home, at least for a few months. Give her something and someone else to think about until she's calmer, until she has accepted Rian's death. We've got at least a few months. Ainsley thinks three, maybe more, and then it will first be the cat in with the pigeons before Beales feels confident enough to strike more directly, with what he thinks will be the killing blow. Once he knows Ainsley is in his sights, we're all in for it."

Valentine nodded his agreement before asking one last question, for Courtland had said something that still nagged at him. "Just tell me this, please. Why would Beales want Ainsley alive?"

Courtland didn't answer for some moments, then said, "None of us knows the answer to that for certain, except Jacko. Beales wants something Ainsley has. We thought that something was Isabella, and she was certainly a part of it. But not all of it. Not all of it...."

CHAPTER TWENTY-TWO

FANNY PLEADED a poor appetite and left the luncheon table set up in the morning room while the others were awaiting the next course, avoiding Callie's suggestion that the younger girl go with her, Mariah's questioning glance and the disapproving tilt of Eleanor's head.

Honestly, for such a huge house, it was sometimes depressingly impossible to be alone. Checking behind her as she went, Fanny made her way to Ainsley's study, knowing that her papa and the other males of the family were taking their luncheon in the main dining room in order to talk strategy, or whatever it was they said they weren't discussing.

She tiptoed across the room, to the large table where Ainsley kept his maps and charts, searching through them to find maps of Europe, and most especially Belgium and France.

What she found first were several hand-drawn maps, all the same except for Ainsley's neat hand with a pen—he'd written names and dates on the maps, as well as drawn lines here and there in both red and blue ink.

Poor Papa, locked up here, both by his own choosing and by circumstance, hiding his face from the world, yet unable to leave it entirely.

She'd seen maps like this before, brought to her by Rian after his lessons on the great battles of Caesar, Alexander the Great, even Nelson's tragic victory at Trafalgar. He'd sit with her, refight the wars, explain strategies to her, just as Ainsley had explained them to him.

Fanny also spared a moment to castigate herself for not listening more closely, for not seeing the lines drawn on the various maps as more than interesting puzzles to solve. She knew now, for certain, that neither she nor Rian had understood the reality of war.

Fanny looked behind her, toward the open doorway, and then turned once more to the maps, knowing what she was planning would upset everyone, if they knew. Brede, most especially.

She'd made so many worthy resolutions last night and early this morning. She'd be good, for Brede. She'd be his supporting prop as he recovered from the horror and trauma of war, mourned the friends he'd lost. All of those fine, generous, unselfish things. She owed him that, and much more. She longed to give him so much more. Give him *all* of herself.

Except…

Except that Rian was out there, somewhere. He had to be. If he truly had died, she'd know it. She'd feel it. Wouldn't she?

Still arguing with herself, her burden of guilt still pressing down hard on her slim shoulders, Fanny bent over the tabletop.

Ainsley had depicted Wellington and the Allied troops in red, Bonaparte's forces in blue, their positions marked on each of the maps, day by day. The names of all the small towns were also there, and Fanny had little trouble locating both the Duke's position on the day of the last battle, as well as that of the Prince of Orange. She slowly traced a line to the South with her index finger.

They wouldn't have been able to travel very far, not with Rian so badly wounded. Not if they wanted to keep him alive. So where would they go? Where would they be safe as the Alliance fanned wide, moved South, relentlessly pushed the remains of Bonaparte's army back onto French soil?

A village? A town? A city? Perhaps a private estate?

Or would they take him to the coast, put him on a ship? Going where? France? England? North, farther into Belgium?

Fanny pressed her palms on the table, looking from map to map, chart to chart.

Where would she take him?

Home. I'd bring him home….

She shut her eyes tight, shook off her melancholy, because that wouldn't help Rian.

She'd set herself an impossible task. The world was so large. Becket Hall had been her home, but it was only an infinitesimal spot on a much larger map, not even large enough to be depicted on any map at all. How on earth could she find Rian? Where would she begin?

"You need to consider him *not* wounded. Consider a plan, already formed before the abduction, an escape route already in place. A destination, a rendezvous point previously chosen."

Fanny turned about so abruptly, her trailing hand swept several of the maps to the floor. "Brede! You know what I'm— That is, um…you *know?*"

"Your penchant for stating—stammering—the obvious bids to lessen my high opinion of your intelligence, my dear. As does realizing that you might actually seriously consider the madness I know you're considering."

"Oh, stubble it," Fanny said, bending to pick up the maps, pretending not to notice that her hands were shaking. "I'm not in the least impressed with your supercilious remarks."

"Supercilious, am I?" Valentine asked, going down on one knee to help her collect the maps. "Arrogant, condescending, disdainful? I'm all of that? You cut me to the quick, madam."

Fanny glared at him as she got to her feet, dumped the maps onto the tabletop. She was frankly amazed to see him looking so well after the night he'd had. He was perhaps slightly *worn* about the edges, but that was only to be expected, she supposed. Mostly, he was still the most ridiculously attractive man she'd ever seen…in his own strange way, of course. Not handsome—almost pretty, the way Rian was—but so uniquely himself. She'd never tire of looking at him.

Then he smiled at her in that lazy, heavy-lidded way he had, and she longed to box his ears for him!

"Yes, Brede, you are all of that, and more. You're also patronizing, pompous, odiously high in the instep, and…and *maddening*. But you no longer frighten me, not even a little bit."

"Now, there's a pity," Valentine said, pulling one of the maps closer to him, to look at Ainsley's notations. "Lucie would be shaking in her expensive slippers, if I were to speak to her that way."

"That's only because your sweet, shallow sister sees no more than you want her to see," Fanny told him. "I know better. And then I feed you. Admit it, Brede. You didn't have your luncheon with Papa and the others, did you? So now you're *chewing* on me."

"Now who is being patronizing? Although

you're correct. Courtland and I were otherwise oc- cupied until just now, and didn't have any luncheon. Or breakfast, for that matter. Are you happy now, to be proved right?"

She looked up at him curiously. He was being more than usually smug. "I believe I'd be consid- erably happier if you told me what kept you and Court *otherwise occupied.*"

"All in good time, sweetings." He longed to take Fanny into his arms, kiss her senseless. Except that doing so might be the one thing he could do to frighten her. So he merely put a fingertip to the map and said, "Here. All things considered, I'd take him here. Valenciennes."

Fanny leaned over the map, her head close to Valentine's. "Why?"

"It's just across the border, for one thing, and I, for one, would much prefer to be clear of Belgium and the proximity of the Allies, hoping for Bonaparte to be victorious, but prepared for either victory or defeat. It's a fairly fine city, and I doubt your Beales stays anywhere the inns tend to present travelers with damp sheets. After all, he could have had to cool his heels there for a week, a month—he would want to be com- fortable as he waited for the battle everyone knew was coming, waited for news on Rian's capture."

"Because *you* would have wanted to be com- fortable."

"That annoys you?" Valentine asked, smiling at her. "And, importantly, Valenciennes is approximately one hundred miles almost directly north of Paris. Close enough, if Bonaparte were to be successful, far enough away if he should fail. With the coast even less than one hundred miles to the West, he'd be within three days' striking distance of where the wind blew fairest. I imagine, listening to Ainsley's description of the man, that Beales is the sort who would feel the need to prepare for all eventualities. Valenciennes is central. Civilized, the Athens of the North, some say, although I'm not among them."

"But, as you said when you first barged in on me, he would suppose that Rian wouldn't be wounded," Fanny said, turning her head, putting herself almost nose-to-nose with Valentine. He was being nice. Why was he being so nice? Well, nice for *him,* at any rate. But why was he being so helpful? Why wasn't he berating her for being a silly, foolish dreamer?

"True. He would have moved Rian somewhere more private to him as soon as possible, some place where he could put questions to him at his leisure."

The moment the words were out of his mouth, he regretted them.

"Torture him, you mean." She felt suddenly dizzy, as if she might faint. "We have to find him."

"Fanny, Rian's undoubtedly dead. God knows I

don't want to believe that, as I'm the one who left him to his fate, even as I don't want to believe Beales has him. But, of the two…Rian would be better off dead."

"I'm going after him," Fanny said as she searched on the tabletop for the best maps of Austria and France. "He'd come after me."

Valentine took hold of her shoulders, ready now to tell her what he'd done, what he and Courtland had done. "No, Fanny, you're not going after him. It's probably futile. It's definitely dangerous. And I won't allow it."

"You won't *allow* it? And who are you to— Don't look at me that way! I know who you are. But Sergeant-Major Hart agrees with me. We can't be left with questions. We have to find him. We have to at least *try*."

"And we've agreed as much ourselves. Ainsley, myself, the others," Valentine said, taking the maps from her hands and placing them back on the tabletop yet again. It was like a tug-of-war, one he was determined to win. "Come to the window, Fanny."

She considered making one last stab for the maps, but then gave it up as a futile effort and allowed him to take her hand, lead her to the window. "What am I supposed to see?"

"It's what you're not going to see, Fanny."

She looked at him, frowned and then turned back

to the window. Her gaze passed over the terrace and beyond, to the empty shoreline, and then once again beyond. "Where's the *Spectre?* Chance's sloop—it's gone."

"And with it your brother Courtland, Sergeant-Major Hart, Clovis Meechum, Billy and a small crew, yes. Thanks to Ainsley's prudent preparedness, any of the three ships is ready to sail at a moment's notice. We only needed to bring fresh food and water on board."

Fanny closed her eyes and let her body sag back against Valentine's. "You did this? You did this for me? I thought…I thought I was the only one. But Court's looking for him now. And he'll find him. I know he will."

Valentine slid his arms around her waist, choosing not to tell her that what Courtland would be looking for was evidence of a body, which would be damned difficult to find, or information that might lead them to Beales or his men. Also difficult to do.

But, as Ainsley had said, what Fanny needed now, what they all needed now, was to feel that they were doing something. Anything.

Rian's death had lent a new urgency to the Beckets, increased their need to find Beales before he found them. There wasn't much of a chance of that, but at least, with Rian, they had some sort of starting point. And it would pass the time as they waited for Beales to find them.

"And now, sweetings, you're free to travel with me to Brede Manor, aren't you?"

Fanny felt an instant panic. She wanted to run, even as she was careful to remain where she was, softly cradled in Valentine's arms. He'd done so much for her. But was she really ready to begin moving forward? When all she could think about was the past? "Brede Manor? I...I hadn't thought... Well, of course. Where else would we go?"

He dropped a kiss on the top of her head and turned her to face him, his hands on her upper arms. "We have a life to begin, Fanny. It's time we began to look for our future. Earlier, Callie volunteered to help the maids pack up your things, and Ainsley has kindly offered me the loan of his traveling coach. We can leave as soon as we've said your farewells. In fact, everyone is waiting in the drawing room."

"Oh, they are, are they? What a busy morning you've had, Brede." Fanny swallowed down hard, hating that she felt so nervous, and so *managed*. "You've, um, already decided that I'd agree? And everyone else has agreed with you?"

"Not to be immodest, but I do believe your family have rather taken to me to their collective bosom." Valentine smiled at her look of exasperation. "But my congenial and appealing self to one side,

Brede Manor is where you asked me to take you when we left Brussels, remember? Courtland's doing all that can be done. A month, Fanny, and we'll be back. A month, possibly two," he promised her, and then watched as she narrowed her eyelids.

Had he overplayed his hand in his haste to get her away from Becket Hall and her memories, get her to himself? It was, he realized, one thing for her to suggest Brede Manor to him, and quite another to have her *portmanteaux* packed and the coach already ordered to the door.

Valentine carefully schooled his features into what he hoped was a look of pleasant neutrality. It seemed safer to do that. Not that he was a coward, but Fanny appeared none too pleased with him at the moment. Oddly, he was still feeling quite pleased with her.

Fanny looked to him for a long moment, opened her mouth to protest, and then finally turned up her hands in a gesture of surrender as she stepped out from beneath his lightly gripping hands. "Very well, Brede, if it's settled, then it's settled. I suppose I know when I'm beaten."

"You *never* know when you're beaten, sweetings. Perverse as it might make me seem to admit this, I find that to be a considerable part of your charm," he said to her departing back, and then followed her down the hallway to the main drawing room, where her family was gathered.

He was, all in all, feeling as if the two of them were making progress together. At last, at last, he'd have her to himself for more than a few hours. They were still near-strangers, for all that had happened between them, and the time had come to remedy that situation.

Jack stepped forward to shake his hand as Fanny went around the enormous room Valentine had earlier admired, knowing it largely had been furnished with the prizes Ainsley had gathered while operating as a privateer.

He looked on as Fanny said her farewells to everyone in turn, kissing Callie on both cheeks, lingering in front of Mariah as that woman spoke quietly to her, and then being detained again when Eleanor made her sit beside her for a few minutes, Fanny's expression becoming increasingly mulish.

"What do you suppose your wife is saying to Fanny that's put that scowl on her face?" Valentine asked Jack.

"I believe she's reminding her that she is now in charge of your exalted household, God help you. Fanny knows as much about running a household as I do, I'm afraid. Ah, look. Eleanor's handing Fanny some books. Probably having to do with proper deportment in society, as well as how often to order the sheets changed and the silver polished."

"Yes, and Fanny's taking the books with all the

cheer of a person being handed a basket filled to overflowing with spiders. She really knows nothing of the domestic arts?"

"Fanny? She knows how to ride. To shoot. She's actually fairly competent with fencing foils. Ainsley seems to believe that a person should be allowed to excel at the things that most interest them. With Fanny, that meant she was interested in anything that interested Rian. I know Fanny's very much a female, Valentine, but she was fairly well-equipped to follow Rian to Brussels. I doubt, however, she could find her way to the linen cupboards here at Becket Hall. I hope you have a competent house-keeper in place at Brede Manor."

Brede attempted to think of his bride frowning over the decisions of daily menus, even of her sitting quietly in a sunny parlor, working a needlepoint pattern into some slippers she'd then force on him as a Christmas present. Both were difficult pictures to hold in his mind, and he dismissed them with relief. "I didn't marry Fanny so that she could run herd on my servants."

"No, of course you didn't. You married her for the same reason I married Eleanor. Humbling, isn't it, to suddenly realize that you've lived per-haps half your life without realizing how empty that life was, until a smile, a certain tilt of the head, a particular voice, turns that empty world like a…well, like a bucket suddenly righted, so that it can begin to fill."

"You've always had such a way with words, Jack, old friend," Valentine said as he watched Fanny hug Ainsley, hold on tight. "First we're men— and then we're empty buckets?"

Jack grinned, embarrassed. "Perhaps I should attempt to put that some other way…."

"Please, old friend, I beg you, we'll leave it at empty buckets. So yours is full now?"

"Overflowing. Eleanor agreed I could tell you, although we won't say anything to anyone else for some time, as this has happened once before, and quickly came to nothing. It would seem I'm to become a father late this year."

"Well, now, my congratulations to you, Jack," Valentine said, truly pleased for his friend, although, putting himself in Jack's shoes for a moment, no more than the mere the idea of starting his own nursery terrified him. Children of the house of Brede had not enjoyed happy childhoods, at least not in his generation. Would he do better with his own children? He couldn't imagine Fanny counting linens, but he could imagine her holding their child….

"Yes, thank you. But remember, Eleanor doesn't want anyone to know."

"A difficult secret to keep, I'd imagine," Valentine said, smiling.

"Here? It's difficult to keep any secret at Becket Hall. I could sneeze in the bowels of the cellars, and at least three people would somehow be close enough to say 'bless you.' Not that I'd be anywhere else. How long will you be gone?"

"You assume I'm coming back?"

Jack nodded. "I know you'll be back. You're as hot to bring Beales down as the rest of us. That's obvious. Because of Fanny. Definitely because of Rian. It wasn't your failure, you know. I put Rian in the best hands I could think of, but no one could have foreseen what happened. What happened was Beales. I saw him, you know, in London."

"No, I didn't know that," Valentine said, watching Fanny try to return the books to Eleanor, who laughed and pushed them back at her. "Tell me."

Jack explained that he'd only seen a glimpse of the man as he entered a coach, and described him as tall, thin, dark. The identification was confirmed by Chance, who'd located one of the man's servants, who had told him that the man chewed leaves. "Coca leaves, Valentine. A habit picked up in the islands, Ainsley tells me. At any rate, he was using the name Nathaniel Beatty."

Valentine turned his head sharply to look at his friend, and then motioned for Jack to follow him into the hallway.

"What's the matter, Valentine? You've heard the name?"

"I *dined* with the man," Valentine said, rubbing at the back of his neck, trying to recall the time, the place. "When I was in attendance at the Congress of Vienna earlier this year? Yes, that's got to be it. I remember now. He was introduced to the rest of us at the table as—let me think a moment—as a financier, by Charles Talleyrand. Pardon me, by the just newly created *Prince* de Talleyrand, much to his delight."

Jack was impressed. "Talleyrand? The man Bonaparte said would sell his own father for profit? We should have realized Beales would cultivate a man like that, one who knows how to play both sides of the fence, and take profit from each side. Ainsley's said more than once that Beales always goes with the winners. This is important, Valentine. We have to tell him immediately."

"You tell him," Valentine said as Fanny walked out into the hallway, clearly having lost the battle of the books. "I'm taking my wife home." He then turned to Fanny, smiling as he held out his hand to her. "Don't you look scholarly, sweetings. Are you ready to leave? As it is, we'll be stopping at an inn for at least the one night, if we don't want to push the horses."

Fanny pulled a face. "It was as if they couldn't wait to see me go," she told him, taking the bonnet one of the maids had left on the foyer table for her, but leaving the shawl. Or she would have, if Valentine hadn't picked it up and settled it over her shoulders. "I wanted to ride Molly, you know."

"Tomorrow, sweetings. For now, let's just be on our way."

Fanny kissed Jack goodbye, turned in a full circle, giving Becket Hall one last look, as if she was leaving it forever, and then stepped out onto the stone porch and looked down the steps. "Odette! I was wondering where you were. I would have come looking for you, to say goodbye, except that this *bear* behind me keeps pushing me out the door."

The older woman waited for Fanny to join her, hug her. She gently pushed Fanny away from her then and traced a small cross on her forehead with the pad of her thumb. "Behave."

Fanny's jaw dropped. "Odette! That's all you can say to me?"

Odette's wide smile showed nearly all of her large, white teeth. "Even that, child, is a mountain you won't find easy to climb."

"Odette, it has been an unique pleasure," Valentine said after speaking to the coachman and joining Fanny. "Ready, sweetings?"

Before she could answer, Valentine had opened the door to the coach and lifted her up into it, not bothering to first lower the steps, and followed her inside, sitting himself beside her on the front-facing seat.

The coach moved off as Valentine slipped his arm behind Fanny's shoulders, and before she could even think what he was doing, he was kissing her, long and hard.

All her protests, all her planned list of complaints, melted from her mind as she lifted her arm up and around his neck, pulling him even closer to her. She sighed into his mouth as he cupped her breast in his palm, dragged his thumb lightly across her nipple through the thin material of her gown.

He took her mouth, again and again, teasing her with his tongue, smiling against her lips as she dueled back at him.

And then he put her from him and turned front on the velvet squabs, his fingers interlaced in his lap.

"What…what do you think you're doing? Did? Brede?"

"What was *necessary,* sweetings," he told her, snaking out his long legs so that his heels rested on the facing seat as he slid lower on his spine, making himself as comfortable as a man can be when he really would like to have his wife sitting on him, rocking back and forth with the motion of the well-sprung coach.

But, no, he couldn't think of that. It was bad enough what he'd done, without thinking of what he wished to do. What he had to do now was control his breathing, his heart rate, his urge to pull Fanny across his waist and undo all the cunning front buttons of her gown.

"Necessary? That again? *Why* was it necessary?"

He turned his head to smile at her. Wickedly. "You'll understand soon enough, sweetings, I hope. Let me just say that some things improve, become more enjoyable, with practice. I spoke to the coachman, and we'll be making our first stop our final stop for the night."

Fanny looked away from him, pretending a concentration on the flat, unchanging view outside the off-window, until she thought she understood what he meant.

Then she turned back to him…and punched him in the stomach.

"Sorry, Brede. It was just…*necessary.*"

She sat back against the squabs, her arms folded, and with a smile on her face that didn't fade for at least another mile, remembered what Mariah had whispered to her: "Remember, Fanny—he's just as nervous about your new, shared situation as you are, just as vulnerable to hurt. Men only hide their feelings better, your husband probably better than most. It's up to you to make him trust you enough to be honest with you…and with himself."

Punching her husband in the stomach probably wasn't what Mariah had in mind.

But did she want him to be honest with her? Yes, she did. Did she want him to have feelings for her? Yes, she did. Did she have…feelings for him?

Yes, she did.

Fanny blinked back unexpected tears. She'd been looking through the window too long, without blinking in the unusually bright sun of a late June Romney Marsh afternoon. That had to be the reason.

"Brede?" she said, still looking at the scenery that never changed, except for number of sheep in any given field.

"No, don't apologize, Fanny," he said, just happy that she was speaking to him again. Jack, anyone of his acquaintance, would double over in laughter if they knew how clumsy and disconcerted this one young woman, his wife, could make him. "I gave in to impulse. You live in a very crowded house, you know, even if it's quite large. This is the first I've been really alone with you since our arrival. I'm sorry."

"You were alone with me last night," she told him, stepping carefully into territory she hadn't planned to visit again once she had awakened that morning to realize he was gone.

"I'm afraid I don't remember much of last night, sweetings. The last thing I can recall, to my ever-lasting shame, is lying on the floor, giggling like the village idiot. I don't even know how or when I managed to crawl onto the bed. I hesitate to ask—was I entirely obnoxious?"

Fanny looked down at her fingers as they twined together, white-knuckled, in her lap. "You don't remember? You *really* don't remember?"

Valentine's heart skipped a beat, then lurched on. "What did I do? Did I…did I attempt to force myself on you?"

She shook her head rather violently. "No, of course not. You're a gentleman."

Valentine couldn't help himself. He laughed out loud. "Hardly, sweetings. I may bear the trappings, but only do so with considerable difficulty. But I did behave myself?"

"You…you *said* some things," Fanny began, and then shook her head again. "You were drunk, Brede."

He watched as she removed her bonnet, shook out her hair that was still unfashionably short, although he admired the way it curled against her cheeks. "What did I say?"

She reached over and took his hand in both of hers, hoping the gesture would soften her words. "You were talking about all the friends you've lost to war, and how happy you are that it's all finally over now. I…I may have lost Rian, and that hurts so terribly, Brede. You lost so many more, so much more."

Brede squeezed her hands. "Edward Pakenham

in New Orleans. I'll always miss him. The stupid loss of a good man in a bad battle. I've had three batmen serving me and all three were killed, so I stopped having them." He looked at her, smiled. "Which explains my always impeccable attire in the field, doesn't it? Ah, Fanny, so many gone yet again. Brunswick at Quatre Bras. Delancy, late in the day at Waterloo, and before we left Brussels I heard that Alexander Gordon had died of his wound. So many more. Too many more. I'm sorry if I was maudlin, as those who dive into bottles often are, I suppose."

She didn't tell him what else he'd said, how he'd hinted, more than hinted, that they should comfort each other, help each other be rid of the nightmares. But she knew she would always hold that thought close to her heart.

"I didn't mind, Brede," she said quietly, easing herself against him, resting her head on his shoulder as the coach continued on to their destination. "I didn't mind…."

CHAPTER TWENTY-THREE

FANNY WOKE AS THE COACH rocked to a stop, her eyes opening all at once when she realized she must have fallen asleep on Valentine's shoulder within moments of resting her head against him.

He sensed the returning tenseness in her body and helped her right herself, for she was no longer propped against his shoulder, but lying with her head in his lap. He'd been stroking her hair, her soft cheek, for more than an hour, thinking random thoughts...those thoughts always returning to Fanny. His bride. His wife.

"I'm sorry, Brede," Fanny apologized as she adjusted her shawl, avoided looking at him. "Why didn't you wake me? Just push me off of you?"

"Onto the floor?" he asked her, and then watched, delighted, as a soft flush of color entered her cheeks. "I will say, Fanny, that when it comes to comfort, you're vastly superior to a warm brick at my feet."

"If that's the case, and since I slept so well, I suppose I should say that you're also very com—"

She clamped her lips shut, knowing there was no way she could end that particular sentence without stumbling over her own tongue, and turned to look out the window. She had to wake up, gather her wits about her, before she said anything else. "Where, um, where are we?"

"I assure you, sweetings, I have absolutely no idea. I will say that either this coach is exceedingly well-sprung, or the roadways in Romney Marsh are well above the quality of those I'm more accustomed to enduring."

Fanny was busy gathering up her bonnet and retying the strings, all while trying not to think about the coming evening, when she'd be alone with Valentine inside the small inn she could see through the window. "With good reason," she said absently. "When we wish to move our loads inland, we can't be worried about bogging down somewhere, so that we're found by the Dragoons when the sun comes up, our wheels stuck in the mud. Oh!"

Valentine bit back a smile. "I already know everything, remember? Shall we?"

"I suppose so. I think I'm done blurting out damning information, at least for the moment. How long have I been asleep?"

"Two hours, I'd say. Why?"

"Nothing. I was just wondering about the

Spectre. They'll be making landfall at Ostend in a few more hours if the wind is fair, won't they?"

"Are you upset that you and I didn't go with them?"

She bit her lips together, shook her head. "No. I won't do that again—cause anyone complications by being the lone female everyone seems to think themselves honor bound to protect, when they should be thinking of themselves. And they'll find Rian and bring him home. I know they will."

"Fanny, you can't—"

"Please, Brede, don't say anything else. I'm not going to give up on Rian. I can't. If I'm being fanciful, at least allow me to deceive myself for as long as possible. It's all I can do."

"You can keep him in your heart, Fanny. He loved you very much," Valentine said, seeing the tears as they gathered in the corners of her eyes.

"Thank you, Brede, for understanding. And now," she said, forcing a smile to her face, "let's feed you, shall we? As I recall, you haven't eaten a single thing all day. I'm surprised you haven't begun gnawing on the leather hand strap you're still holding on to," she said, waiting for him to open the door and let down the steps, and then taking his hand as he helped her to the ground.

She stood in the innyard as Valentine directed Jacob Whiting and the ostler who'd run out from the stables to have their baggage off-loaded before seeing to the horses, and then escorted Fanny into the small, dark hallway of *The Golden Fleece*, a misnomer if ever he'd encountered one.

But the landlord seemed duly impressed with their appearance, and when Jacob popped his head in the door to ask "milord" if there was anything else he needed, the landlord visibly straightened another inch and began bellowing for his wife to come take "her ladyship" to the private dining room while the best bedchamber was made up with fresh sheets.

Clearly, the "quality" didn't make it a point to stop at *The Golden Fleece* with any regularity.

Fanny looked to Valentine, slightly bemused, and then realized that *she* was "her ladyship." In point of fact, she was now the Countess of Brede. Goodness! She struggled to keep her expression blank— knowing *haughty* was too far above her limited reach—but when Valentine caught her eye, and winked at her, sharing in the joke, she had to hide her giggle with a cough.

"Would her ladyship be so pleased as to follow me?" the landlord's plump, rosy-cheeked wife inquired nervously, dropping into a curtsey and then gesturing toward the rear of the hallway.

Fanny tipped her head slightly from side-to-side and grinned at Valentine. "Why, yes, I imagine her ladyship would like that very much, thank you," she said, and brushed past her husband...who gave her a surreptitious pat on the backside to send her on her way.

By the time he'd joined her, Fanny had time to whisper in the landlady's ear, be led to the rude but clean facilities, and return to the private dining room to find the table piled with bread, ham and cheese.

She pointed to the food as she chewed on a marvelous bite of sweet country ham, and watched as he sat down across the table from her. Neither of them said anything else until the landlord himself had served Valentine a mug of home-brewed beer and placed a pitcher of lemonade so fresh its tart aroma filled the air on the table for Fanny.

The man then quit the room, bowing himself out, his broad rump making contact with the doorjamb so that he had to step to his left before bowing one last time and closing the door.

Fanny swallowed the ham, choked on a giggle and motioned for Valentine to quickly pour some lemonade for her. She drank thirstily before using her serviette to wipe at her streaming eyes, and then finally sat back in her chair, neatly folding her hands on the edge of the tabletop. "Does this always happen?"

"Does what always happen, Fanny?" Valentine asked her, pretending not to understand the question.

She spread her hands. "You know—*that*. The… the bowing…the scraping. It's rather embarrassing, don't you think? Not for me, actually, as I'm rather enjoying it, but for people like our good innkeeper. I imagine he's still bowing, out there somewhere."

"Hmm, yes. Bowing, scraping, gleefully weighting our bill to suit what he believes is the size of my pocketbook. But you're a countess now, sweetings. Laden with consequence. Positively *dripping* with it, actually, if I count the lemonade on your chin. Expected to behave as befits your station. Why, you'll be presented to the Prince Regent when we travel to London for the season. Although that might be considered a dubious honor."

After quickly dabbing at her chin with the serviette, Fanny picked up another slice of ham, took a bite out of it and then chewed on it thoughtfully, her elbow propped on the table.

"And you'll be expected to use your fork," Valentine added before taking a sip of his wine.

"I know how to use a fork," Fanny told him, dropping the ham onto her plate and then sucking on her fingertips. "Elly gave us all lessons in deportment, etiquette at table, all of those dreary things. Repeatedly."

"And books. She also gave you books." The girl had all the makings of a minx, when she applied herself, and Valentine was fairly certain she was applying herself at the moment, deliberately shaking herself out of her doldrums. Really, he hadn't enjoyed himself so much in years. "With all of that taken together, I can only suppose that you're being deliberately *un*mannerly at the moment. Is there any special reason, or are you just being perverse?"

She lifted the fork, stabbed a piece of ham. "My family would be happy to tell you it's the latter. Oh, all right, yes. Yes, there's a special reason. I'm attempting to show you what a grave mistake you made, marrying me. I don't know why I'm doing that, but I am. I'll stop now. See? I'm even using the fork again."

"Oh, don't, not on my account. Or have you never read Fielding's *Tom Jones,* and his recounting of Tom's dinner with the delectable Mrs. Waters? Ah, you're frowning, and I'm a lout to be speaking of such things with my lady wife."

"Even if said lady wife doesn't have the faintest idea what you're saying?" Fanny asked, remembering Odette's parting warning and deciding that she really should continue using her fork, as she'd made her point. "I'm really woefully stupid, you know. Nothing more than a simple country girl, a bumpkin. I'll bore you to flinders within a week."

"Or I could take on the role of mentor. We could sit together in the evenings, and I can read to you. I think you might like *Tom Jones.* I know I'd be interested in your reactions to the book."

"I said I was stupid, Brede. I didn't say I don't know how to *read.*" Then she sighed, dramatically.

"But I don't paint, I don't play the harp and I don't sing. Oh, and I don't sew. I'd go mad, if anyone asked me to do any of those things."

Now it was Valentine who propped his elbow on the tabletop as he smiled at her. "Are you applying for the position of my wife, or attempting to talk me out of keeping you as my wife? All while remembering, sweetings, that we're already very much married."

"I know that, you poor thing. I'm simply warning you, Brede. It was one thing, in Brussels, or even at Becket Hall. But now you're all but *dragging* me into your world, and you should be aware that I won't fit. Lucie said I'm as suited for polite society as she is for penury, whatever she meant by that."

"She meant, sweetings, that she doesn't know how to be poor. And she doesn't. What prompted her to say this to you, I wonder."

Fanny broke off a bit of the fresh, crusty loaf and began breaking it apart with her fingers, popping small bits into her mouth. "When she refused to leave Wellington's headquarters after you were so cutting to me, I threatened to stand up in the carriage and recite every vile word I know."

Valentine coughed, dislodging a bit of ham from his throat, as he'd been swallowing as Fanny spoke. "And did you?"

"No," she said, crumbling more of the bread.

"But I did, at her request, recite those words to her later."

"My stars," Valentine said, chuckling.

"Yes, definitely," Fanny agreed, grinning, "that's exactly what Lucie said, several times. Then she tossed at least three of those words back at me when I told her what I'd said to Miss Pitney, who continued to dance at Lady Richmond's ball, even as the bugles were sounding."

Valentine rubbed his hand over his mouth, trying to subdue his grin. "And you said to Miss Pitney…"

"I told her she was a silly, heartless twit, I believe." She blinked at him, feigning country bumpkin innocence. "Are you aware that Miss Pitney is rather closely related to the Duke of somewhere-or-other?"

"Yes, I believe I do know that. A fine family, by and large, and able to trace themselves back to the Flood, although the current generation leaves much to be desired, obviously. Anything else? Did you show too much ankle? Walk outside unaccompanied? Dump porridge on anyone's head in a fit of pique?"

"No, none of that, I'm afraid. I was only with your sister for a few days before…before the battle. I didn't have time to be more of a trial to her. But, Brede, if that's what I can accomplish in only a few days, think of the havoc I could create in London."

"Yes, I'm doing that now. It could end with irreparable damage done to the family escutcheon, couldn't it?"

Fanny tilted her head to one side as she looked across the table at him. His eyes were positively dancing in his head. "Why, shame on you! You're thinking of your father's warning to you as you left for war all those years ago, aren't you? And *delighting* in the thought."

"I know. I'm horribly ashamed. Why, the old tyrant is probably already spinning like a top in the Brede mausoleum, just in anticipation of the disgrace. Would you like more lemonade, sweetings?"

Fanny's mouth dropped open in mock shock, while, inwardly, she was delighting in the teasing. "You married me in hopes I'd make a cake of myself in London?"

Valentine put down the pitcher, careful to keep it out of Fanny's reach. "No, sweetings, I did not marry you for that reason. But, speaking with you now, I am beginning to see the potential for entertainment in what is usually a pitifully boring Season. I never boasted of being a nice man, remember?"

"So you'd let me disgrace myself? You're really despicable, aren't you? For shame."

No missish young debutante, not his Fanny. "Yes, but I'm bound to be thwarted in my plan, as you'd never disgrace yourself, or me, for that matter. London will take one look at you and be as entranced as I am."

"You're…entranced?" Fanny's heart skipped at least two beats.

He got to his feet and walked around the table to her, held out his hand to her. "Utterly."

Suddenly Fanny, who had been finding it so easy to talk to Valentine, banter back and forth with him, couldn't think of a single thing to say to the man. She looked at his extended hand for a moment, and then slipped her hand into his, allowed him to gently raise her to her feet.

They were still standing like that, looking deeply into each other's eyes, when the landlord knocked on the door and, not waiting to be begged to enter, barged into the room, wringing his hands at his ample waist. "There's…a thousand pardons, my lord. But there's a…a *personage* to see you. Well, two of them, actually. And neither seems willing to take no for—"

"*There* you are! I was so worried we wouldn't be able to catch you, which would be ridiculous, as Jacob held the reins, and Lord knows he's a sweet man, but he couldn't push more than five miles an hour out of horses twice as fine as Papa's, and Papa's are very fine. We'd only just arrived when we learned that you were gone, so we *tossed* the babies at Elly and set out to hunt you down. And here you are!"

Fanny's eyes were open wide as she goggled at

the vision in burgundy silk that had just pushed past the innkeeper. *"Morgan?"*

"Obviously, and Ethan's with me, as well," Fanny's sister said, coming to a halt after sweeping into the room, to hold her arms out to her. "And you're married. I can't believe it."

Valentine watched, a bemused smile on his face, as Fanny ran to her sister, who was as night to her day, her hair as black as midnight, her features bright, vibrant, rather exotic. They were both tall and slim, but Morgan had a rich lushness about her curves that did much more than simply whisper at her femininity. She was, in short, about as subtle in her beauty as a stiff wind knocking your hat off and whirling it down the street.

"Brede," the Earl of Aylesford said quietly as he entered the room behind his wife, still beating road dust off his sleeve with his riding gloves. He was dressed impeccably, as was his reputation, his dark blond hair combed severely off his face and caught in a black riband at his nape. The same silly Aylesford Valentine remembered, except that, thanks to explanations from Ainsley and the others, he now knew better. The man was as much a Becket now as if he'd born to the brood.

"Aylesford," Valentine returned, bowing to the man. "An unexpected pleasure."

"Oh, I doubt that," Ethan Tanner said, grinning

at him. "What man wants to be chased down in the first blush of his honeymoon? I did have time to hear of your hasty escape from Becket Hall, before my wife dragged me after you." He held out his hand to Valentine. "My felicitations, friend, and a bit of tongue-in-cheek sympathy. Fanny will keep you on your toes."

"Oh, stop teasing him, Ethan," Morgan warned her husband, laughing as she pulled out of Fanny's rather watery embrace. She walked over to Valentine and held out her hands to him. "Welcome to the family, Valentine. I only, as do we all, regret the circumstances."

Morgan's words sent a pall over the small room for a few moments, until Fanny said, "But it's all right, Morgie. Courtland's gone to find Rian, and bring him home."

Morgan shot Valentine a quick, questioning look, then slipped an arm around Fanny's shoulders and directed her out into the hallway, saying, "I'm sure there's a nice path outside somewhere. Let's take a walk, sweetheart, shall we?"

Valentine watched them go before shouting for the innkeeper, ordering a second tankard and pitcher of beer. "Sit, Ethan. She…she's dealing with Rian's death in her own way. By degrees, I guess you'd say."

Ethan sat himself in the chair Fanny had lately vacated, placing his gloves on the tabletop. "Yes.

Spencer quickly told me what's going on, as I waited for Morgan to change into her riding habit. Damn, I can't believe the boy's gone. How's Ainsley taking it? It's difficult to tell with him, as he's very much his own man."

Valentine shrugged, silently allowing the landlord to scurry in, then scurry out again, clearly overwhelmed by the presence of not two but four members of the quality deigning to visit his humble establishment. "I don't know the man well enough to say, having first met him a few days ago. But he agreed to send Courtland to follow the trail I described to them. Hope dies hard, Ethan. We all know that. More especially, I'd imagine, when it's your child."

Ethan nodded his agreement. "I can't even imagine his pain. I look at my own children and—no, I can't even imagine it. So, let's put that aside, shall we? You know about Edmund Beales? I'll assume you do, since he seems to have sent someone after Rian."

Valentine took a deep drink of the cold beer as he collected his thoughts. "I don't understand the depth of the man's hatred—Beales, that is. And Court said something to me. Beales, if he finds them, if he comes after them, will want Ainsley alive. Do you know why?"

"No, and don't think I haven't asked. What happened was terrible, but it was, what, seventeen or so years ago? Beales was certainly the victor in that encounter, the bastard. What else would he want from Ainsley? He killed the man's wife, he killed the man's people, *destroyed* them. I've learned that he carried away Ainsley's share of whatever plunder they still had there on the island. What else could he want? Want badly enough to interrupt his own life now, all these years later?"

"I saw him, you know, earlier this year, in Vienna. The man had a diamond on his hand the size of a goose egg. And he was rigged out like a prince. He had a small black page, as I recall it, forced to stand behind him for the full three hours we sat at table. That's probably why I remember him—for the callous way he treated that boy. I didn't care for him, but others at the table were fawning all over him. He's rich, he's been careful to keep himself aligned with the winning side. What does he need with an old grievance?"

"He still can't know for certain that Ainsley's still alive, remember," Ethan pointed out, slicing himself a piece of bread from the loaf and wrapping it around a slice of ham. "All he knows now, at least as far as we've considered the thing, is that his lucrative smuggling operation, funneling English gold to him, was destroyed by someone named Becket. Unless Spencer's wrong, and someone was left alive last August when he had that small dustup in London with Beales's men. There is that. In any case, Beales is a careful man, and we're a complication, a loose end at this point, one he must like to see snipped."

"So that he can come back here, to England, without worrying that someone might expose him?" Valentine leaned his elbows on the tabletop, as all the pieces suddenly fell into place for him. "That's it, Ethan. That's got to be it. Beales is planning a return to London."

"A *triumphant* return, yes." Ethan lifted his tankard in salute. "I always thought I'd like you. And now that we're settled that between us, let me drink to you and your lovely bride, and then drag Morgan out of here and back to Becket Hall. After all, you've only just escaped us, haven't you?"

CHAPTER TWENTY-FOUR

FANNY SAT ALONE on the low stone wall in the stand of trees about one hundred yards away from the stable behind the *The Golden Fleece,* thinking about all that Morgan had said to her before kissing her goodbye and going off to rouse her husband from his coze with Valentine. They needed to start back to Becket Hall while the sky was still light, if they didn't want to push their mounts too hard, and that's one thing neither Morgan nor Ethan would ever do.

Her married sisters and Mariah all had given her advice now. Mariah had advised her to be careful of Valentine's feelings. Eleanor had urged her to remember that she was now in charge of her husband's comforts.

But it was left to Morgan to tell her that a gentleman might desire a lady in his drawing room, but he much preferred that lady to leave all of her fine manners and gently reared inhibitions at the bedchamber door.

"I saw the way he was looking at you when I

came crashing into the room," Morgan had said to her, squeezing her fingers in her own. "He looked as if he could eat you up. I've seen Brede a time or two, you know, in London, and I never thought I'd live to see such a warm, caring look on his homely face."

"How can you say such a thing? He doesn't have a homely face," Fanny had protested in real shock. "He's…he's quite handsome. He's just…well, he's just Brede. When he's tired, when he's…when he's mussed, when he isn't being so concerned with his consequence, why, he's just like a little boy, Morgie. His hair falls in his face, and he looks at a person from beneath those droopy eyelids he employs to such great advantage when he thinks he's being intimidating. And…and when he smiles—when he laughs? How can you call him homely? Shame on you. He's…why, he's *beautiful*."

Morgan had laughed at that, and then shaken her head. "I suppose that's it—I've never seen the man smile. But that's what you see, Fanny? You see Brede as beautiful? Then, of course, you're right, and he is just that—beautiful. Oh, this is wonderful. You're in love with him, aren't you, little sister? Elly was worried you might not be, that you might have simply run to him when Rian— Well, see how wrong our resident worrywort was, hmm?"

In love with him? In love with Brede?

Fanny played the words over and over inside her

head as she worked at the pretty yellow-centered wild daisies she and Morgan had picked as they'd walked along, one completed daisy chain resting on her hair, the remainder of the pile in her lap as she fussed with the blooms, absently slitting their stems with her thumbnail, then lacing them together.

It was so peaceful here, sitting beneath the trees, sunlight filtering through the leaves and onto the ground around her. They'd traveled only about ten miles inland, always heading to the West, but the landscape had already begun to change. Become more lush, greener.

She'd lived her entire life close beside the water, looked out over an endless vista of sea and sky, and had never really imagined living anywhere else. Brede Manor was inland, she knew that. Would she be happy there? Or would she miss the sound of the waves, the smell of the saltwater?

As long as Valentine was there with her, did it really matter where she was, what sort of scenery lay outside her window?

Fanny loved Becket Hall, the wide, wild, mysterious Marsh. But there was an entire world out there she'd never seen, the beginnings of that different world only miles from her own doorstep. She hadn't cared about that; she'd been content. Her world had been Romney Marsh. How was a person to know she'd enjoy flying, until she'd spread her wings?

Fanny lifted her head slightly, sniffed at the air and smiled. "Where are you?" she asked, turning her head this way, then that, looking for Valentine somewhere in the trees.

"So much for my legendary stealth," he said from somewhere behind her, and she quickly turned completely about, to see him standing with one arm raised and leaning against a tree trunk.

He'd rid himself of his jacket and waistcoat, and his untied cravat hung around his neck the way the silk scarf had done the first time she'd seen him. He bit down on the lit cheroot clamped in the corner of his mouth and pushed at the hair that had been snared by a leafy branch, only making more of it slide forward, now caught in the clutches of the sweet breeze.

Fanny's heart did a small, fluttering flip in her chest. Morgan should see him now, then she'd understand. Mussed, rumpled, his eyes alive with humor. "I smelled your cheroot," she told him, watching as he pushed himself away from the tree and came to sit down beside her on the stone wall.

"Here," she said, finishing the second daisy chain and holding it up, intending to put it on his head.

"Oh, I think not," he told her, taking the chain from her and putting it with the one already on her head. "There. I crown you Queen of the Daisies. Long live the Queen."

Fanny looked up, as if she could see the flowers on her head. "That's silly. Are they gone? Morgan and Ethan, I mean, not the daisies."

"Yes, I know who you meant. I waved them on their way myself, just to be certain they were. Fine horseflesh they're riding, the two of them. And your sister sits a horse quite well, although she doesn't have a patch on you, when you're astride in your uniform trousers."

Fanny bent her head, feeling warmth creep into her cheeks. "We weren't going to talk about that anymore, remember?"

"Ah, but I insist that you must at least allow me my fond memories, sweetings," he said, grinning around the cheroot. "Shall we walk?"

Fanny got to her feet quickly, hoping she hadn't let him see how anxious she was to be doing something other than sitting close beside him, wondering what he'd think of her if she were to lean toward him, only slightly, push at the hair loosely framing one side of his face, and then perhaps press her lips against his smiling mouth. "Morgan and I walked back this way," she said, pointing to her left. "There's a well back there. Morgan called it picturesque."

"And did you call *down* it? Listen to hear if there's a member of the Waterguard desperately clinging to the slippery sides by his fingernails, hoping to be rescued?"

"That doesn't really happen," Fanny told him, taking his hand without thought and leading him along a narrow path leading to the old stone well. "At least not for years. And not here. Chance's wife, Julia, told me all about those terrible times. That was the Hawkhurst Gang, and others, who were so violent, and they've all long since gone to their rewards."

"Or the hangman," Valentine said as they stopped beside the well. "Still, we should at least try," he added, bending over the opening, *"Hall-oo!"*

Hall-oo… Hall- oo… echoed back at them, and Fanny giggled.

"Let me try." She leaned in over the well, Valentine hastily grabbing at the sash of her gown to steady her, and she cupped her hands around her mouth. She thought for a moment, frowned and, her hands still up at her face, turned to him. "What shall I say, Brede?"

"Valentine," he told her quietly. "Say Valentine."

"But I—" Fanny allowed her hands to drop to her sides. "Valentine," she said softly. Then she said his name again, more strongly this time. "Valentine."

It was his turn to cup his hands around her small face. "Again. And this time, say it like this. Valentine…kiss me."

Fanny's heart was beating wildly in her ears. Could he hear it, too? She laid her hands on his arms, needing to hold on to him or else her knees might give way. "Valentine. Please kiss me."

"Ah, even a *please*. How can I possibly refuse?"

"Refuse?" She dug her fingertips into his forearms. "Wretch. You were the one who asked me to—"

But that's as far as she got, because he was kissing her now, his mouth warm and possessive and seemingly hungry for her, and she had closed her eyes and was eagerly kissing him back.

Holding each other, they slowly subsided onto to the wide stone wall surrounding the well, sitting with their knees touching, Valentine's arms slipping around her, Fanny tightly holding on to the ends of his untied neck cloth as she pulled him closer. After all, hadn't Morgan told her that husbands didn't want dainty little misses in their beds?

When Valentine moved his hands to cup her breasts, Fanny realized something. She wasn't in her husband's bed. She was here, not one hundred yards from a busy inn, being wonderfully mauled by that same husband.

And then she realized something else.

She didn't care.

Her hands went to the buttons of his shirt, undoing them, one after the other, until she could slip inside, run her fingers over his heated skin, and he rather groaned against her mouth, most especially when she lightly rubbed her fingers over his flat male nipples.

But fair was only fair, and that's what he was doing to her, wasn't he? Oh, yes, he was.

Even through the fine lawn of her gown, her chemise, she could feel his touch, feel her body responding to that touch, her nipples hardening, so that he was able to actually take them between his thumb and forefinger, squeeze her gently, draw a soft moan from her own lips.

His mouth left hers as he trailed kisses along her jawline, lightly licked the sensitive skin behind her ear, nipped at the side of her throat as she tipped back her head and opened her eyes, looked up through the canopy of trees, at the sunlight streaming down through the leaves.

It was a wide, wonderful world, filled with new sights, even new sounds…and most definitely new experiences. Wonderful experiences. Fresh, exciting. Heady. Heart-poundingly beautiful.

Her eyes opened wider as Valentine continued to kiss her, now licking at the skin exposed above the modest neckline of her gown…now fastening on her nipple through the stuff of her gown. Sucking. Teasing…

She felt his right hand move to her knee, easing up the material of her skirt. Felt the warm sun and soft breeze against her leg as he raised that hem up and over her knee, then placed his hand on her thigh. Stroked her, inched up higher…higher…found his way beneath her smallclothes and all the way to the warm, moist place between her legs.

She felt his fingers there, gently opening her, seeking out the small bud of her womanhood, his touch sending waves of sensation throughout her body, causing the blood to pound in her ears, her breath to catch in her throat.

Closing her eyes, she concentrated all of her being on what Valentine was doing to her, and the way her body was responding to him, opening for him, straining toward him.

"Valentine…"

There was nothing else to say. Because he seemed to know. Know everything she needed, everything she wanted, even as she didn't know, could never have imagined…

"Valentine…"

He held her close, whispered against her ear. "Yes, sweetings, yes. It's all right, it's all right." He caught her startled cry with his mouth as her body began to convulse around him, and held on tight until she melted against him, her breathing swift and shallow, her body seemingly gone boneless.

Fanny slowly collapsed against his shoulder as he held her, gently smoothed her skirt back down over her knee, ran his fingers through her sun-warmed hair, pressed light kisses on her forehead and cheeks, and finally put her from him, smiling into her face.

"Well, that was an odd reaction to hearing you

say my name," Valentine said, letting out a long breath. "You might not want to do that too often, and most especially not when we're out in public."

"Valentine," Fanny said, moving toward him once more, only to have him put his hands on her shoulders, keeping his distance. "What's wrong?"

He chuckled softly. "You'll understand one day. But for now, wife, I can only ask you to sit here with me for a while as we admire the flowers and the trees and listen to the birds, and I think about draining fields, and if my steward planted the wheat at the proper time, and…" He let his voice fall off as Fanny looked at him, and a hot blush ran into her cheeks.

"Oh, Brede, I'm so sorry." Fanny hopped up from the side of the well and stood back a good three paces, wrapping her shawl tightly about herself, as if that would help him to somehow see her as less than what he knew she was, which was as the most beautiful, desirable creature he could ever hope to see.

This probably wasn't the moment to tell her that all he wanted was to lie her down among that nearby patch of daisies and make love to her until her eyes rolled back in her head, find the release he craved to the core of his being. "It's all right, Fanny. Just give me a few moments. I'm confident I'll survive."

"But it's not all right." It had taken her some moments, lost as she was in her own pleasure, but she now felt she understood his dilemma. "I'm so stupidly selfish. I just take and take, don't I? I never *give*."

"Fanny, no—" he began, but she had already turned on her heels and was walking quickly back down the path, and then running toward the inn, the two daisy chains still, remarkably, crowning her white-blond hair.

She'd be all right. There really wasn't much trouble she could get into at the inn, at any rate. And she'd calm down, she always did, always saw reason. He just had to give her some time to collect herself, that's all. And, once she did, there was the matter of how she'd attempt to make it up to him. There was always that, he thought, various possibilities playing through his mind, making him smile.

So he sat there, at the well, and thought his own thoughts, and then eventually found his way back to the inn, to find the innkeeper and order what he hoped would be a memorable meal served in his and Fanny's shared bedchamber in a few hours.

"Yes, my lord," the innkeeper said once he and Valentine had exhausted the inn's simple yet fairly extensive menu, choosing several dishes he hoped would please his bride. "And would you be wanting a tub as well, my lord?"

"As well?"

"Yes, my lord. My wife and daughters are in the

kitchens heating up water for one now, for your lady wife. We've another chamber free. Would you be wanting a tub?"

Valentine put his arm around the smaller man's shoulders and walked him toward the taproom. "Ah, my good sir, what a splendid idea. But with a few minor adjustments in the logistics of the thing, hmm?"

For the space of the hour he and the innkeeper had decided on, Valentine remained in the taproom, reading a few of the barely out-of-date London newspapers the inn could boast of, learning that the Prince Regent had elevated the heroic Uxbridge to the new title of Marquess of Anglesey, while Wellington, already laden with titles, had been awarded the Knight Grand Cross of the Order of the Bath, with other honors doubtless to follow.

He'd also read down a depressingly long list of casualties, to discover he'd lost even more good friends to Bonaparte's ambitions, as well as a listing of the wounded, some of them now returning from Brussels, to be welcomed as the heroes they were.

The war seemed so far away now, a memory that was blessedly fading, although always to be a part of him. But there was a future now, for Fanny and himself, one he would protect with his last breath.

That thought took him to Edmund Beales, and that man's ambition.

He'd been surprised to hear the name Nathaniel

Beatty and realize that this was the man who had wreaked such havoc on the Beckets and their crew, the families whose survivors now made up the inhabitants of Becket Village.

As he sipped at a second tankard of warm ale, he cast back in his memory, putting together bits and pieces of the conversation that had gone round that dinner table so many months ago.

Talleyrand had been his usual prepossessing self, pleasant, ingratiating, yet always aware, alert, measuring those around him as if considering their relative worth and importance—and how they could be of use to him.

Beatty—Beales—on the other hand, had rather taken control of the conversation for the length of at least three courses, giving his thoughts on Bonaparte, Wellington, the role of the Alliance. And, oddly, as Valentine recalled, he'd spoken long and passionately about the writings of Machiavelli, comparing the Congress of Vienna to that man's approach to governing, that man's observations about power and its divisions, its pitfalls and its benefits.

In short, the man had been a bloody bore, in love with the sound of his own voice, and Valentine had made his excuses early and quit the room before anyone suggested they all retire for cigars and brandy. He had, in fact, decided that this was a man who'd never had to pick up a weapon and put himself personally in the path of danger.

He'd been wrong about that. The man certainly had picked up a weapon.

And employed it to do his utmost to destroy his supposed best friend and all that man held dear.

Valentine put down the tankard, no longer thirsty, and glanced at the clock on the mantel over the large, now cold, fireplace. Tossing a few coins on the tabletop, he got to his feet, stretched and headed for the hallway and the stairs leading up to where his bride waited, most probably impatiently, and not in the best of humors.

He reached the landing just as the innkeeper's wife and two young girls who most depressingly resembled her both in face and figure stepped into the hallway, closing the door behind them. He waited until they were gone, heading for the rear stairway, he supposed, and then approached the room, knocking on the door.

Fanny's voice came to him through the heavy wooden door. "As I said before, her ladyship is fine, thank you. She doesn't need anything else."

"It's only your husband, Lady Brede," he called back to her, and then smiled, as he was sure he heard a slight splash from the other side of the door. He could picture her, stepping none too daintily into the tub.

"Brede? *Now?* Where were you? No, never mind. Go away. I'm having a bath."

"Yes," he said, extracting the key the innkeeper had given him and slipping it into the lock, "that was the plan."

Fanny heard the key turn in the lock and reached frantically for the towel that had been draped over a nearby chair. Which was how Valentine first saw her as he entered the low-ceilinged room to catch her half in, half out of the tub, her fair skin glistening with a thin layer of bubbles.

Fanny fell back into the bath with more haste than care, sending water sloshing over the sides of the tub, to soak into the wide-planked floor. "Brede! Go away!"

He slid his untied neck cloth out from around his neck, tossing it in the general direction of the high, wide bed. "You don't mean that, sweetings."

She goggled at him, simply goggled, as he began unbuttoning his shirt. "I most certainly *do* mean it. And stop grinning like that."

"Grinning in what way, sweetings?" he asked her, slipping his arms free of the shirt and tossing that the way of the neck cloth. "I'm an earl, if you'll recall. I am beaten down by the mighty weight of my considerable consequence, and I most assuredly don't *grin.*"

"You do and you are," Fanny said, at last locating

the small—too small—sea sponge in the bottom of the tub and holding it up against her breasts. "You also giggle like the village idiot. You said so yourself." She narrowed her eyelids as he walked to a corner of the room and used the bootjack bolted to the floor to rid himself of his boots. "Stop that!"

But he wasn't listening. He was sitting in a chair he'd pulled out from a small desk in front of the window, and he was rolling down his hose, removing them, one by one. In another moment he'd be as naked as the day he was born, just as she was at the moment.

She was helpless, trapped in the tub.

So she closed her eyes.

"Yes, that's probably a good idea, sweetings," Valentine said as he stood up, walked around the tub so that he stood behind it. "It's rather early days for too much familiarity."

"If that's true, why don't you just leave?" Fanny said, then squealed involuntarily as Valentine reached past her to take the sea sponge from her nerveless fingers and begin running it over her bare back. "Oh, Valentine…"

"Shh, sweetings, and let me tell you something very important. The greatest pleasure I can think of in this world is in giving you pleasure. Never think otherwise, my dearest Fanny, all right?"

My dearest Fanny.

Fanny bit her bottom lip between her teeth as she

nodded, acknowledged that she'd heard him, and that she understood.

"Valentine," she said, doing her best to ignore the way he seemed to be drawing lazy circles on her back with the soapy sea sponge, "Morgan said that you love me."

Valentine's hand stopped, and a slow smile came to his face. "Oh, she did, did she? One might have thought she'd leave that sort of happy confession to the persons involved, rather than spilling the beans that way."

Fanny half turned in the tub, to see that he was still wearing his pantaloons—not that it mattered. "Then you do? You love me?"

"Did I say that?" he asked her, frowning comically.

"Now you're making fun of me!" And then, because she was Fanny, and she'd probably never learn to be entirely civilized, no matter how many books Elly gave her or how many times she did her best to behave, she grabbed on to the waistband of those pantaloons and pulled him into the tub.

He rather twisted in the air and landed on his rump, his legs sticking straight in the air, water and soapy bubbles splashing everywhere.

She daringly reached below the surface of the water, to attempt to open the buttons on his pantaloons. After all, she was naked, and what was good for the goose…

"Do you know, Brede, that Morgan told me something else? She thinks you're homely."

Brede was attempting to right himself, pull his legs fully into the tub so that he could face his wife. So far, as romance went, his idea wasn't going all that well. "Really? An astute woman, although I would have said that she is very pretty, if anyone should ask."

"But she's wrong, Brede. I find you eminently adorable."

"Oh, good, I'm now the *adorable* Earl of Brede. I'll be laughed out of my clubs," he said, struggling out of his wet pantaloons and tossing them across the room. "You mean, like a kitten, Fanny, or a puppy? Charmed, I'm sure."

"Don't go all starchy on me, Brede. You're not at all like a kitten."

"A puppy, then?" he asked, at last able to put his back against the tub, slip his arm around Fanny, pull her close against his side.

"All right," Fanny said, running the sea sponge over his broad chest. "Perhaps a hound? With those adorably droopy eyes of yours."

"This gets worse and worse," Brede told her, taking the sponge from her, dipping it into the warm water, and then watching closely as he made lazy, soapy circles on the rise of her breasts. "I'd say I feel my dignity taking a strong hit, except that I've already been unceremoniously pulled into m'lady's tub, and it's too late now to worry about my dignity. I had a much different scenario planned when I came in here, you know."

"Really?" Fanny was all but bubbling herself, even as her insides began to melt under the heat of her growing pleasure. Morgan had been right. Definitely not about her adorable Brede, but about leaving the *lady* at the bedroom door. "And exactly what had you planned?"

"Hmm…well, let me see," he said, moving the sponge lower. "I believe I planned to begin by kneeling outside the tub—*outside the tub,* I said—kissing you as you sat here, warm and rosy. Gently kneading all the tension from your neck and shoulders as you purred beneath my touch."

"Oh…" Fanny said, quite aware that the sponge was now floating on the surface of the water, but Brede's hand had not surfaced with it. Indeed, it was quite busy elsewhere. "And…and then…"

"And then? Why, I suppose I would have washed your hair for you. But, of course, you would first have to get your hair wet for me."

"Yes, I suppose I—" When she surfaced again it was sputtering, and with arms flailing, trying to hit him for having shoved her beneath the water, only to have him catch her wrists, holding her arms wide as he put his smiling mouth to hers. "Beast," she mumbled against his lips even as he let her go and she wrapped her arms tightly around his bare shoulders.

"Sorry, sweetings, but turnabout is fair play, or so they say." Then he caught her at the knees and back, lifting her high in his arms, the two of them dripping water and bubbles as he stepped out of the tub, nearly slipping on the wet floor.

"We're causing a flood, Brede," Fanny pointed out unnecessarily.

"Some things, sweetings, are more workable in theory than in practice," he told her as he stood her on her feet and reached for one of the large white towels. "My tub at Brede Manor is more suited for what I'd planned."

Fanny hung on to him, her eyes closed tight. Perhaps she hadn't as yet left *all* of the lady at the bedroom door? But she did open her eyes for just a second, to peek. Then quickly shut them again. *My goodness!*

"Would, um, would that statement, Brede, be more in the way of a threat than a promise?" she asked him as he wrapped her in the toweling and picked her up once more, this time heading for the bed.

The man seemed to have adjusted his plan accordingly, and it was very much in agreement with her own.

"You can open your eyes now, sweetings," Brede

said once he had laid her on the bed and joined her beneath the covers.

"Not if you're laughing at me, no. I'm all wet and must look terrible."

"The proverbial drowned rat, I'm sure," he told her as he pulled the towel from beneath her. "And chilled, as well, perhaps?"

"Yes, I am. There's no end to the flaws in your plan, Brede."

He trailed kisses down the side of her throat and onto the curve of her breast. "I feel like a raw, bumbling youth, I agree. My dignity has quite deserted me, and I blame you entirely, wife."

Fanny moved beneath him as he slid one long leg over her lower body. "I like you this way. Not perfect. People shouldn't be perfect."

"Perfect? Far from it, Fanny. What's perfect is lying here with you beside me. Life, with you beside me."

"Oh, Brede, you make me want to cry."

He grinned. "Because you've just realized you'll be spending your life at my side?"

"No, because you're so smart. How did you know that at your side is exactly where I would want to be?"

"As I had been about to tell you earlier, before the aforementioned Morgan burst in on us, I knew so—I *hoped* so—my dearest wife, because I love you. Completely and utterly. I will love you until the day I die, and probably even after that."

"Because it's *necessary?*" Fanny asked him, her heart singing.

"Very necessary, sweetings."

Fanny sighed as he slid his warm hand over her midriff, spread his long fingers, slowly moving his thumb back and forth between her breasts. He was so big, all of him, so very much the man. She felt small and fragile beneath him. And very much the female. Protected. Even cherished. And yet his equal.

"I find it necessary, too, Valentine. To love you, that is. Because I do, I really, really do love you. I know now what it means to say that, what it means to be in love with a man, and I am completely and absolutely in love with you." She sighed against his chest. "You poor thing."

Brede gave a shout of laughter, light, carefree, even *young,* and pulled Fanny on top of him, to kiss her and to hold her and to make love to her, with her, both of their hearts at last free to give each other all that they had to give….

* * * * *

The *Regency*

LORDS & LADIES
COLLECTION

More Glittering Regency Love Affairs

Volume 17 – 4th January 2008
One Night with a Rake by Louise Allen
The Dutiful Rake by Elizabeth Rolls

Volume 18 – 1st February 2008
A Matter of Honour by Anne Herries
The Chivalrous Rake by Elizabeth Rolls

Volume 19 – 7th March 2008
Tavern Wench by Anne Ashley
The Incomparable Countess by Mary Nichols

Volume 20 – 4th April 2008
Prudence by Elizabeth Bailey
Lady Lavinia's Match by Mary Nichols

Volume 21 – 2nd May 2008
The Rebellious Bride by Francesca Shaw
The Duke's Mistress by Ann Elizabeth Cree

Volume 22 – 6th June 2008
Carnival of Love by Helen Dickson
The Viscount's Bride by Ann Elizabeth Cree

www.millsandboon.co.uk

M&B

A delicious addition to the Moreland family novels!

Gloucestershire, 1878

Ever since Anna Holcombe refused his proposal, Reed Moreland has been unable to set foot in the home that was the backdrop to their romance – Winterset.

But when Reed has dreams about Anna being in danger, he heads back to Winterset, determined to protect the woman he still loves. Once again passion flares between them, but the murder of a servant girl draws them deep into deadly legends of Winterset…and a destiny neither Anna nor Reed can escape.

Available 18th April 2008

Celebrate 100 years of pure reading pleasure with Mills & Boon®

To mark our centenary, each month we're publishing a special 100th Birthday Edition. These celebratory editions are packed with extra features and include a FREE bonus story.

Plus, starting in February you'll have the chance to enter a fabulous monthly prize draw. See 100th Birthday Edition books for details.

Now that's worth celebrating!

15th February 2008

Raintree: Inferno by Linda Howard

Includes FREE bonus story Loving Evangeline
A double dose of Linda Howard's heady mix of passion and adventure

4th April 2008

The Guardian's Forbidden Mistress by Miranda Lee

Includes FREE bonus story The Magnate's Mistress
Two glamorous and sensual reads from favourite author Miranda Lee!

2nd May 2008

The Last Rake in London by Nicola Cornick

Includes FREE bonus story The Notorious Lord
Lose yourself in two tales of high society and rakish seduction!

Look for Mills & Boon 100th Birthday Editions at your favourite bookseller or visit
www.millsandboon.co.uk